Earl of Every Sin

Sins and Scoundrels
Book Four

Scarlett Scott

© Copyright 2019 by Scarlett Scott
Text by Scarlett Scott
Cover by Wicked Smart Designs

Dragonblade Publishing, Inc. is an imprint of Kathryn Le Veque Novels, Inc.
P.O. Box 7968
La Verne CA 91750
ceo@dragonbladepublishing.com

Produced in the United States of America

First Edition November 2019
Print Edition

Reproduction of any kind except where it pertains to short quotes in relation to advertising or promotion is strictly prohibited.

All Rights Reserved.

The characters and events portrayed in this book are fictitious. Any similarity to real persons, living or dead, is purely coincidental and not intended by the author.

ARE YOU SIGNED UP FOR DRAGONBLADE'S BLOG?

You'll get the latest news and information on exclusive giveaways, exclusive excerpts, coming releases, sales, free books, cover reveals and more.

Check out our complete list of authors, too!

No spam, no junk. That's a promise!

Sign Up Here

www.dragonbladepublishing.com

Dearest Reader;

Thank you for your support of a small press. At Dragonblade Publishing, we strive to bring you the highest quality Historical Romance from the some of the best authors in the business. Without your support, there is no 'us', so we sincerely hope you adore these stories and find some new favorite authors along the way.

Happy Reading!

CEO, Dragonblade Publishing

Additional Dragonblade books by Author Scarlett Scott

The Sins and Scoundrels Series
Duke of Depravity
Prince of Persuasion
Marquess of Mayhem
Earl of Every Sin

*** Please visit Dragonblade's website for a full list of books and authors. Sign up for Dragonblade's blog for sneak peeks, interviews, and more: ***
www.dragonbladepublishing.com

When Alessandro, the half-Spanish Earl of Rayne, settles upon a marriage of convenience with Lady Catriona Hamilton, the terms are clear: an heir in exchange for her freedom. Still haunted by his painful past, he has no intention of entertaining a true marriage with his new wife or remaining in England.

A ruined lady brought back from her banishment for a second chance, Catriona is practical and determined. There's no stronger lure than the prospect of her independence. Except for the earl himself, that is.

Saddled with a scapegrace brother-in-law, a mouse-toting ward, a Spanish-speaking butler, and a wife he cannot stop wanting, Alessandro is about to learn life is best when it does not go according to plan. But if he doesn't let go of the past, he'll lose everything.

The darkest hearts fall the hardest...

Chapter One

Alessandro Diego Christopher Forsythe, ninth Earl of Rayne, had only been in England for one month, and already, he had shot a man and acquired a betrothed.

To be fair, he had shot the Duke of Montrose when defending himself from the drunken fool, who had been hell-bent upon shooting him in the head. And the betrothal had yet to become official because Lady Catriona Hamilton, sister to the fool he had wounded, was proving a most recalcitrant future countess.

"I am sorry, my lord," apologized the dowager Duchess of Montrose for the fourth time. "I cannot imagine Lady Catriona will be much longer."

They were seated in a formal salon, a full tea service spread before them, awaiting the arrival of the lady he had promised to wed after shooting Montrose. In truth, Montrose had demanded the obligation from him as a debt of honor.

Rayne intended to leave England and return to Spain with as much haste as possible, but he also recognized he had a duty to the title and the entail. Marrying Lady Catriona had seemed, at the time, an efficient solution to two problems. He could satisfy a bleeding—and highly drunken—man's demand, and he could also obtain a bride without being required to court her.

Provided Lady Catriona could meet his requirements in a bride.

Which was becoming less and less likely by the moment.

"Perhaps she is ill once more, Your Grace," he said at last, unable to keep the irritation from lacing his voice.

This was his third visit to the Duke of Montrose's townhome to visit his prospective betrothed. On his first attempt at meeting her, she had been suffering from a severe case of megrims. On his second try, Lady Catriona had fallen ill with a lung infection.

He drummed his fingers against his thigh, the sound falling heavily in the silence that had descended between himself and Lady Catriona's mother, who wore the look of a woman disappointed with the world beneath her white cap. And he could hardly blame the dowager for such a sentiment.

Her son, the Duke of Montrose, was a scapegrace drunkard who dipped his prick in every willing female in London. And if gossip was to be believed, her daughter had been ruined and summarily sent to Scotland by Montrose to hide from the scandal she had created. She had then been rescued by her brother's stupidity, but refused to meet the man who would be her savior and pluck her from the maws of said ruination.

The duchess's eyes fell upon Alessandro's tapping fingers.

He stilled them.

"Please accept my sincere apologies, Lord Rayne," she whispered, sounding mortified.

"I believe I shall take my leave now, Your Grace," he announced.

Alessandro had wasted enough time being made a fool by Lady Catriona. Montrose would have to settle upon some other answer for his debt of honor. He would find a different wife, one who was not the scandalous, minx sister of a drunkard duke.

The dowager made her apologies as he offered her a curt bow and saw himself out. Irritation mingled with fury as he stalked down the hall. He did not appreciate his precious time being wasted by a spoiled girl. Time was a luxury he could not afford to waste, for each day he lingered in England was a day that could have been meaningful in

Spain, his mother's homeland. The homeland of his heart.

A flutter of movement caught his eye, giving him pause. It had been, he thought, the swish of a lady's pale, rose gown disappearing over the threshold of a chamber down the hall. Instinct told him it was *her*. And whilst he knew he ought to take his leave as he had announced he would do and see himself to the door, he found himself spinning on his heel and pursuing that gown.

Pursuing that maddening creature who had dared to refuse to be introduced to him. He followed her without thought for propriety or even sanity. What did it matter if he eschewed convention and sought out Lady Catriona alone? She was already ruined, and he was already known as the mad Earl of Rayne. As rarely as he returned to England, even Alessandro knew his unflattering sobriquet.

He reached the closed door into which she had disappeared and opened it, striding through without hesitation, closing the portal at his back. The room in question was a library. A rather small affair, lined with two levels of shelves, flanked at each end by a set of overstuffed chairs. But Alessandro did not linger on the books or the chairs.

He had eyes only for the woman, her chestnut hair pulled into a simple chignon that put the graceful column of her throat on display. Her back was to him, and he took a moment to drink in the sight of her at last.

"Lady Catriona." He spoke her name into the silence, gratified when she spun about, a hand fluttering over her heart, and emitted a most unladylike squeal.

For a moment, she stared at him, and he stared back, confounded. Lady Catriona was not at all as he had imagined she would be. She looked nothing like her immense clod-of-a-brother—thank the Lord for that mercy—her form curvaceous in bosom and hips, just as he preferred. Small ringlets framed her heart-shaped face, and her eyes were the blue of the ocean, her lips a pink Cupid's bow that begged for kisses.

Fortunately, he was not the kissing sort of man. Nor was he the sort who was easily swayed by beauty, for Lady Catriona undeniably possessed more than her share of it. She was stunning, her loveliness not just ethereal but unusual, so unique he could not deny his initial reaction to her.

At least, not until he tamped it down and reminded himself, she had made an ass of him on no less than three occasions.

"Have you nothing to say for yourself, my lady?" he asked, stalking nearer to her, though he knew he ought to simply leave. "You look remarkably hale for a lady possessed of such a delicate constitution. First megrims, then a lung infection. Your sainted mother did not even bother to offer an excuse for your absence today. Tell me, what was it, my lady? A stomach ailment? A scrape? Perhaps you stubbed your toe."

Her eyes narrowed upon him, her bearing seizing up, as if the sight of him was loathsome to her. "You were meant to be gone by now. Why are you still here, Lord Rayne? And why have you followed me?"

He almost laughed at her daring. But he was not amused by her impudence. He stopped only when he was close enough in proximity to touch her. To note how thick and long her lashes were, how her eyes held untold depths of gray within them.

"I came here to propose marriage to you, just as I have done on the previous two occasions when you were also too struck with illness to see me," he said coolly, whisking an assessing gaze over her. "But now I confess, I am grateful for your discretion, Lady Catriona."

She frowned, and even in her expression of confused distraction, she was lovely. "I am afraid I do not understand, my lord. Precisely what is it you express gratitude for?"

"For saving me from an untenable fate." He chose his words with care, enjoying himself for the first time since his arrival. A worthy opponent, Lady Catriona. "I can see clearly now we would never suit."

Her frown deepened. "Why not, Lord Rayne?"

He would have felt a hint of compunction for what he was about to do had not Lady Catriona begun this battle between them. But she had fired the first volley of cannon, and Alessandro was declaring war. Lady Catriona Hamilton was a menace, just as her brother was. Her insolence spurred him on. He had been gone from the battlefields too long, and his endless thirst for vengeance would only be quenched in one fashion.

"I require a wife with mettle," he said, "not a girl who hides from me like a mouse."

Her shoulders stiffened as his taunt found its mark with ease. "I was not hiding from you, Rayne. I merely had no wish to take part in whatever madness you hatched with my brother. If you owe him a debt, surely you may find another manner in which to repay it."

He ought not to toy with her. There was something about Montrose's defiant sister that would not allow him to go. If she was a mouse, he was the cat, pawing at her for his own amusement, tricking her into believing she could escape before sinking in his claws and making her bleed.

He moved one step closer to her, near enough now to not just touch but to note faint details, such as the flecks of violet in her eyes, the freckles on the bridge of her nose. "You have been hiding from me on three occasions. I can understand a pale, timid English lady such as yourself cowering in fear. I must terrify you, no?"

"No." She pursed her lips, remaining where she stood rather than retreating. "I do not, nor have I ever, cowered, Lord Rayne. Nor am I a mouse, I assure you. If I were, I would not have returned to England at all."

Ah, the suggestion of her past. He had not bothered to ask for a full accounting of the scandal, for it had not mattered to him. Her innocence was immaterial. He was not attempting to woo her, after all, but to get her with child and return to his life. She was a duty, nothing more.

He did not even require a wife to be faithful after she produced the necessary heir, for *Cristo* knew he had no intention of upholding English vows when he was at home in Spain, where he belonged. And when the only vows that would ever bind him had already been spoken and shattered by death.

But now that Lady Catriona was at last standing before him, he found himself curious. He could well understand an English fop losing his head over her. And he wanted to know more about this vexing creature herself.

"If you are not hiding from me, then who is it you are hiding from, Lady Catriona?" he probed. "Your lover?"

Her face drained of color, her sensual lips compressing into a harsh line. "How dare you?"

He should have felt pity, he knew, but he had spent the past few years witnessing horrors greater than the beautiful, spoiled aristocrat before him could possibly comprehend. He had lost everyone he loved except his half-sister Leonora.

His compassion was gone. So, too, his ability to feel. There was a reason for his name, *El Corazón Oscuro,* the dark heart. His soul was even darker. Death and murder had a way of making their claim upon a man. Though he had not committed a quarter of the atrocities which it had been rumored he had throughout Spain, he had indeed killed and wounded his enemies.

He had needed to in a land where it had become either kill or be killed.

Alessandro flashed her a feral smile. "I dare everything, my lady. You are ruined, are you not?"

"You are a brutish boor to dare utter such a hateful thing to me," she snapped.

Still cold, still haughty.

He could not resist goading her, for she had made a fool of him, and Alessandro was no one's fool, *maldición*. "Do not look so surprised, Lady Catriona. I may have been gone from these putrid English shores the last few years, but I am not stupid. Montrose wanted me to wed you because no other man will have you, and he wishes to free himself of the burden of a spinster sister."

Cruel of him, perhaps. Honest, too, however. He had endured a lifetime of being treated as if he did not belong, and he would be damned before he would allow a beautiful duke's sister who had never known a bit of struggle in her life to look down her nose at him. If she was making a fool of him because of who his mother had been, he would return the favor by reminding her she was no angel.

Her nostrils flared, the only sign his words had affected her at all. "Yes, I am ruined. Is that what you wish to hear, Lord Rayne?"

The bitterness lacing her words was not lost upon him. "What happened?"

"Why are you still here, my lord?" she returned coldly. "I have made my opinion of a betrothal between us apparent, I believe. There is no reason for you to linger."

Lady Catriona Hamilton nettled him. He wanted to oppose her. To match her in wits and wills. Some unfettered part of him was enjoying this battle between them after all. Enjoying it more than he had enjoyed anything for as long as he could recall. He was not ready for it to come to an end.

"Mayhap I have decided to take pity on you and wed you despite the insults you have paid me, Lady Catriona," he said.

"And mayhap I neither want nor need your pity, Lord Rayne." Her manner was regal as any queen's. "Nor do I wish to become your countess."

"You are prideful for a ruined woman," he observed.

In spite of himself, he admired her courage. Her defiance was appealing. The sparks of interest developed into a searing flame within him. If he must wed—and he must, though the notion still displeased him mightily—he wanted to wed a woman who at least possessed a modicum of spirit.

Maria would have appreciated that, for she had been not just spirited but giving and loving. She had been an angel on earth, which was why she had been taken from him so soon. He had not deserved her or her love.

"You are vulgar and cruel, just as I expected you to be," Lady Catriona said, her cutting words biting through his thoughts. Her chin tipped up. "You may go now, my lord."

He clenched his jaw at her boldness. He raked her form with a searching stare. Her dress was demure. Her décolletage revealed little beyond the hint of lush breasts. Against his will, Lady Catriona Hamilton stirred him.

"Do you know why I promised your brother I would wed you?" he asked, banishing his unwanted reaction to her.

He was still not certain he *wished* to marry this impudent chit. But his reluctant trip to the land of his birth had reminded him he had responsibilities here, and if he did not fulfill them, a man who had disparaged Alessandro's mother would one day inherit his title. He did not give a damn about the title or the estates, but he did care about thwarting a hateful bastard like Henry Abbott.

"You shot him, Lord Rayne." She tilted her head. "Did you imagine Montrose would neglect to share such a salient detail with me? Perhaps you thought to shock me, my lord. As you can see, I neither fear you nor wish to continue this audience. Please excuse me."

She made to sweep past him, but he caught her arm, staying her in a grip that was firm but not punishing. "I shot him in a duel, Lady Catriona. Your brother was drunk, and he almost killed me. I saved myself, making certain to only wound him. So, you see? I am not always cruel. I can be forgiving when I wish."

"Release me," she demanded through gritted teeth.

"No." He smiled, for he was enjoying himself even more now.

The more she fought him, the more he wanted to keep her. He

could settle for far worse as his bride. And she was an expedient solution to his problems. More than that, he liked her fire. Even her scorn fascinated him.

"Lord Rayne," she said, jerking her arm in a useless effort to free herself. "I demand you unhand me."

"I have not finished speaking with you, Lady Catriona."

He could not seem to stop staring at her mouth, so pale and pink, the Cupid's bow taunting him. He had not kissed the lips of another woman since Maria, and it displeased him to realize the first to tempt him was an Englishwoman.

This Englishwoman.

Perhaps he should let her go after all.

"But *I* have finished with you, my lord," she snapped.

Sí, he should release her and walk away. Obey the urge which had first overwhelmed him, to inform Montrose he needed to find a new means of satisfying his debt of honor. But he could not.

He needed a wife. He required an heir. More than anything, he had to return to Spain. Lady Catriona Hamilton could enable him to accomplish all three. He told himself that was the only reason he lingered.

"What will become of you if you do not wed me, my lady?" he asked her then. "Shall you return to Scotland? Be dependent upon the munificence of your drunkard brother? Become a companion? A governess?"

"Why should you care?" she asked bitterly.

She could not be more different from Maria. She was ice where Maria had been fire, and that pleased him.

He released her arm, gambling she would remain. "I care because I owe Montrose a debt of honor, and I intend to uphold my obligation. But I am also in need of a wife and heir. You will do after all."

Her brows arched. But she did not go. "I will *do*, Lord Rayne?"

"*Sí*." Her outrage was almost palpable.

"How generous of you, my lord." Her voice was acidic. "However, I have no desire to wed."

He had expected Lady Catriona objected to him because of his Spanish mother and his reputation as the mad earl. But for the first time, it occurred to him that she truly did not want to marry.

"A marriage with me could benefit you greatly, my lady," he told her, trying a different tactic. "I require a wife and an heir, but I must return to Spain. I will not be living here, which means being my countess will afford you great freedom."

Her blue eyes narrowed. "You do not intend to live in England?"

Cristo. Never.

"No."

Her countenance changed, growing curious. "You would require me to…share the marriage bed with you until I…"

"I do not expect it would take long," he said, taking pity on her. "A few weeks, no more. When I am assured you are with child, I will return to Spain, leaving you with a generous stipend to dispose of as you wish. You will also be free to do as you like after the birth of my heir. I will not expect fidelity from you. Nor should you expect it from me."

A flush stained her pale cheeks. "What you propose is very cold indeed, sir."

He shrugged. "It is what I am offering you, and far better than the life you have been leading, hidden away like a shameful secret. But you must decide, Lady Catriona, here and now."

She was silent for a beat, searching his gaze as if seeking the answer to a great mystery.

"What if I bear you a daughter?" she asked at last.

"I will return." The prospect aggrieved him mightily, for he would prefer to never have to return to English shores again. "I will be candid. The sole reason I require an heir is to prevent my cousin from inheriting the earldom. When that objective has been reached, you will be free to live your life as you choose."

"What of your child? Would you not wish to meet him?"

He swallowed down a knot of the grief which refused to leave him. "I do not care for children."

"Why, Lord Rayne?"

He thought of Francisco, pale and still in his arms. Of Maria, quietly bleeding to death before the fever set in. "I do not care for children," he repeated. "The child will be your responsibility. One heir, that is all I require."

Her lips compressed, her expression implacable. For a moment, he became convinced she would deny him. If she did, he would accept her refusal. His pride would allow nothing less.

"Yes," she said at last. "Very well. I will marry you, Lord Rayne."

Victory.

But a hollow one, nonetheless. How different his last proposal of marriage had been from this one. It had been a lifetime ago, when he had been younger, more innocent. When he had blindly believed in the hope of a future which had never come.

He bowed. "*Excelente*, my lady. I will see to the rest with Montrose."

Chapter Two

"When I heard the news, I almost did not believe it. Tell me, is it true? Have you truly agreed to wed the Earl of Rayne?" the Honorable Miss Hattie Lethbridge demanded, sounding horrified.

They were seated in the drawing room of Hamilton House, enjoying tea as they had on hundreds of other occasions in the past. But this time was different.

Catriona sent her best friend an attempt at a reassuring smile, though she was sure she failed miserably. "It is."

Thanks to the friendship between their disreputable brothers, Hattie and Catriona had become as close as sisters over the years. She was more grateful than ever to see her friend now, when she was drowning in misery over the fate to which she had consigned herself the day before.

She had scarcely even slept.

Or eaten.

"Oh, dear heavens, Catriona," Hattie said, her eyes going wide and anxious. "Montrose is not forcing you into it, is he? He is a rogue of the worst order, but surely not even he would do something so dissolute."

"No," she said swiftly. "Monty would never force me."

Her relationship with her brother was...strained in the wake of her ruination. But he would never make her marry anyone. He did not have it in him.

"He did banish you to Scotland," Hattie pointed out, her lips compressed in a grim, unimpressed twist.

Hattie's rancor for Monty was no secret. She thought he was a disreputable scoundrel. And, well, Monty *was* a disreputable scoundrel. There was a reason he was known as the Duke of Debauchery. His reputation was as depraved as it was legendary, and though Catriona loved her brother, she knew he was no angel.

Of course, neither was she.

Far from it, as all fashionable London so painfully was aware.

"You know why he banished me," she said quietly, though it pained her to speak of the reason.

And most especially of the man who had caused it.

A man she had believed—quite foolishly—loved her.

But as it turned out, she had been wrong. Indeed, she had been wrong about a great many things. She could only hope agreeing to wed the Earl of Rayne would not prove one of them. Lord knew her history in trusting men spoke for itself.

"Do not remind me of that insufferable reprobate, Shrewsbury." Hattie's glower made her opinion of the marquess quite apparent. "Montrose ought to have met him on the field of honor and put a bullet in his black heart. I know Montrose is your brother, Catriona, and you love him, but I find nothing redeeming in him whatsoever. There is a rumor he has three mistresses. Three!"

Knowing Monty, he probably did.

"Hattie, I begged Monty not to do it," she defended her brother, suppressing a shudder as she recalled the row which had ultimately ended in her being sent away to Scotland. "You know that."

"And the coward took you at your word, sending you away instead of making Shrewsbury pay for what he had done," Hattie said, settling her teacup in its saucer with more force than necessary. "How can you forgive him for it, my dear? Your heart is far purer than mine, I will own. When someone betrays me, I cannot rest until the injustice is somehow accounted for."

Monty was not a coward, Catriona well knew. He had been determined to meet Shrewsbury at Battersea Fields to satisfy Catriona's honor. But she had fallen upon her knees before her brother, begging him not to challenge the marquess to a duel, for the marquess was a notoriously excellent shot, and Monty was a notoriously in-his-cups ne'er-do-well. Her brother would not have survived, and Catriona could not have borne his blood on her hands.

Far better to live with her own shame.

"He did what I asked him to, Hattie," she told her friend, grateful for her unending allegiance, but reluctant to relive her own ignominy. "I did not want Shrewsbury to kill him."

"You saved his life, and in return, he banished you to Scotland." Hattie harrumphed. "Fine brother he is. Bad enough he forced you to leave Town as if you were responsible for that cad Shrewsbury's actions. But now, he is making you marry the Earl of Rayne."

Hattie shuddered for effect.

Inwardly, Catriona was shuddering as well, but it was for different reasons than her beloved friend. It was because the Earl of Rayne affected her in a way no man ever had. In a way not even Shrewsbury had.

And she could not like it, nor trust it, any more than she could like or trust the Earl of Rayne himself.

She took a calming sip of her tea, realizing belatedly she had scarcely touched it and that it was growing cold. "Hattie, dearest, I have already told you, Monty is not forcing me to marry Rayne. I made the decision myself."

"That is nonsense, and I refuse to believe it. Montrose brought you back to London expressly to see you betrothed to the earl. He told Torrington as much, and Torrington told me. You know how the two of them are when they are drinking together at their club. Worse than a pair of dowagers at a ball."

Hattie's brother, Viscount Torrington, was one of Monty's oldest and closest friends. For all that he was an incorrigible scoundrel and rakehell, Torrington's love for Hattie was boundless. It was the only redeeming quality he possessed. Monty and Torrington together were nothing but trouble.

All London knew it.

Just as they knew she, Lady Catriona Hamilton, had been caught kissing the Marquess of Shrewsbury at the Mansfield ball.

"You are right that Monty brought me back to London because of the earl," Catriona said. "But he did not issue a demand. He told me he had found a means of restoring my reputation, and he urged me to accept Rayne's suit."

What she did not say was that she had only returned to London because Mama had been adamant that she must. And that she had instead launched her own campaign of avoidance, hoping Rayne would cry off.

Only, he had not.

He had returned on three occasions.

She shivered as she recalled her first sight of him in the library. Because he spent so little time in England, she had never before had occasion to meet him. She had imagined him to be older. And uglier.

But he was near enough in age to her, only in his mid-thirties, she would judge. And he was the furthest one could reasonably get from being unattractive.

He was the most glorious man she had ever beheld.

"They say he is mad," Hattie said.

It was entirely possible, for only a mad man would have pursued Catriona into the library as he had. Only a mad man would want to marry a woman and then never see her again after she bore him an heir.

"He did not seem mad," she said rather unconvincingly.

"On how many occasions have you spoken with him?" Hattie

asked knowingly.

"One," she admitted, wetting her lips.

Her friend pursed her lips. "Was he a gentleman?"

"Yes." And also, somehow, no.

He had held her elbow, keeping her captive during their heated exchange, and his touch—the warmth he exuded, along with the potent allure—had branded her through her dress. Worst of all, and much to her shame, he had released her at some point during their dialogue, leaving her free to go, and she had not noticed. Instead, she had remained tethered to him by some strange connection she could not yet comprehend.

Hattie's eyes narrowed. "You say that in a most unconvincing fashion."

"He was a gentleman," she argued. "Far more of a gentleman than others I have had occasion to be courted by."

That was not entirely true either, but the bitterness in her voice was meant for one man alone: Shrewsbury.

"If you are telling me the truth, and Montrose did not oblige you to betroth yourself to Rayne, then the earl must have changed your mind," Hattie observed shrewdly. "You were set against wedding him when you first returned."

"I know." Dear, sweet Hattie had called upon her the moment she arrived in London despite the potential damage it would cause to her own reputation. "Rayne was…I cannot explain him adequately."

Handsome did not do him justice.

Gorgeous could not convey the sizzling magnetism of the man.

He had stolen all the air from her lungs. From the chamber. For a heartbeat, she had not been able to think of a single, coherent sentence when she had first seen him. Not even one word.

"He is fine-looking," Hattie guessed.

"More than that," Catriona admitted, flushing. "But that is not the reason why I accepted his proposal."

And indeed, it was not. Even if he was beautiful, from his dark hair and eyes to his olive skin, to his broad shoulders, lean hips, and long, muscular legs encased in breeches that fit him like a second skin, to his finely sculpted lips and brooding countenance, she had been determined to send him away.

Until he had changed everything.

"What is the reason?" Hattie sighed. "Catriona, do not, I beg you, try to convince me you have somehow developed tender feelings for the mad earl after meeting him on only one occasion. I know you far too well to believe it."

Catriona smiled, then took another sip of tea.

It was completely cold.

"He promised me freedom, Hattie," she said, aware, as she revealed it to her friend, just how foolish Rayne's proposal seemed.

His words returned to her. *When I am assured you are with child, I will return to Spain, leaving you with a generous stipend to dispose of as you wish. You will also be free to do as you wish after the birth of my heir.*

"Freedom," Hattie repeated, raising a brow. "What manner of freedom can he possibly offer you if you are forced to become his wife?"

"I am not being forced," she reminded. "He wants to carry on his line, but he does not wish to live here. I will provide him with an heir, and he will give me leave to live my life as I see fit."

Hattie frowned. "And what of Rayne? Where shall he be, and what shall he be doing whilst you are living your life as you see fit?"

"He will be living in Spain," she said simply.

Unbidden, the rest of what he had said returned to her as well. *I will not expect fidelity from you. Nor should you expect it from me.*

And suddenly, something about his admission he would be taking a lover or lovers in Spain needled her. Perhaps he already had a mistress awaiting him in Spain. Someone he loved. It would make sense given the cold manner in which he intended to leave his wife and child in England, having no part of their lives.

But she told herself this was just the manner of husband she preferred, a man who would wed her and leave her. She would not have to answer to him or be disappointed or betrayed by him.

"You mean to suggest Rayne expects you to bear him an heir, and when you have done so, he will disappear to Spain?" Hattie sounded perplexed. And outraged.

"It is an odd arrangement, I know," she conceded. "But it is not so very different from many arrangements between husband and wife in our set. Only think of it this way, I will be able to regain my reputation in society over time, having become a countess in my own right. And I will have a child to dote upon. I will be free to live my life as I wish."

She had always wanted children of her own. It had been one of the most painful realizations she'd had to make in accepting her ruination and banishment, that she may never find a man willing to overlook her transgressions and make her his wife so she could have a family.

"I understand, my dear, and do not think otherwise," Hattie said. "But I am concerned for you. You have suffered enough heartbreak at the hands of a scoundrel. This marriage Rayne proposes to share with you sounds as if it will only produce more pain for you."

That was where her friend was wrong. "A man cannot break your heart if it is never his to break."

Catriona did not love the Earl of Rayne, nor was she in danger of ever developing feelings for him, which meant marrying him would not cost her anything. She had learned her lesson well with Shrewsbury. She would never again allow her heart to be vulnerable to a man. She had trusted and loved with blinding loyalty, and he had repaid her by leading her onto a balcony and ramming his tongue down her throat.

All in the name of winning a bet at White's.

He had never loved her at all. Nor had he been courting her. His entire pursuit of her had been a lark. A stupid, foolish game.

He had collected his winnings, and so, too, had she in the form of a life's lesson learned.

"Are you saying you are certain you will not fall in love with him?" Hattie asked.

"I am saying I will never again fall in love with another man," Catriona answered with utmost confidence. "The Earl of Rayne will never be able to hurt me, because I will never feel anything for him. He will be a means to an end, and that is all. If I wed him, I will have my life back. If I do not, I am doomed to either try to find a husband who will have me although I was compromised, or become a companion or a governess."

Rayne had not been wrong about her potential fate. It was indeed grim.

"So you see, Hattie dearest," she pressed on with a bright smile she did not feel, "marrying the earl is the best decision for me."

Her friend gave her a searching look, her mien grim. "I pray you are right about that, Catriona, for you deserve only happiness."

Happiness.

The word held a different meaning for her now than it once had. And she hoped she could rediscover it as the Countess of Rayne.

ALESSANDRO SAT OPPOSITE the Duke of Montrose in a private room at The Duke's Bastard. Montrose had a half-consumed glass of contraband Scottish whisky at his elbow. Contrary to his previous meetings with the duke, this time, Montrose did not appear to be thoroughly sotted.

A welcome improvement, that. One would only hope the blackguard would remain sober enough to discuss the marriage contract for his only sister.

"I will provide her with a more than generous allotment of pin money," he told Montrose, continuing his list of provisions for his future wife.

Wife.

Cristo, how the word stung. He remembered whispering it to Maria after they had first wed, in awe that she was his. Only, he had spoken it to her in their language. *Esposa*.

Lady Catriona Hamilton would never be his true wife.

She would be the woman he married. The way to settle his duties. The conveyance for his freedom and return to the country and people he loved.

"I have read the contracts," Montrose said. "I find them all in order. Your allowances for Lady Catriona are fair. Fairer than need be, given her reduced status. Most men in your position would not accept her."

He hissed out a sigh of annoyance. "I am not most men. And thank *Cristo* for that. I have already procured a special license, Montrose. What else did you wish to discuss? To my knowledge, the contract is plain, and it benefits Lady Catriona in the extreme. What reason have you for tarrying over it?"

Montrose took a long swig from his glass of whisky before settling it back upon the table with an indelicate thump. "Damn it, this is my *sister*, Rayne."

He was unmoved. "Your sister who you insisted I wed?"

The duke scowled at him. "To save her. Because I love her. But I also acknowledge I was a trifle cupshot at the time I made the request to you."

Alessandro pinned him with an unimpressed glare. "And every instance afterward, including now."

"I am not in my cups now, devil take you," Montrose denied.

He flashed the duke an insincere smile. "The devil has already taken me. That is why I am here, sitting opposite you in this glorified pleasure palace, watching you swill smuggled whisky and bluster over the marriage contract."

It was also why he had lost the only two people he had ever loved. Why Maria was gone, why their son had never taken a breath in this world.

"Do you want to marry her or not, damn it?" Montrose demanded.

Here was his chance. He could say *no*. One syllable, so succinct, so easy. The same in both his languages.

"Yes," he bit out instead. Because it was the only answer he could give. His duty loomed, now more than it ever had since his return. Lady Catriona was the answer he needed.

"And will you promise to treat her well?" Montrose pressed. "She is difficult and stubborn, but her heart is soft, Rayne. It has already been broken. She has endured a great deal."

Alessandro almost laughed. If the duke knew what *he* had endured over the last few years, he would imbibe an entire bottle of whisky just to chase away the memories of it. He had not been ruined. He had been devastated. The man he had once been had been forever changed. Losing Maria and Francisco, fighting in the war, the horrors he had witnessed and partaken in, melded in his mind into one sickening blur of agony.

"I understand, Montrose," he forced himself to say. "Believe me, I understand better than you think, and I promise to treat her as I would expect to be treated in turn."

Which meant after she provided him with an heir, she could fuck anyone she chose.

And so could he.

Why this now filled him with a bitterness he could not seem to dispel was a question he would seek to answer later. Another day. A day when he was not signing his life away as he sat opposite the Duke of Montrose.

"You would not harm her, would you?" the duke asked next. "Or force her? If she is not willing? I am aware of this business you have with wanting an heir. Cat told me herself after your meeting. Before I agree to your nuptials, I need to be certain you will always…treat her with care."

Cristo, what did Montrose think he was, a monster?

"I will not force myself upon her, Montrose," he said coldly. "You can sleep soundly knowing you have not foisted your scandalous sister off on a man who would hurt her."

He would not hurt her, of course. He was not a man given to violence against women. Against men, yes. He had committed a shocking number of sins at war. All of which he would carry to his grave and answer for one day. And he knew it.

But Lady Catriona Hamilton would not be one of them.

Of this, he was certain.

"I am not foisting her, damn you," Montrose said then, before draining the remnants of his whisky from his glass and slamming it back on the table. "I am trying to save her."

Alessandro gave a grim bark of laughter at such a pronouncement. "Ah, Montrose. None of us can be saved, and the sooner we accept our fates, the better we all shall be. Now, I trust all your concerns have been met, and the nuptials are to proceed as planned?"

Montrose looked as if he were about to argue, but instead, he nodded. "We shall proceed."

Chapter Three

THE GARDEN AT Hamilton House was small.

But the Earl of Rayne made it feel even smaller as he walked at Catriona's side. It was not his impressive height or the barely leashed strength hidden in his lean form. It was not even the austere colors of his jacket and breeches.

Rather, it was his presence.

There was something dark and dangerous, breath-arresting, and stomach-clenching about him. Only he could make the out of doors seem like a confined space.

"I prefer for the wedding to occur quickly," Rayne said as they reached a small stone bench bracketed by hedges.

His lightly accented English trailed over her like warm honey. The years he had spent in Spain had marked his speech, and she found it alluring.

"How quickly, my lord?" she asked, recalling his statement, the first he had made to her since his arrival that did not pertain to pleasantries.

Because of their betrothal, Mama had allowed the two of them an unchaperoned walk in the garden, but they were to remain within view of the drawing room windows. The part of the garden they had reached was decidedly not visible from where they had left her mother.

"Would you like to sit, Lady Catriona?" he asked solicitously.

His tone was so polite, it was difficult indeed to believe he was the same man who had prowled into the library three days before, upending her life as she knew it. She searched his gaze, wondering if it was wise to linger here with him, where Mama could not see them.

His lips quirked into a half-smile. "There is no need to fear me. I promise not to compromise you."

She drew back her shoulders. "I do not fear you, Lord Rayne. I merely did not wish to sully my gown."

It was a lie, of course. He did incite an inkling of something much like fear deep within her. Nor did she particularly care for the state of her gown. The bench looked clean enough.

He turned toward her, so they stood chest to chest, and he looked down at her, his stare scouring her face. He was solemn. "Are you certain? The look in your eyes tells me otherwise."

He saw too much. More than she wished for him to see. She looked away, severing the connection of their gazes, settling her eyes upon the hedges surrounding them with their twin walls of greenery.

"I am certain." But this, too, was a prevarication. He made her feel...unsettled. He was an intense man. "You did not answer my question, my lord. How quickly do you wish to wed?"

The notion of marrying him at all still left her with the same feeling she had experienced once when she had taken out a horse Monty had prohibited her from riding. She had known the beast was dangerous and unpredictable, but she had been too tempted by the forbidden. The ride had been exhilarating and terrifying all at once.

He studied her, his smile fading. "Three days hence."

Three days.

"Surely you jest, my lord," she sputtered, finding her tongue. "I require time to prepare."

"What do you have to prepare?" he asked dispassionately. "All I need is a bride."

How coolly he spoke of their marriage, as if she could be anyone.

As if any woman would do for the role of his countess. Though he had presented their nuptials to her in just such a bloodless manner, and she ought not to be surprised, she could not quite quell the spear of disappointment his detached manner produced in her.

"I need to prepare my trousseau," she said. *And myself.*

"You shall want for nothing as my wife."

"Nevertheless," she insisted, "three days is not sufficient time for me to plan."

He clenched his jaw, and even sullen, he was beautiful. "Five days."

"I am afraid that is still not long enough—"

"*Maldición*," he interrupted her. "A sennight. No more, Lady Catriona. I cannot linger here in England forever. The sooner we are wed, the sooner I will have an heir."

The sooner he would bed her, he meant.

She felt hot and cold at once. "I am sorry, Lord Rayne, but when I agreed to become your wife, you did not make it clear you were desirous of such a hasty wedding. If that is what you require, perhaps it is best for you to find another bride. Our betrothal has yet to be announced, so ending it will not cause any undue consequences for you."

His full lips compressed. "You are being stubborn, my lady. The marriage contract has already been made. You are mine."

Mine.

His pronouncement chased away the ice within her, leaving only fire in its wake. Languid, licking through her, settling in her belly, and lower still, between her thighs. What would belonging to this somber, fascinating man mean?

"I am not yours yet," she cautioned, chasing her unwanted reaction to him with common sense. "If we cannot agree upon marrying, I will not be yours at all."

He touched her, gently holding her chin captive with his gloved thumb and forefinger. "Do not fool yourself, *querida*. You have been mine from the moment you agreed to marry me."

She thought, for a breathtaking moment, he would kiss her. Catriona held still, refusing to wrest her gaze from his. She had only been kissed by one man, and the longing to dispel those kisses forever, to chase away their painful memory with the Earl of Rayne's sinful lips rushed over her.

"My lord," she forced herself to protest, but she was breathless. Helpless. Held captive by his intense regard. She *wanted* his kiss, and the knowledge frightened her more than anything else could.

But he did not bring his mouth to hers.

"A sennight is the longest I am willing to wait, Lady Catriona," he said, still holding her chin in a gentle grip.

Slowly, he released her, only to trail his touch down her throat until his fingertips rested over her pounding pulse.

The ache between her thighs intensified. His proximity was intoxicating. His scent drifted to her on a soft breeze. Bay with a hint of spice. She inhaled slowly, attempting to gather her wits, but he had her desperately flustered.

There was something about this man—not just his attractiveness—but something indefinable and yet so heady. No gentleman had ever looked at her as Rayne was now. Nor had he ever touched her thus—just the ghost of a caress, and yet enough to set her pulse pounding and turn the trepidation inside her into flame.

"A fortnight," she made herself argue, and only because her pride refused to allow him to see how greatly he affected her.

"What are you afraid of, my lady?" he asked, his baritone sending a delicious frisson through her. "Your heart beats so fast."

She reminded herself the only reason he wanted to marry her in haste was so he could also leave her in equal haste. "Perhaps I require time to adjust to the notion of becoming a wife."

His dark brows furrowed, his expression turning fierce. "Is it because of me? Because of who my mother was?"

Her heart gave a pang at the realization he must have been reviled before, by someone else. "No," she reassured him. "That is not the reason."

The true reason was the way he made her feel.

She was afraid of herself.

"Why, then?" Slowly, he removed his touch from her neck.

She mourned the loss. Her skin cried out for more. The connection had been so visceral, so profound, even though it had been just the faintest hint of a caress. But then, as she watched, his lips parted and he caught the tip of his glove in his teeth, removing it in an ungentlemanly gesture that somehow made her heart beat faster still.

"I have only just met you, Lord Rayne," she forced herself to explain. "If I am to be your wife, I should prefer some time to get more acquainted with you first."

He took his discarded glove in his left hand, and then his right hand—bare, swarthy, long-fingered, and enthralling as the rest of him—cupped her cheek. "There. The touch of flesh to flesh. Mine to yours, yours to mine."

"My lord," she meant to scold, but in truth, the words left her as a hushed murmur without any bite. "You ought not to flout propriety in such a bold fashion. If my mother were to see..."

"You would be ruined again," he finished for her, flashing her a smile. "By me, the man who intends to wed you. You need not worry, *querida*. Your mama was not even watching from the window when we first entered the garden. No one shall see."

His thumb traced her cheek.

She forgot to breathe.

Think, you fool, she urged herself. *Put an end to this.*

She clasped a hand over his, intending to remove it. But somehow, she could not force herself to do so. She liked the way his hand felt. Liked the sear of his caress. A rush of longing swept over her.

"What are you doing, Lord Rayne?" she asked him instead.

His smile deepened. "Acquainting us. Your body tells me one sennight is more than enough time, Lady Catriona."

She swallowed. "My lord, you grow too bold."

"I do not live by your society's rules."

"It is your society, too, is it not?" she dared to challenge. "You are half English. An earl."

"This is the land of my birth, and that is the title I inherited, neither of which can be helped." He paused. "But I do not belong here. I never did. I do not look like an *Inglés*, I do not think like one, and I do not act like one. My heart belongs in *España*. It is where I choose to make my home, in spite of what I lost there."

His admission was impassioned, and she could not help but to feel this was the first time he was being completely honest with her. That this was the first time she was witnessing the real Earl of Rayne. But even so, there was much of himself he held apart, refusing to reveal.

"What did you lose there?" she asked, her hand still covering his.

It was as if they were locked together, as if they were the only two people in the world. She looked into his eyes, and she saw the devastation there. The stark pain. She saw the man.

But that quickly, his countenance changed, growing closed. The glimpse she had been given died like an ember cast from a fire.

"Everything," he gritted.

His response left her with more questions than it answered.

What was *everything*? Was there someone he loved?

The knot inside her grew.

I will not expect fidelity from you. Nor should you expect it from me.

Or perhaps, he only wanted to marry an Englishwoman for the sake of his title, but he would return to Spain and the woman he loved. The notion ought not to send a pang straight to her heart, but it did.

She removed her hand from his and took a step back, putting some necessary distance between them. "And yet, you choose to return there," she said coolly. "Why?"

His eyes remained flat, his expression like a mask. "It is the home of my heart."

Of course he would not confide in her. Why had she imagined he would? More questions swarmed her. What manner of husband would he be? Whilst he intended to return to Spain as quickly as possible, she would be living with him. Sharing her body with him.

The foreboding increased.

"A fortnight," she repeated. "That is how much time I require, Lord Rayne."

His jaw tensed. "That is simply not possible. Seven days, Lady Catriona. No more."

And here was a discovery about both of them, they were equally stubborn.

They stared at each other, at an impasse.

He made no effort to move closer to her, and neither did she to him. The chasm between them seemed to grow by the moment.

"I know nothing of you," she said.

He raised a brow. "What do you wish to know, *querida*? Ask and I shall answer."

If only she believed that. "I already asked, and you refused."

He slapped his glove against his thigh. "*Maldición*, I do not want to speak of my past. Ask any other question, and the answer will be yours."

His acknowledgment did not stay the chill threatening to sweep through her, chasing away the heat. The questions she longed to pose most were the ones he would not satisfy.

She forced herself to offer another, which had also been eating at her. "Does it not bother you that I have been compromised?"

His gaze darkened. "I already told you, I do not observe the rules of your society. They mean less than nothing to me. I govern my life in the manner I choose."

Something else occurred to her then. "If you think to rush the marriage because I am ruined, my lord, you need not do so."

"I am not rushing the marriage," he denied swiftly. "One week is ample time. But please explain yourself, my lady. What sin is it you suppose me guilty of now?"

Her skin went hot. Her cheeks were bathed in flames. The place between her thighs ached anew. And even her breasts tingled.

If only she were not so painfully aware of him.

"Do you want to marry me in haste because you imagine me…experienced, Lord Rayne?" she asked, gathering her courage.

He considered her. "Whether or not you have shared another's bed before does not signify. All I ask is that you remain faithful to me until you bear my heir. We have discussed such matters already. Our discourse grows tired."

She did not like the bite of his tone, or the suggestion she was boring him.

How could he be so unaffected, so cool, when merely being in his presence had her in a tumult?

Another question arose within her, one which needed to be spoken. "Will you remain faithful to me in turn before I bear you heir?"

He stilled. "Would you like me to be, Lady Catriona?"

"Yes." Her own vehemence surprised her, but there was no calling it back once her admission had been made.

A small smile returned to his lips. This time, he moved, taking a step in her direction at last. The scent of him drifted to her once more. She could not quell her reaction regardless of how hard she tried.

"Then I shall be," he told her softly, stopping when there was once more an improper distance between them.

Scarcely any.

She could touch his chest.

Or his broad shoulders.

Or, *good heavens*, his lips.

She wanted to do all those things. To touch him everywhere.

"I will not be made a fool," she added, disconcerted anew by his proximity. "I have already been mocked and scorned enough."

"I will not bring shame upon you, *querida*." He touched her chin once more. "We are to be each other's allies in this war. I am not like the other man you knew, the one who hurt you."

She pressed her lips together. Perhaps he knew more of the scandal than he had previously suggested.

"How do you know I was hurt?" she asked.

"It is there, in your eyes." His gaze seemed to bore into hers, dark and consuming. "Do you want to tell me what happened?"

She shook her head. "No."

She did not want to relive her foolishness. The naïve ease with which she had been led to believe Shrewsbury's affections were true. That when he told her he loved her, he had meant those words.

"Did he force you?" There was a punishing edge in his voice now.

"No," she hastened to say. "He merely misled me. I was fool enough to believe his lies."

And she had vowed to herself then and there that she would never again believe the lies of another man. That she would never again find herself at another man's mercy. Yet, here she was, on the cusp of being at the mercy of the Earl of Rayne.

"I will never lie to you," Rayne said, "and that is a promise. Nor will I mislead you. I am being honest about what I want from you, just as I expect you to always be truthful with me. Allies, Lady Catriona."

"Allies," she repeated, liking the sound of the word.

A man with secrets.

Perhaps she would learn them one day.

He leaned toward her, dipping his head. She held her breath once more, supposing his mouth would claim hers. But it did not. His lips brushed over her cheek in a chaste kiss.

"One sennight," he repeated when he raised his head.

It was not a query but a statement.

With that one, tender gesture, he had eased her misgiving. "Seven days," she relented at last. "I will marry you seven days from today."

His smile was blinding. "Yes, you will, *querida*."

She thought of one more question. "What does that word mean, *querida*?"

Her knowledge of Spanish was frightfully sparse. The way he spoke it, in his mellifluous, accented voice, made it sound beautiful. Almost tender. But for all she knew, he was calling her a spoiled chit.

He sobered, releasing her chin before sliding his glove back on. "Dear. It means dear."

Rayne bowed, and with those final, parting words, he was gone from the garden, leaving her to watch his imposing form stride away. When he was out of sight, she allowed herself to settle quite soundly upon the bench she had derided for being dirty.

A sennight.

As she sat alone in the garden, staring into the blossoming clumps of Sweet William at her feet, she could not stop thinking of the sadness in his eyes. Nor could she stop thinking about the manner in which he had touched her. The velvet roughness of his bare skin upon hers.

One whole week.

It hardly seemed time enough to prepare herself.

But somehow, it also seemed like a lifetime away.

Chapter Four

ALESSANDRO HAD GONE mad.

That was the only reason he had agreed to wait seven days to make Lady Catriona Hamilton his.

Seven damned days.

What had he been thinking?

Madness was also the sole explanation for his presence at a *ball*. A boring society ball, being held by the Marquess of Searle and his marchioness, who was Alessandro's half-sister, Leonora. Balls were nothing but a pestilence. There was nothing more inane than lords and ladies preening about and dancing. He suppressed a shudder and sipped his ratafia, which was decidedly not strong enough to quell his rising temper.

For nothing, it seemed, could spur his ire quite like the sight of Lady Catriona dancing with another partner. He watched her on the dance floor beneath the glittering chandeliers, smiling as she elegantly made her way down the line before twirling about with a man Alessandro did not recognize. He did not like it. *Maldición*, not one bit.

Leonora appeared at his side suddenly, smiling and looking radiant. "Alessandro," she greeted him. "I am so pleased you decided to join us this evening."

He did his best not to glower at his sister, for she was beloved to him. "It was not of my own volition, I assure you."

Leonora's smile faded. "I know you dislike balls."

"I would prefer to have my eyes pecked out by ravens," he said.

In Spain, he had witnessed ravens feasting upon the bodies of soldiers. He would never forget the sight. Such a strange dichotomy between the man he was in Spain, the *guerrillero*, and the man he was supposed to be here in England, the Earl of Rayne. He scarcely even knew who he was any longer.

Both men, it was certain, were devils.

His sister blanched. "You must not say such things in society, Alessandro."

No, he must not. Far better to pretend there was not a war waging on the Continent, ravaging his home and his people.

Bitterness made his lips curl in a grim twist. "Forgive me, *hermanita*."

"Lady Catriona is beautiful," Leonora observed, "and quite kind and intelligent as well. I do approve of her."

He approved of her, too. His gaze flitted back to the dance floor where she was once more twirling with the blond-haired fool whose cravat had been tied into a ridiculously elaborate affair. He looked like a cake.

Alessandro scowled. "She was an expedient solution to my problem."

Leonora tapped his arm with her fan. "You need not be so grim. If you had not shot Monty—"

"Leonora," he interrupted her with a suffering sigh, still not able to tear his gaze from his future bride. "Need I remind you of the reason for the incident to which you refer?"

Leonora sighed at his side. "No, you do not."

Her husband, the Marquess of Searle, had been hell-bent on dueling with Alessandro because he believed him responsible for his imprisonment by enemy soldiers. Alessandro had been leading a band of guerrilla soldiers against the French when he had been charged with taking Searle behind enemy lines. The men he had chosen for the incredibly difficult operation had been overtaken by the French themselves. Searle had been taken captive and tortured.

But after falling in love with Leonora, Searle had decided to abandon his quest for vengeance. Only, he had failed to inform Alessandro himself, instead relying upon his second, the drunken reprobate Duke of Montrose. Montrose had stood in Searle's stead, and in the sotted state he had been in, waving a pistol, Alessandro had been given no choice but to be the first to inflict a wound.

"We will leave the past where it belongs," he told his sister tightly as the dance came to a conclusion and Lady Catriona dropped into a pretty curtsy. "Thank you for helping to ensure my betrothed an entrée back into society."

Though he wanted nothing to do with the pompous lords and ladies of the *beau monde*, Lady Catriona would be remaining in England as his countess. He had no wish for her to suffer in his absence, nor did he want his heir raised in ignominy. Knowing she would have a staunch ally in Leonora pleased him.

"It is my pleasure," Leonora said genuinely, for his sister had a heart as pure as an angel's. "I am so pleased you are deciding to wed, Alessandro. I have missed you these past few years."

Guilt pricked him. "I am not remaining in England for long, *hermanita*."

But still, his gaze would not leave the graceful figure of his future countess across the chamber. Lady Catriona had a partner for the next dance as well, it would seem. *Perdición*.

"But you will have a wife," Leonora protested, her voice steeped in disappointment.

"I will," he acknowledged, "but that will not alter my intentions."

He had not had the heart to tell her his stay in England was only predicated upon getting an heir on his wife. That he had every intention of returning to Spain—and the war—as soon as he could. He had known his sister would disapprove, and he wanted nothing more than to avoid exchanging words with her.

He loved Leonora far too much for that.

She was all he had left.

Until he had Lady Catriona.

But he did not have her yet. And she was currently smiling at yet another pallid, English fop. Resentment boiled within him. Old fears and feelings he had thought long banished returned.

"What do you mean having a wife will not alter your intentions?" Leonora demanded. "Alessandro! You cannot mean to return to Spain after you wed. Surely not."

He forced his gaze back to his sister at last, knowing the irritation inside him would only swell to a dangerous crescendo if he continued watching his betrothed dance with other gentlemen. Gentlemen who would have been only too pleased to cut her, given her damaged reputation, before she had become his betrothed, and Leonora had launched a campaign to see Lady Catriona's reputation restored.

The scandal tainting her was not gone completely, it was to be sure. But tonight was a beginning.

Leonora was frowning at him.

"Spain is where I belong, *hermanita*," he said simply. "You know this."

"You belong at your wife's side," she countered. "You cannot abandon her."

He gritted his teeth. "She will not be abandoned. She will want for nothing as my countess. Her pin money will be more than generous, and she will have you and my heir as her family."

"Your heir," Leonora repeated. "Alessandro, if you have a child, you must remain."

He had already had a child. But not even Leonora knew about Maria and Francisco.

He said nothing. On this, he would not be moved.

"Alessandro," his sister prodded, condemnation dripping from her voice.

"All will be well," he told her simply. "You shall see."

In truth, nothing would ever be well, including Alessandro, again. But there was no point in dwelling upon that which could not be changed. His wife and son were buried beneath the red, Spanish clay. He had died along with them. The shell that remained, bitter and broken, would carry on. War was all that was left for him.

He knew how to fight. How to kill.

He had become a monster, and he knew it.

He was spared from making further conversation by the appearance of Leonora's husband, the Marquess of Searle. They bowed to each other. The marquess's expression was wary. And well it should be, for the bastard had used Alessandro's sister as a pawn in his game of revenge. If it weren't for Leonora's gentle disposition and obvious love for Searle, Alessandro would have torn him limb from limb.

"Rayne," Searle bit out grimly.

"Searle," he returned with equal rancor.

"Husband and brother," Leonora said warningly. "I do expect you both to be courteous on my account. I know how very much the both of you love me."

"It is his only redeeming quality," Alessandro and Searle both muttered at the same time.

Disgruntled, he could do nothing but meet the equally peeved gaze of his former nemesis. Perhaps they were not as different as they believed. *Dios* knew they ought to have been friends, would have been allies, had not the campaign to land Searle behind enemy lines gone so hopelessly awry.

"Oh, how fortuitous," Leonora said then, giving them a quelling look before turning her attention in the direction of the dancers Alessandro had been doing his damnedest to ignore. "Here comes Lady Catriona now."

At last.

But his betrothed was not alone. Rather, she was accompanied by the sallow Englishman who had been her partner in the last dance. Alessandro stared at the man, who was either too stupid or too self-important to care he was inciting Alessandro's wrath.

Pleasantries were exchanged as Lady Catriona and the man—Viscount Dutton—added themselves to the circle. Alessandro ignored most of the drivel the man spouted.

Two days had passed since he had touched Catriona in the garden, and all he could think about was touching her again. The softness of her skin. The way she smelled sweetly of jasmine. How she had tipped her head back, her blue eyes melting into his. Or how her lips had parted, an invitation he resisted with only the greatest exertion of control.

He had almost kissed her.

He hungered for her lips beneath his, even now, when he had sworn to never again take another woman's mouth with his. It was shameful, the way his body had reacted to hers. He hated it, and yet he also craved it. He could not help but wonder what it would be like between them, whether or not their lovemaking would be as fiery as he believed it would be.

Her eyes flitted to his then, as the fool escorting her began a dialogue with Searle. The pink flush blossoming in her cheeks told him she was recalling their shared moment in the garden as well.

He suddenly wished they were back in the garden rather than surrounded by two hundred sets of curious eyes and gossiping tongues.

"You have come," Lady Catriona said to him softly so the others could not overhear. There was approval in her voice.

Had she doubted him?

He inclined his head. "I am always true to my word."

A small smile flirted with her lips. "I am glad to hear it, Lord Rayne."

The strangest urge hit him then, like a fist to the jaw landing out of nowhere.

He wanted to dance with her.

Perdición.

He had not danced at a society event since he had been obliged to obey his sire and forced to become a proper English lad. The only trouble with his father's plan was Alessandro was the half-Spanish son of his Spaniard wife, a woman who had been his mistress. Alessandro, with his dark hair, eyes, and skin, and scandalous mother, had been an outcast from the moment he had been born into this cursed world.

On principle, he had eschewed all English customs from the moment he had been old enough to have a choice. He had immersed himself in the land of his mother's birth, using the language she had taught him before her death instead of English. Why, then, would he wish to engage in niceties at a ball?

The faint strains of the next dance reached him.

A waltz.

He had danced it before, on the Continent. The English had considered it far too fast, but he supposed times were changing. And fortunate for him, too, for there was nothing he would like more in that moment than holding Lady Catriona in his arms. He had five more days to wait, after all.

He bowed to her. "Will you do me the honor, Lady Catriona?"

Her brows rose. "I thought you did not dance."

He cast a glare in the direction of his sister, who had obviously been responsible for relaying that salient bit of information to his future bride. But Leonora was chattering animatedly with the viscount and her husband, ignoring him. Just as well. At least the fop was occupied.

He returned his attention to his betrothed. "I do tonight. With you, my lady."

Only you, he wanted to say, but refrained. It would not do to make her think he harbored feelings for her. He most assuredly did not.

"Yes," she said.

They excused themselves from Leonora, Dutton, and Searle. Alessandro was acutely aware of the woman at his side as they made their way to assemble with the other dancers. The faint hint of jasmine sent a powerful rush of need surging straight through him.

But he was also feeling churlish. He had not liked suffering through watching her dance with a procession of fops. Their betrothal had only just been announced, and he wanted all the world to know she was his. It was to be expected that she dance with others at a ball, for not even a betrothed could claim each dance as his own, but the irritation mounting within him did not know that.

"You seem to be enjoying your return to society, my lady," he observed, not without a tinge of bitterness.

He wanted her to be accepted, of course he did. For he did not wish to cast his heir into the same abysmal position in which he had found himself—reviled for who his mother was and the way he looked.

"I am treading with care," she said, surprising him. "These are the very same people who turned their backs on me and called me ruined. Nothing has changed except your sister's very generous sponsorship and my future place as the Countess of Rayne."

They took up their positions on the dance floor.

"I find it difficult to believe becoming my countess would be a boon to anyone," he remarked. "The *beau monde* has scorned me all my life, and I, in turn, have despised them all with the burning hatred of a thousand suns."

The dance began in truth, and she was in his arms, their hands joined. Though it had been years since he had last danced, his body recalled with ease. Steps and twirls. Lady Catriona moving with him, one with his body felt...natural. *Right.* He was forced to realize the coldness which had been his constant companion since Maria's death had been warmed, just a small bit, by the woman he was about to wed.

He did not like it.

"Why not five thousand?" asked Lady Catriona as they made their way around the parquet floor, whirling in tandem with their fellow dancers.

"Five thousand?" he repeated, searching her upturned face for the answer he sought. Perhaps the twirling about was rendering her dizzy. He could not make sense of her query.

"Suns," she elaborated, giving him a teasing smile that made more warmth trickle into his cold heart. "Why only one thousand? Why not more?"

She was teasing him. He could not recall the last time anyone had spoken to him with levity. The last time anyone had *dared*.

Against his will, a laugh burst from him.

Perdición, laughter.

Mayhap the waltz was making *him* lightheaded.

"Perhaps five is a more apt number," he said.

"Why?" she queried next, her eyes almost violet tonight, glittering beneath the burning candles and against the demure lilac of her evening gown.

Though her décolletage was modest, the hint of creamy swells rising beneath the draped satin of her bodice was a temptation he had not missed. She was lovely, white beads studding her gown *à la militaire*, Vandyke lace adorning her hem. A sprig of white flowers accented her lustrous brown locks, which had been swept into a pile of curls on her crown, with a few tendrils framing her face.

"My lord," she prompted, undaunted by his silence. "You did not answer my question. Why do you despise society so much?"

"They did not accept my mother," he bit out, "and nor did they accept me."

His mother had been the Earl of Rayne's third wife, and he had met her in Spain, where she had become his mistress whilst he was still married to his second wife. After the second Lady Rayne's death, Alessandro's father had wed his mother. Though he had been born on the right side of the blanket, it had never mattered to society.

"Why did they not accept her?" Lady Catriona wanted to know.

Her voice was soft, and it would not carry to their fellow dancers, but this was hardly a dialogue he wished to have with her now. Or ever, for that matter.

"Why do you think, my lady?" he asked curtly instead. "You need only look at me for your answer."

"Oh, Rayne," she said, her gaze searching his. "I am sorry."

He did not want her pity. He wanted…

Cristo, he knew not what he wanted. He had meant to dance with her, to seize upon an excuse to touch her, to show the lords and ladies of the ballroom crush she was his. But now they were waltzing, and it was somehow far more intimate than he could have imagined. The last woman he had held in his arms thus had been Maria. Her brown eyes had been glistening, her head tipped back. She had been beautiful, as always.

For their honeymoon, they had traveled to Germany. And she had been happy, so happy. The recollection returned to him. Had it truly been years? Yes, it had, and he had been so young and foolish, incapable of understanding how fortunate he had been to have been given a small glimpse of paradise. Alessandro had thought his happiness would last forever, but instead, it had been devastatingly short. He had spent more years alive since her death than he had with her.

How could time have been so cruel, passing by so quickly without her?

Disgust sliced through him, mingling with despair. He had been so enamored with the notion of staking his claim upon Lady Catriona, he had failed to realize how greatly dancing with her would affect him. Perhaps he had been wrong about himself. He was a shell, but sometimes, even a shell could still feel.

"My lord," Lady Catriona pressed, her expression anxious as he mindlessly led them in another series of steps. "What is wrong? You look troubled."

Troubled did not begin to describe him.

He forced a smile to his lips. This cursed waltz could not end soon enough. "I am well, Lady Catriona."

Her lips compressed. "If you do not wish to tell me, I understand. I do hope, after our marriage, you may confide in me, my lord."

"There is nothing to confide," he bit out.

What would she have him tell her? How much he missed his wife and son? What it had felt like to hold his lifeless infant in his arms? To watch the woman who owned his heart die before him while he was helpless to do anything to save her?

Or would she like to know how he had been spending the time since his wife and son's death, throwing himself headlong into war? He was not even a soldier. Never had been. He was merely a man who believed in defending his home, in taking a stand for what was right.

But blood was on his hands. Staining his soul. His men had committed atrocities under his watch.

"I am sorry," Lady Catriona whispered to him.

Their ill-fated dance was coming to an end. Inside, Alessandro was beginning to unravel like a ball of string which had been poorly wound. "You need not feel sorry for me, my lady," he told her coolly. "If anyone is in need of compassion and sympathy, it is you, for I am to be your husband."

Her gaze was stoic, unwavering. "Until you leave."

"Until then," he agreed, wishing he knew why the words felt so damned hollow as he spoke them. They ought to have filled him with a sense of reassurance. The knowledge he would soon be back where he belonged.

Her smile was sad. "You could always choose to stay, Rayne."

Bitterness sifted through him. She did not understand. But he did not expect her to. No one ever had.

"Neither one of us would want that, Lady Catriona," he said, his tone harsh. "Trust me on this matter. I am no good for anyone, yourself included."

He could not bear to live in England. The longer he lingered, the more desperate he became to break free. Undoubtedly, it was part of the reason he was so eager to wed and bed her. The sooner he did both, the sooner he could find the relief of emptying his ballocks and returning to the land he loved. Returning to the war he was determined to win.

"You are hurting," she said. "I can see it in your eyes."

More than she could ever comprehend.

"Do not pretend to know my anguish." He gritted his teeth. "If you think your life was difficult, being exiled to Scotland by Montrose, you know nothing of life, my lady. I have spent the last few years living in a hell from which I cannot escape."

Her brow furrowed as they concluded a final turn. "In Spain? I do not understand. Why would you return there if it is a place which has caused you great misery?"

"Because it is my home," he answered. "Sometimes, my lady, we cannot undo the ties which bind us. I am inextricably bound to Spain."

"Is there someone else in Spain?" she pressed, determined to have her answers when they were not the answers she would want.

When they were not the answers he was prepared to give. But there was freedom in honesty, if not a cure.

"Yes," he admitted.

"A woman you love?"

He did not miss the stricken expression which had come over her lovely face. Nor did he allow it to keep him from telling her the truth. "*Sí*."

Of course, he loved Maria. He always would. Death did not extinguish love, for love was not a flame, quick to sputter out and dissipate. Rather, love was a hot coal, always ready to form a spark.

Lady Catriona missed a step.

With an arm snugly clasped about her waist, he held her steady, guiding her through the final strains of the waltz. He could have lied to her, of course. And perhaps he should have. He could have fed her any number of false stories. Pretty stories. Or he could have said nothing at all.

"This woman," Lady Catriona said haltingly, drawing his attention to the fullness of her lips once more. "Why do you not marry her if you are desirous of an heir and in love with her? Why marry me, Lord Rayne?"

The music ended. They bowed and curtsied to each other, and he offered her his arm. Strictly polite.

"I already did marry her, Lady Catriona," he revealed before he could think better of the admission.

He had not meant to make the disclosure. But once spoken, the words could not be retracted.

"I am afraid I do not understand, my lord." Lady Catriona was matching his lengthy strides despite their difference in height.

He ought to take pity on her. Slow his gait.

He did not. And nor did he blunt the starkness of his next words. She was going to marry him, after all. It was best she knew what manner of monster would soon be hers.

"I married her, Lady Catriona," he elaborated. "And she is dead."

Before he said anything else, he took his leave of her, abandoning her in the midst of the ball. From the periphery of his gaze, he saw Leonora moving toward him, but this, too, he ignored. He stalked from the ballroom, desperate for escape.

He did not stop until he reached his carriage.

"To The Duke's Bastard," he ordered his coachman.

He required whisky.

And oblivion.

Chapter Five

Catriona was attending her second ball in as many evenings. But unlike the previous night, her heart was heavy, weighed down by the revelation the Earl of Rayne had made to her the night before, prior to making an abrupt departure.

She had not seen or heard from him since.

Catriona watched the crush of dancers from her vantage point beside a potted palm. She had pled a headache for the last dance, seeking a refreshment and a respite instead. How had she forgotten how wearying the social whirl could be? She had not forced this many false smiles to her lips or dipped into as many curtsies in the last year as she had in the past two days.

Being back amidst the ranks of men and women who had considered her a social pariah before her engagement was discomfiting. Not one of her friends had sent her letters whilst she was in Scotland, save Hattie, which had forced Catriona into the uncomfortable realization that most of her friends had not, in fact, been friends at all.

Hattie was dancing with the Marquess of Lindsey, who looked undeniably smitten whenever his gaze settled upon her friend. Catriona felt a twinge of something uncomfortably akin to jealousy, knowing the man she was marrying in four days' time would never look at her with such frank adoration.

Because he loved another woman.

His first wife.

The knowledge Rayne had been married before still shocked her. He had never previously made mention of such an important fact, though she supposed he would not have. The earl had made it quite clear what he expected of her, and their marriage would not involve tender sentiments or romance. He intended to share as little of himself with her as possible before returning to Spain.

Either way, her waltz with Rayne had left her shaken. Following his abrupt departure, she had been left to agonize over the stark pain she had seen in his expression before he had stalked away from her. He must have loved his wife deeply. Catriona was filled with questions.

When had he been married? When had his wife died? Why? How? She could only suppose he had not had any children, for he had not mentioned them to her. And he was quite explicit in his need for an heir. All through the remainder of the ball, and then through the night as she had been unable to fall asleep, questions had continued to assail her.

With the morning light, they had not stopped. They were teeming inside her now, along with a riot of emotions she did not dare make sense of. On a sigh, Catriona looked about the ballroom for her mother, who was deeply engaged in a discussion with her bosom bow, Lady Creeley. Although Monty had escorted them to the ball, he was nowhere to be seen. Catriona had a suspicion he had already fled in favor of his club as he was wont to do, leaving the carriage behind and hiring a hack to take him to one of his favorite dens of iniquity.

On account of all the guests and the candles, not to mention the general warmth of the air this evening, the ballroom was stifling. She fanned herself, but it did precious little to cool her. Two sets of doors led to the balcony, and Catriona could not resist the temptation to seek escape there.

Just a moment of restorative air to clear her thoughts and chase the moroseness from her, she thought as she made her way there. With the guests distracted from all the festivities within, she found the balcony blessedly empty. She settled her hands upon the stone balustrade and tipped her head back to look at the sky. A few stars twinkled down at her, nestled amongst the velvety darkness of the night.

She took a deep breath, telling herself it hardly mattered if the Earl of Rayne had been married before. That it was of no import whatsoever that he had loved his wife. That his lack of appearance this evening was meaningless and entirely unrelated to the confusing waltz they had shared at the Marquess and Marchioness of Searle's ball.

"Lady Catriona."

The low voice at her back—familiar and unwanted—stiffened her spine. She spun about to face the Marquess of Shrewsbury. *Dear heavens*, she had somehow failed to realize he was in attendance this evening. Had she known he would be present, she would never have come. She had not seen him since the awful night he had ruined her with a kiss and a wager.

Even in the moonlight, he was still as handsome as she remembered. Tall, lean, and elegant. But seeing him now, she felt none of the yearning she had once felt. None of the silly fluttering in her belly that had led her to allow him to lure her into a chamber and kiss her.

Instead, she felt only anger.

"I have nothing to say to you, my lord," she told him coldly. "If you will excuse me, I must return to the ball before I am missed and before you lead me into another scandal."

He stepped in front of her, blocking her, though he made no effort to touch her. "Wait, my lady. Please. I would ask for a minute of your time. Nothing more."

"You do not deserve a *moment* of my time." The resentment she still harbored over the callous way he had treated her boiled, making her hands tremble. "You have already done enough damage to my reputation. I will not allow you the opportunity to do more."

"I want to apologize, Lady Catriona," he startled her by saying.

It was not what she had expected, and she told herself that was the reason she lingered rather than fleeing when she should have.

She considered him. "You are far too late in offering your contrition, Lord Shrewsbury, if indeed you have any."

Which she doubted.

This was the man who courted her and wooed her, who sent her posies and took her driving, who danced with her and sought her out at every society function before arranging for a group of others to witness him kissing her. He had known she would be ruined. And he had not cared.

She could still recall the expression on his face after they were caught.

Triumph.

It had only been the next morning that she had discovered the extent of his betrayal after Monty had informed her of the wager. The bet had not been common knowledge until Shrewsbury had claimed his winnings.

And Catriona had been sent to Scotland. Monty had given her a choice: wed Shrewsbury or be banished. She had chosen banishment.

"I tried to call on you a number of times," the marquess persisted. "I wanted to explain."

"There is no explanation you have which will ameliorate your actions," she told him, and she had never meant words more. "Your actions spoke well enough for you."

"I accepted the wager before I knew you," he said, stepping closer to her.

Once, she would have relished his nearness. She would have longed for the slant of his lips over hers. No longer.

"I do not care to hear your reasons," she snapped, aware the longer she lingered here with him, the greater their chances of being caught once more.

And she had only begun to reclaim her life. She could ill afford another scandal. Not even becoming the Countess of Rayne would help her if she was once more ruined by the Marquess of Shrewsbury, to say nothing of what her betrothed would do. Or Monty.

"I offered for you," Shrewsbury continued, ignoring her protestations. "I would have been happy to make you my marchioness. Montrose refused my suit, and he would not allow me to see you. I…I never meant for you to be hurt, Lady Catriona. I beg you to believe me."

She did not know what to believe.

"I refused your suit myself," she told him. "I would sooner be ruined than to become the wife of a man who would so callously betray me. You arranged for witnesses. You intended for me to be ruined."

"After the bet had begun, I realized I wanted you as my wife." He paused, reaching out and taking her hands in his. "I still do, Lady Catriona. I know you are betrothed to Rayne now, but it is not too late for us. You can cry off and marry me instead."

She could not have been more shocked if he had leapt from the balcony before her.

She tried to tug her hands free, but he held fast. "Lord Shrewsbury, I have no intention of calling off my engagement. You are forgetting that I do not want to marry you, regardless of the feelings you claim to have."

"I do not claim," he insisted. "I know. I am in love with you, Lady Catriona. You hold my heart in your hands."

"You are too late in making such confessions." His protestations of feelings for her left her oddly unmoved. Whatever his motivations, he had betrayed her. She could not forgive a man so willing to use her for his own gain. Some hurts simply ran too deep to be dispelled.

"I tried to tell you before," Shrewsbury said. "I made every effort to see you, and after you left London, I sent you letters."

She had returned them all, unopened.

"Because I did not care to hear what you had to say, my lord," she told him resolutely. "If you will excuse me, I must return to the ball before my absence is noted. Thanks to you, I am already treading upon the thinnest ice in society."

But his grip on her hands only tightened.

"My lady—"

"I recommend you release my betrothed," interrupted a deep, accented baritone.

Catriona turned to find the familiar silhouette of the earl prowling toward them. Relief warred with misgiving at his appearance. Shrewsbury still held her hands in his, and the scene must look damning. She could only wonder how long Rayne had been in the shadows, how much of her dialogue with the marquess he had overheard.

"Unless you would like to name your second and meet me at dawn?" Rayne persisted, his voice laced with danger.

Shrewsbury dropped her hands as if they had been fashioned of flame, but instead of fleeing the balcony as she had supposed he might, he turned to face the earl.

"I am an excellent marksman, Rayne," the marquess said. "If you wish to take such a foolish risk, I welcome it, especially since your demise will leave Lady Catriona free once more."

Catriona inserted herself between the two men, facing Rayne with Shrewsbury at her back. "Please, my lords, stop this nonsense. It ill becomes the both of you. Bloodshed and further scandal will not solve anything."

Rayne's dark eyes glittered. "He was touching you."

"My hands, nothing more," she promised. "I was leaving the balcony when you arrived, my lord. Nothing untoward occurred, nor would it have, I assure you."

"You are damned right it will not," Rayne growled. "If this puppy so much as looks in your direction again, I will gut him."

"How dare you?" Shrewsbury cried out at her back. "I ought to challenge *you* to a duel instead for such an insult."

Rayne smiled, but there was no mirth or levity, only menace. "Be my guest, *bellaco*. I will not challenge you to pistols, but swords, and then I will make good on my word to slit you from your navel to your chin. No one dishonors my family. Do you understand? *No one.*"

Catriona shuddered at the suppressed rage in the earl's voice before making the disquieting realization he had just referred to her as his family. "Rayne," she said pleadingly. "I do not want violence. Please."

Rayne's lips tightened, and his shoulders were still tensed, as if he were a man about to go to battle. "You are a *cobarde*, a coward, to use a woman to get what you want and then expect her to fall upon you with gratitude. Do not dare to ever so much as look in her direction again."

"I will not be threatened by you," Shrewsbury said.

A change came over Rayne then. Catriona could not define it, for it was so subtle, someone less observant may have missed the manner in which his shoulders went back, the sudden stillness with which he held himself. But she noticed, and a new kind of fear crept into her heart.

It occurred to her she did not know what he was capable of any more than she had known what Shrewsbury would do. And yet, she was entrusting herself to him. To this stranger who was at times smoldering, at times cold. This man whose heart belonged to a dead woman. This man who intended to wed her, bed her, and leave her.

"Go inside now, Lady Catriona," Rayne ordered her. "I will find you within."

She did not want to leave. Misgiving held her in place. She feared what the two men would do to each other. "Lord Rayne, I do not think it wise for the two of you to remain here alone. Let us all return to the ball separately and forget this discourse ever happened."

"Go," Rayne said, and though his tone was gentle, it was edged in stone.

He would not bend.

There would be no forgetting.

She swallowed down a knot of dread. Both men had left her with little choice. First, Shrewsbury had kept her on the balcony far too long, increasing the odds of discovery. Now, Rayne had come as well, as distant, cold, and angry as he had ever been. The longer she lingered, the sooner her mother would look for her, the greater the chances of someone else seeking the cooler air of the outdoors.

"Promise me you will not hurt him," she begged.

A grim smile twisted the earl's lips. "Such pretty concern for the man who ruined you. Your heart is too good, my lady. But never fear. I have no intention of maiming this *bellaco* unless he forces me to. You must return to the ball before you are missed."

Still filled with a grim sense of foreboding, she curtsied, the formality ingrained in her, and left the men behind. Slipping back into the ball, she searched for a friendly face and found Hattie near the potted palm she had abandoned not long before. She made her way through the revelers, all too aware of the conversation between the earl and the marquess she had left. What would Rayne do? What would Shrewsbury say?

By the time she reached Hattie's side, her inner misery must have been written all over her face, for her friend took one look at her and frowned.

"What is the matter, dearest? You look as if you saw a ghost," Hattie said.

In a way, she had.

A ghost from her past meeting the grim wraith of her future.

"Shrewsbury and Rayne are on the balcony," she said, biting her lip.

Hattie's brows shot up. "Shrewsbury and the earl?"

She nodded miserably. "I fear they are going to either break into a bout of fisticuffs or challenge each other to a duel."

"Oh dear." Hattie sighed. "That is rather unfortunate, but if anyone deserves to be shot, it is the Marquess of Shrewsbury."

Unfortunate did not begin to adequately express the situation.

"Shrewsbury asked me to cry off my betrothal to Rayne," she revealed. "Rayne found us. He was most displeased."

"How dare Shrewsbury?" Hattie fumed on her behalf. "Has he not already done enough damage? If Rayne does not plant him a facer, I will be more than happy to do so on your behalf."

The notion of Hattie walloping the Marquess of Shrewsbury spurred a reluctant smile to Catriona's lips. Her beloved friend's ceaseless championing of her was heartening, though it did little to put her mind at ease. Her eyes remained upon the doors to the balcony until at last, Rayne stalked back into the ballroom. His expression was thunderous.

There was so much about the earl she did not know. He was an enigma. A mystery.

And soon, he would be her husband.

Chapter Six

ALESSANDRO ATE HIS turbot with lobster sauce and pretended to listen to the Marquess of Searle.

Lady Catriona was seated across from him, but she may as well have been an ocean away. Just as well, for if she were nearer in proximity, he would be tempted to touch her. And if he touched her, he would not be able to control himself.

As it was, he was already a wild, ravening beast, hungering for her in a way that perplexed him. Three days until she was his.

Purgatorio.

"Where shall you and Lady Catriona go after the wedding?" Leonora asked, stealing Alessandro's attention away.

Dinner tonight was, blessedly, a small affair, attended by only family and close friends. Leonora, her mother, Searle—who he reluctantly counted as family—Lady Catriona, her mother, Montrose, and the Honorable Miss Harriet Lethbridge and her mother. Miss Lethbridge was a friend of his betrothed's who had the good sense to scowl at Montrose as if he were lower than a louse.

Which he was.

"We will honeymoon in Wiltshire," Alessandro told his sister.

Although this was to be a marriage of convenience, he had not been to his country seat in several years. Since he was to be landlocked in England until Lady Catriona was with child, it stood to reason he may as well see Marchmont himself rather than continuing to rely on the reports of his steward. Especially since Searle had warned him his steward had been badly mismanaging the estate.

"How lovely that shall be," Leonora said, giving him a look of sisterly approval.

"I deemed it best to ascertain the state of things myself before I return to Spain," he said, needing to undercut any hopes his sister harbored that he had changed his mind.

It would not do for either Leonora or Lady Catriona to imagine he had any intention to remain in England. The approval in his sister's countenance was replaced by a frown. "I do hope you shall change your mind about Spain. You are needed here."

He inclined his head and proceeded to continue eating his fish. There was nothing he could say which would please his sister, and he was not going to change his mind. Wedding Lady Catriona would not alter the course of his future.

After an awkward pause, Montrose began a conversation about the weather.

"I confess, I am shocked you have been outdoors enough of late to realize there is weather at all," Miss Lethbridge told the duke tartly, her condemnation almost palpable.

Montrose sent Miss Lethbridge a quelling look. "Of course I have been outdoors, m'dear. How else is one to travel to amusements?"

The sly emphasis in the duke's voice as he said the word *amusements* left no question as to what he referred to. Even as rusty as Alessandro's manners were after being gone so long from English shores, he knew better than to allude to Cyprians at the dinner table. Either Montrose had never learned how to behave as a proper gentleman, he was too soused to care, or he was intentionally nettling Miss Lethbridge.

The lady in question's eyes narrowed to an undisguised glare. "How excellent to hear you have been enjoying your *amusements*, Your Grace. I am quite gratified on your behalf."

In truth, Miss Lethbridge sounded rather the opposite.

Alessandro was grateful for the distraction of the boorish Montrose and his betrothed's prickly friend. Far better to watch the consternation of others than to wallow in his own.

And of his own, he had plenty.

The evening before, he had almost courted scandal by beating the Marquess of Shrewsbury to a pulp for her. No man had ever deserved a drubbing more. Alessandro had arrived late to the ball, having spent the previous evening determined to find the bottom of a bottle of whisky.

He had watched from afar as she slipped onto the balcony. And watched as a few moments later, the marquess had followed her. His legs had taken him to her, eating up the distance. But part of him had been curious enough to linger in the shadows and eavesdrop upon their exchange.

At first, he had not realized Shrewsbury was the man responsible for compromising Lady Catriona. But it had become quickly, appallingly apparent to him just who the man was.

The daring of the *bastardo*, ruining a woman over a wager and then expecting her to wed him. Lady Catriona should have clubbed the blighter. An answering spark of jealousy had been lit within him. Jealousy he had no right to feel, let alone act upon. Though she was his, their relationship was to be temporary in nature. Just as he wanted it to be. And there had been another instinct, rising like a tide, the urge to feel her lips beneath his. To kiss away her every memory of the arrogant lord who had seduced and betrayed her.

He still did not know the details of his future bride's ruination. If Shrewsbury had taken her innocence, all in the name of a wager…

Alessandro would duel him after all. He would not rest until the *bellaco* was as dead as any enemy soldier he had faced in Spain.

The next course arrived, glazed Westmoreland ham and greens. Like every other part of society, Alessandro had forgotten how tedious a dinner and all its courses could be. Soups, removes, entrées, entremets, an endless procession of food and falsely polite conversation, all drowned in wine.

Speaking of which, he needed more. Such dullness was not to be borne without the gentle warmth of incipient inebriation. He quaffed the remainder of his wine, and a footman appeared at his elbow to refill his glass.

Say what you might of Searle, the fellow had efficient domestics.

Alessandro noted then that Lady Catriona was scarcely touching the food on her plate. His gaze lifted to her lovely face. Their stares meshed for a brief moment, and the connection hit him with the force of a blow to the midsection. Already, he felt responsible for this woman.

He wanted to be the man who claimed her, and the man who shielded her from every hurt. He wanted to be the man who made her forget whatever it was that had happened with Shrewsbury.

But how could this be when he was also the man who would leave her?

"Wiltshire," she said softly.

"It is my country seat," he offered as it occurred to him he had not discussed a honeymoon with her. "You are displeased at the notion, my lady?"

"No." A smile pulled at her lips.

The urge to taste them anew hit him, shocking him. Would they be as soft as they looked? Would they part for him? Move in response against his? Surely it was the wine he had consumed which led him to wonder.

He drank some more. "Marchmont was originally built in the sixteenth century, though my father employed an architect to modernize it."

"I should like to see it," she surprised him by saying, and still her gaze lingered upon him, searching.

Whatever she was looking for, he did not possess it.

"See it you shall." He poured a bit more wine down his throat. *Cristo*, he was turning into Montrose. He returned his wine glass to the snowy table linen with a grimace. "We will stay a month's time. Perhaps longer, depending upon the state of affairs."

And how quickly she was breeding.

But he did not say that.

"How very agreeable, Lord Rayne," said the dowager Duchess of Montrose then.

Since the early stages of his courtship with Lady Catriona—namely the three occasions upon which she refused to see him—the dowager had spoken few words to him. Her expression now was one of intense relief.

He could not blame her, for at least one of her erstwhile offspring would be well settled now. As for the other…the Duke of Debauchery was decidedly not Alessandro's problem.

"Lord Rayne is a most agreeable fellow," Searle added to the conversation then, his tone grim as Charlotte of apples with apricot was brought round.

Alessandro gritted his teeth at the subtle jibe. Perhaps he and his brother-in-law would never achieve a true peace. But as long as the marquess kept Leonora happy, Alessandro was willing to accept every veiled insult aimed in his direction.

He deserved them all, and worse.

He ate the rest of the meal in self-imposed silence.

AFTER DINNER, CATRIONA and the other ladies settled in the drawing room. Hattie and the Marchioness of Searle flanked her whilst her mother, the dowager Countess of Rayne, and Hattie's mother chatted to each other quietly on the other side of the chamber.

"I cannot believe you shall be gone an entire month," Hattie said. "I will miss you, my dearest. What shall I do in your absence?"

"Perhaps you can browbeat Monty," Catriona suggested impishly, relieved for the opportunity to think of something lighter.

"He requires a beating with more than just my brows," Hattie grumbled, *sotto voce* so the mothers would not overhear.

"I agree," the Marchioness of Searle chimed in. "I love Monty like a brother, but someone needs to take him in hand. A wife, perhaps."

Catriona did not miss the way Hattie stiffened at the mentioning of Monty taking a duchess. *Interesting.*

"Marriage would likely do him good," Catriona added, watching her friend closely. "Monty is too much like our father, I fear. But with a duchess at his side, preferably one who is intelligent and strong, the sort of lady who is unwilling to allow him to run roughshod over her, perhaps he could change."

Hattie let out a dismissive puff of air. "Forgive me, dearest friend, but the Duke of Montrose will no sooner change his roguish ways than the sky shall trade places with the earth."

"Your opinion of poor Monty is hopelessly grim," she observed.

Perhaps too grim. Her friend was protesting just a bit too much.

"Love can change a man," the Marchioness of Searle said, her bright gaze pinned upon Catriona. "Marriage to the right woman can exert all manner of transformation."

Catriona thought of the Earl of Rayne and how impenetrable he was, how confusing. He was more intense than any gentleman she had ever known, and yet there was some part of her that could not deny she longed to be the right woman for him.

But of course, theirs was not to be a true marriage. It was to be a marriage of convenience, nothing more. Moreover, he had already found that woman and lost her. She thought then of his first wife, and sadness blossomed inside her, replacing the trepidation.

"Will you tell me about the previous Lady Rayne?" she asked the marchioness before she could stifle the impulse.

Knowing more about her predecessor was unnecessary, but she was curious all the same. What kind of woman had stolen the inscrutable Rayne's heart?

The Marchioness of Searle frowned at her. "Rayne's mother, you mean? I know little of her, aside from her position as my father's third wife. Rayne tells me she was a kind woman, loving hearted and sweet. She taught him to speak Spanish before he learned English, much to the dismay of our father."

That would explain the lingering hint of an accent in the earl's speech.

But it did not explain anything of the wife Rayne had loved.

Perhaps Lady Searle did not wish to speak of an upsetting subject.

Guilt skewered her. "Forgive me, my lady. I ought not to have mentioned Rayne's first wife. It was not my place to ask."

"Rayne's first wife?" Lady Searle was looking at her as if she had just announced she was taking a walk to the moon.

"Yes," Catriona said hesitantly. "He mentioned her to me previously, and he indicated theirs was a love match. I did not wish to pry with him, but I do admit to wondering what sort of woman she was, for him to have loved her so deeply."

"Rayne told you he was married?" the marchioness asked.

"Yes." Confusion filtered through her. Lady Searle seemed genuinely perplexed. "Did you not know her, my lady?"

"I did not know *of* her," Lady Searle revealed. "Rayne is terribly quiet about his life in Spain. I... He never mentioned a wife. I had no idea he had wed."

Catriona did not know precisely what to make of such a revelation.

The earl's words returned to her, the bitterness in his voice, the hollowness in his stare, the desolation on his countenance. The raw emotion haunted her still. *I married her, Lady Catriona. And she is dead.*

Her heart ached for him, even as she remained wary of him.

Terribly nervous at the prospect of wedding him.

"When did he tell you, Lady Catriona?" Lady Searle asked.

"At your ball," she answered, "just before he left. I am sorry, my lady, to foist such news upon you. I would never have mentioned it to you—indeed, I ought not to have, and I know it. What Rayne's first wife was like is no business of mine. But you are his sister, and I thought perhaps you might give me some insight, some hope of understanding him."

"That explains the hasty manner in which he departed," said the marchioness, her tone careful. "I had wondered. Rayne does not prefer society, and I thought it merely the need to escape that prompted him."

"Dear heavens," Hattie said, echoing Catriona's sentiments exactly. "What a muddle."

"A muddle of my brother's making." Lady Searle's expression was grim.

"And mine," Catriona added, feeling miserable for upsetting her hostess. "Lord Rayne did not indicate his marriage was a secret. I am so very sorry, my lady."

"I am grateful he told you, Lady Catriona," the marchioness said. "Rayne is a law unto himself. He refuses to be bound by propriety and rules, and he has always felt more at home abroad than he ever has here. If he is already opening up to you, divulging facets of his life he has withheld from others, it is a good sign indeed. He is not an easy man to know."

She sighed, for it seemed to her as if Lady Searle was placing a great deal of hope upon Catriona's impending nuptials with Rayne. "I wish I had your confidence, my lady."

"Only think of this," Hattie said, "you have a far better chance of taming Rayne than anyone has of bringing your disreputable brother to heel."

She wondered if that were true.

Her chance seemed small.

And then she wondered if she *wanted* to tame Rayne. If he returned to Spain, she would have her freedom, after all. She would have money, independence, and clout. Everything she needed.

Except for him, she thought. *You would not have the Earl of Rayne.*

Then again, very likely no mere mortal ever could.

Chapter Seven

One day until she was his.

In the morning, he would take his second wife.

He had not seen Lady Catriona since dinner several nights before. Some distance between them had been necessary, and his desire to suffer through one more dinner or yet another ball had waned to infinitesimal. In short, he could not bear it. Alessandro had exhausted the art of nicety.

Instead, he was borrowing a page from the Duke of Montrose and busying himself with drinking. He was nicely in his cups now, half a bottle of brandy already consumed to keep him from his thoughts.

Thoughts of Maria.

He held the bottle to his lips and drank. Why bother with a glass or even a decanter when the direct source was so much more efficient?

Thoughts of Francisco.

Another sip of brandy. This one burned all the way to his gut.

Thoughts of a violet-eyed minx who made him feel too much. The woman who would become his wife in less than twelve hours.

A knock sounded at the library door. *Maldición*. Had he not told the butler he had no wish to be disturbed this evening?

"*Vete*," he called. *Go away.* Speaking to his staff in Spanish left them wearing aggrieved expressions as they attempted to decipher what he had said.

"My lord," came the long-suffering voice of his butler. "You have a visitor."

Alessandro raised the bottle back to his lips, taking another swig. "*Al diablo con el.*"

"Ahem." The butler cleared his throat. "Are you certain that you wish me to convey to your future countess she ought to go to the devil?"

Mierda.

Either he was more sotted than he thought, or his butler had been studying the Spanish language, and his betrothed was paying him a call at ten o'clock in the evening. He placed the bottle upon a table alongside a book he had been trying—and failing—to read before he had settled for the distraction of spirits instead.

And then he rose. "You are certain it is my future countess?" he asked.

"May I open the door, sir?"

He sighed, then stalked across the room and yanked open the portal himself. "Where is she?"

"In the guest parlor, my lord," his butler said, his countenance stoic and unruffled as ever.

"Is she alone?" he demanded next, despite suspecting he already knew the answer.

"Yes, my lord."

What in the hell did she think she was doing, venturing out in the night—alone, no less—one day before their wedding? Had she no respect for herself? No inkling of how much unnecessary danger she was placing herself in?

Moreover, why had she come?

What could possibly be the reason?

He wanted answers, *maldición*, and he wanted them now.

But every thought churning through his brandy-soaked mind fled when he crossed the threshold of the parlor and saw Lady Catriona standing there with a tear-stained face. Something seized inside his chest. He had never before seen her upset, and the stricken expression on her face was enough to make fear clamp down on him, along with a sudden rush of protectiveness.

"Lady Catriona," he said, closing the distance between them. "What is wrong?"

"Monty," she said on a sob, hurtling herself into his chest as if it were where she belonged.

Dios, what had the scapegrace done now?

"Montrose?" His arms came around her, which felt alarmingly natural.

Right, taunted a voice within him.

Wrong, he corrected. What he felt for her was the instinctive reaction of a male body to a feminine body pressed against it. Their union was temporary in nature. He would not sully Maria's memory by fooling himself into thinking he possessed tender feelings for a woman he scarcely knew.

Lady Catriona nodded against his chest, sobbing enough to saturate the fine lawn of his shirt. He was not wearing a cravat, coat, or waistcoat, leaving precious few layers to separate them. "There was an accident."

Cristo. Montrose was not *dead*, was he?

"What sort of accident, *querida*?" His hand traveled up and down her spine in soothing strokes.

"He was racing Viscount Torrington," she explained, her breath catching on another wave of sobs. "They were both in their cups, and they settled upon some foolish wager."

"Racing?" What a pair of addle pates. He may be halfway sotted himself, but he had nowhere to go but his bedchamber. And if he knew Montrose, the racing would have been breakneck. "Is Montrose…"

"He is injured, Rayne," she said, winding her arms around his waist. "But Hattie's brother, Lord Torrington is far worse. H-he may not live."

The depth of Lady Catriona's distress made sense now. He frowned, a surge of anger coursing through him at Montrose's recklessness. Would the fool's stupidity know no end?

Her presence at his home, however, remained a mystery.

"When did this happen, my lady?" he asked, still smoothing his hand over her back in gentle motions.

"A-a few hours ago, but he and Torrington were brought to our home just now, and both are in a bad way," she said on a fresh wave of sobs. "I am so s-sorry to intrude. Mama is away for the evening, and I have sent for doctors, b-but I am frightened. I did not know where else to go."

Dios. It made sense now. Lady Catriona was on her own, playing nursemaid to two drunken, broken lords. And she had come to him for aid. The knowledge sent a course of warmth through his chest that not even the urgency of the circumstances could chase.

She needed him.

"I will accompany you," he told her without hesitation. "How did you come to be here?"

"I b-brought my own carriage. My lady's maid attended me, and she is awaiting me within it." She tipped her head back. "Oh, Rayne. I am so frightened for Monty and for Hattie's brother. If anything should happen to them…"

It would be deserved, he thought grimly. Any man who would go racing whilst thoroughly in his cups was only tempting the devil.

But he did not dare say as much to the distraught woman in his arms.

Instead, he cupped her face, the best way he could imagine comforting her. Her cheek was silken and wet, and the jolt that skipped up his arm, past his elbow at the contact of his skin upon hers was undeniable. "Nothing will happen. And if it should, you have me now, Lady Catriona. I will make certain you are taken care of."

He had been about to say he would make certain she was not alone, but it was not a promise he could keep. For one day, he reminded himself sternly, he must leave her. That day, however, had not yet come.

"Thank you, Rayne." The smile she gave him was tremulous.

But then she shocked him by turning her head and pressing a kiss to the center of his palm. An unwanted arrow of heat stole through him. Her gesture had been innocent and unthinking. It meant nothing.

"You need not thank me, *querida*," he said grimly, for she was his duty. He was obligated to protect her. Or, at least, she would be his duty tomorrow.

Tomorrow.

The wedding.

Cristo, if he had to wait to marry her, he would thrash Montrose in spite of his injuries.

"Allow me to retrieve my coat, and I will meet you at the door," he said, forcing himself to release her and take a step back.

She nodded, biting her lip, looking so forlorn, the place in his heart where he had been certain only a dried husk remained, ached. She hugged herself. "As you wish, my lord."

To hell with it.

Instead of striding away from her, he took a step forward. The subtle hint of jasmine, already familiar, hit him. He clasped her hand in his. "Forget the coat. I do not want to leave your side."

The words left him before he could contemplate the wisdom of their utterance.

But they were the truth.

Clearly, he ought to have finished the other half of the brandy bottle.

CATRIONA WAS PACING in the corridor outside Monty's bedchamber when the door opened and Rayne emerged. His dark hair was disheveled, as if he had been running his fingers through it, and his lawn shirt was rumpled. He looked disreputable *sans* cravat and waistcoat, but she had never seen a more welcome sight.

"How is Monty?" she asked on a rush, feeling as if she had spent the last hour holding her breath.

"Montrose is settling now with the aid of some laudanum," Rayne said. "It was fortunate I came. Dr. Croydon required my aid in holding him down to set the bone. He has a broken ankle, and he is an abysmal patient, but that appears to be the worst of it."

Relief washed over her, along with gratitude. "Thank you, my lord. I am indebted to you."

"Correction, *querida*," he said in his beautifully accented voice. "*Montrose* is indebted to me. This is the second time I have been present at his sickbed. Fortunately, this time, I am not the man responsible for his injuries. The fool himself is. Although, one could certainly argue he was responsible for his own injuries when I shot him as well."

She shuddered at the recollection of Monty's attempt to duel the earl on behalf of the Marquess of Searle. Catriona had been in Scotland at the time, and she had only received word through a letter from Hattie.

At least her brother would once again survive a scrape. She could only pray the same could be said for Hattie's brother. Worry churned through her. Torrington's own physician had been sent to aid him, and he had yet to emerge from the guest chamber where the viscount had been carried.

"I am relieved if Monty shall recover," she said to Rayne then. "But I fear for Torrington."

Rayne's countenance remained stern. "From what I understand, Torrington suffered a blow to the head. It may be days until the full extent of his injuries are revealed."

Hattie would be beside herself with worry when she discovered what her n'er-do-well brother had been about this evening. She frowned. "Perhaps there is something the doctor needs."

"The servants are more than capable of providing the physician with anything he should require," Rayne said. "Come, my lady. You are overwrought. Let us find a place to sit."

"Very well." Sitting sounded excellent. After all the pacing she had done in her slippers this evening, her feet were sore. Worry had left her exhausted.

She allowed Rayne to escort her down to the salon on the floor below. He directed a maid to bring them tea and biscuits, then led her to a divan. The door to the room remained open—she supposed out of deference to her reputation. Noting it, she could not stifle the almost wild peal of laughter that fled her.

"My lady?" Rayne had seated himself opposite her. "Are you well?"

"I expect not." It was either laugh or cry, it seemed. The madness of the last few weeks was finally settling in. "Forgive me, Rayne. It is merely the door being left open, as if I have a shred of reputation left to fret over."

He frowned. "I take your reputation seriously, Lady Catriona. You have never been ruined in my eyes."

And somehow, the slight tenderness in his statement made her vacillate to the opposite side of the emotional tree. Tears pricked at her eyes. Before tonight, she had not cried often. Indeed, she had not cried in the wake of her ruination. Not even when the full implications of her kiss with Shrewsbury, along with knowledge of how complete his betrayal had been, had set in. Nor when she had been banished to Scotland.

But the brooding Earl of Rayne had only to say one moderately kind sentence, and she turned into a watering pot.

Strike that, not one moderately kind sentence but *two*. Sobbing over Monty and Hattie's brother was one thing. Weeping over the Earl of Rayne showing compassion… it was not done.

Either way, she was saved from having to respond—or beginning to cry in truth—by the arrival of the tea tray Rayne had requested. When the maid curtseyed and took her leave as if it was perfectly ordinary for the lady of the house and her suitor to sit about alone at midnight having tea, Catriona moved to pour.

"No," Rayne said gently, with just enough bite in his tone to make her listen. "Allow me, Lady Catriona. You are overset."

Yes, she was overset. Having a madcap brother who seemed intent upon achieving his own demise had that sort of effect upon one.

But she did not say that aloud either.

"You have been very kind today," she observed instead.

For it was true. He had. He had shown a side she had not previously imagined existed. Through the clamor of the situation, he had been a calming, cool influence. He had known just what to say, what to do.

And he had helped in the setting of Monty's bone, all while worrying after her welfare.

Rayne's lips flattened. "I am not kind, Lady Catriona. It is not in me. What I am is a man concerned with his best interests. If your fool brother would have died tonight, I would not have been able to wed you on the morrow."

She did not believe him. She knew the difference between genuine concern and self-interest when she saw it. Catriona was not as naïve as she had once been. Time, disappointment, and betrayal had seen to that.

"Nevertheless," she persisted, "I am thankful for your assistance. I cannot imagine the butler or a footman could have held Monty in place for the bone to be set. Perhaps two or three of our most burly servants at once."

Rayne's tall, imposing build emanated strength.

A strength she suddenly, desperately longed for.

"Anyone could have done as well," Rayne dismissed. "And I am compelled to warn you, I cannot say I will appear at Montrose's bedside a third time. Thrice is not a charm in this instance."

"I hope he will change his ways." She was worried for her brother, and she could not deny it. His drinking and carousing were out of control.

Rayne snorted. "Montrose will not change his ways, my lady. I have seen his kind before. The best you can hope for is this latest injury tames his hunger for recklessness to the extent that he will no longer drown himself in drink and then make the sort of mistakes a man cannot undo."

The earl was the second person in the last few days to tell her Monty would never change. The first had been Hattie. *Lord in heaven*, she shuddered to think what Hattie's opinion of Monty would be after this. She prayed Lord Torrington recovered swiftly and fully.

"I believe everyone is capable of change," she felt the need to offer, not just on Monty's behalf. She truly did believe it. She had to, or she would lose faith in all mankind. "Do you not think it so, Lord Rayne?"

His face was inscrutable, but his gaze, the color of hot cocoa with flecks of gold she had not noticed before, was intense. It warmed her from the inside out. "I think we are, all of us, what our lives have made us. There is no escaping that."

She swallowed, knowing he was thinking of his wife.

Missing her.

Catriona resented the intrusion of the past, of the ghost who was never far from his thoughts. But then, the resentment was chased swiftly by shame. She had no right to envy a dead woman.

"What if we can be more than our lives have made us?" she asked quietly.

It was the closest she could bear to asking him if there was ever a hope he may find love again. With *her*.

"Impossible, my lady," he told her flatly. "The sooner you accept it, the happier you will be."

Well, that rather explained his stance on the matter in crushing clarity. It had been a foolish longing on her part, anyway. She did not know where it had emerged from. Likely the shock of the day and the lateness of the hour.

"Or you can continue to have hope and faith," she offered anyway.

"And be endlessly disappointed." His voice was hard yet smooth, like a stone from a river bed. "Milk? Sugar?"

His change of subject was so abrupt, she blinked, struggling to find her way in their dialogue. Ah yes, he referred to the tea. "Both, if you please."

With efficient movements that seemed at odds with his large hands, brawny body, and aura of danger, he prepared a cup of tea for her. When he held the finished product out to her, their fingers brushed.

Neither of them wore gloves.

She almost shook at the contact. Nothing much, just the brush of his callused fingers over hers. As it was, her heart pounded with so much force, she feared he would hear it, seated as he was on the adjacent settee. His skin was hot. He made *her* hot.

And flushed. "Thank you, my lord."

And clumsy. Her composure was badly shaken by her reaction to him, even after such an obvious rejection. She fumbled her saucer, then made an effort to right her cup, which only resulted in her spilling her tea all over her gown.

"Oh dear," she muttered, looking about for a napkin and finding none. She lifted her skirt away from her thighs, where the dark stain had begun to spread on her pale muslin.

"*Cristo*," Rayne bit out in his decadent voice.

She could not be certain what he had said, but she could easily venture a guess.

Likely, she had disgusted him with her late-night dash to his townhome, followed by the buckets of tears she had cried into his shirt. Now this. She could not even have a proper cup of tea without dumping it into her lap.

All because the Earl of Rayne's fingers had grazed hers.

What was the matter with her? It was true he was the most gorgeous creature the Lord had ever fashioned—so beautiful he made her ache—but he was also the Earl of Rayne. He was cynical, detached, in love with a dead woman, set upon getting her with child and then leaving her...

But then, he was on his knees before her, a snow-white linen handkerchief in hand, dabbing at her drenched skirts. His head was bent.

"*Maldición*, the tea was hot," he growled. "Did you burn yourself, *querida*?"

Dear.

Why did he insist upon calling her that? It made resisting his obvious charms so very impossible. She was staring at his thick, dark hair now, noting how it glistened in the candlelight, wondering what it would feel like, ever so tempted to tunnel her fingers through the wavy lengths.

Even his hair was handsome.

Of course it was.

She ought to answer him, she knew. Indeed, she had meant to, but she was rather distracted by his sudden nearness, the way he called her *querida* in his velvet-gruff voice...

"Are you injured?" he asked again.

Her mouth opened to tell him no, that the tea had not been scalding, that her gown was merely sodden and stained and her pride tattered, but his hands—those elegant hands—were sliding beneath the hem of her gown. Beneath her chemise, too. Over her stockings, up her calves. Caressing her knees.

She could not speak.

His hands traveled all the way to the tops of her thighs, lingering there. His touch was gentle. Hesitant. No lighter than the landing of a butterfly on a flower. But oh, how she felt it. She felt it to her core. Felt an answering ache pulse to life there.

Even the air around them seemed to change, growing heavy. Thick with possibility, with suppressed desires. Her every inhalation was of him, his scent, bay and spice and man.

Him.

Breathing became an erotic art with his fingers skimming over her damp flesh.

"Lady Catriona?" At last, he tipped back his head to meet her gaze.

She fell headlong into his eyes, his brooding beauty.

"Yes," she managed to say. It was the answer to every question he could possibly ask her, she was sure of it.

May I keep touching you?

May I kiss you?

May I raise your skirts higher?

Her wild imagination conjured up an endless number of questions he might pose, all of which would have received the same response, a resounding *yes*.

He did not ask her any of those questions, however.

"Does it hurt?" he asked, his gaze roaming hungrily over her face.

Yes, but not where you think it might.

She swallowed. "No."

His hands stilled in their gentle exploration. "The tea did not burn you? I can have a servant fetch you a soothing salve if it did."

The tea had not burned her. But his fingers on her skin most assuredly did.

"I am..." *Dear heavens*, what was it about the earl that made it so impossible for her to maintain her wits? She scrambled for something to say. The truth would be best, if only she could force her tongue to cooperate. "I am perfectly fine, my lord. The tea was not hot enough to do damage. Indeed, the only damage inflicted was upon my pride."

His concern for her wellbeing did not go unnoticed. With any other man, she may have suspected an impure motive for such a personal inspection of her body. With Rayne, she had no such concern. Of course, within a few hours, he would be her husband anyway, and her body would be his to touch as he liked.

Whenever he liked.

She hoped it would be everywhere and frequently.

"Good. That is very…that is *excelente*. I am relieved if you were not injured, my lady." He removed his hands from beneath her skirts with the haste of a man who had been caught committing a crime. Her hem was flipped back down once more, and he was on his feet in no time, returning to the settee.

"Forgive my carelessness," she said, still embarrassed by her lack of grace.

His gaze bored into hers, his countenance once more impenetrable. "If you wish to postpone our nuptials tomorrow, given the unfortunate events of today, I understand, Lady Catriona."

What? He did not want to marry her after all?

"No." Her response fled her before she could rethink it. Or form it into something more elegant, more refined. It was simply how she felt.

"No?" he asked, a raven-black brow raised. "Are you telling me no, you no longer wish to marry me, or no, you do not wish to reschedule the nuptials on a different day?"

"The latter," she answered with ease. Too much ease, she knew, and far too quickly as well. "What I am telling you, Lord Rayne, is that I want to marry you tomorrow morning, just as we have discussed. I do not wish to tarry any longer."

His sensual lips flattened into a thin line of determination. "And yet, you initially objected to the abbreviated nature of our betrothal. What has changed, my lady?"

Everything.

You.

Me.

The way you make me feel. Your hands beneath my skirts.

She blinked. "Nothing has changed, and that is the reason why we ought to carry on as planned. I have prepared myself according to the nature of our agreement, my lord. I do not wish to wait any longer. Doing so would not benefit either one of us. We both are eager to move on with our lives."

Deny it, she begged him inwardly. *Tell me you have no intention of moving on without me. Tell me your intentions have altered.*

Instead, he nodded. "This is true, my lady. The sooner you are with child, the sooner I can return to Spain."

She suppressed a flinch at his words. She had known, all along, what he wanted from her. Why had she dared to think he might change his mind? Because he had shown her a modicum of concern? Because he seemed to care? Because he had run his delicious hands over her thighs?

"Of course," she forced herself to say brightly, as if the reminder of his plan to callously abandon her and his child were not the verbal equivalent of sinking a dagger deep into her heart. "If we marry tomorrow as planned, we will both be much nearer to accomplishing our goals."

"Our goals," he repeated.

Ah. He believed he was the only one in their marriage with goals. How very man-like of him.

"Yes," she said. "*Our* goals, my lord. You wish to return to Spain, assured of an heir who will keep your odious cousin from inheriting your estates and title. I wish to secure my freedom and to hold my head high in society. To never again have to suffer banishment. I will admit, I am most eager to return to my friends and the social whirl."

His jaw had tensed. She did not miss the signs. Something about what she had just said had displeased him. But she could not fathom what it would be.

"Which friends are you eager to return to, Lady Catriona?" he asked coolly. "I will remind you that you are a reflection of me. And further, that you will remain faithful to me until you produce me a healthy heir. Not a moment sooner."

How dare he suppose she only wanted to marry him so she could take a lover or otherwise bring scandal and condemnation down upon him? When he was the one who was so hell-bent upon returning to Spain and abandoning her and their child in England?

Catriona's first instinct was to rail against him and such an unwarranted judgment.

She forced her indignation aside, however, for the night had been a long and trying one for the both of them. And she was still thankful for the way he had come running to aid her, Monty, and even Torrington.

"I am more than aware of the responsibilities I will be undertaking as your countess, Lord Rayne," she informed him, her voice equally frigid. "I may have been ruined, but I have no intention of flouting the vows we speak."

She could only hope he would not.

He nodded. "Thank you, Lady Catriona. I will take you at your word."

"And I will thank you for honoring my word," she said, even though she was certain he doubted her. Perhaps few people in his life had ever been worthy of his trust, or something had happened to make him so quick to be suspicious.

At odds with the sudden vein of their conversation, he proceeded to pour her a fresh cup of tea, adding sugar and milk accordingly. He offered it to her with a wry smile. "Tea, Lady Catriona?"

"Thank you." This time, when she accepted the cup and saucer, she took great care to keep her fingers from brushing his. Spurred by a persistent voice inside her, she continued. "You promised me freedom, Lord Rayne. After I bear your heir, I am to have free reign over my own life. You assured me that much when you asked me to become your wife, and if you are seeking to rescind the offer now, please say so."

He poured himself a tea—no sugar, no milk—with effortless elegance. "One life in exchange for another," he said. "That is what I promised you, my lady. I trust you are still willing?"

One life in exchange for another.

How cold it sounded.

How emotionless.

He had no wish to meet his child or have a role in his upbringing. She must not forget that.

She met the gaze of the man who would become her husband in a few hours' time. "I am still willing, Lord Rayne."

The tension seemed to ease from him before her eyes. He nodded. "*Bueno.*"

Catriona sipped her tea, forcing a smile she did not feel. "*Bueno.*"

She could only hope it was a promise which would come to fruition.

Chapter Eight

THE WEDDING WAS going to be delayed.

Alessandro understood this undeniable, unwanted fact the moment he received a missive from Hamilton House, before he even bothered to open it and scan its contents. The Duke of Montrose, foolish *bastardo* that he was, had moved in the night, no doubt attempting to find some liquor to pour down his worthless gullet, and had ruined the setting of his bone. Another attempt would need to be made this morning.

But worse news still, Viscount Torrington had yet to regain consciousness.

Alessandro's betrothed wrote prettily, in the unhurried scrawl of a lady who had learned from a governess and who had never needed to worry over the cost of paper or the time penning such a note would take from her day. Of all the things he was to fixate upon, the penmanship of Lady Catriona seemed the most unlikely.

And yet, it was another reminder of how different the woman he was about to marry was from the first woman he had married. Maria had not been born to the life of an elegant lady. Her scrawl had been small and concise, the hallmark of a woman who needed to conserve both her paper and her time. Her father had been a wealthy merchant, but drink and the loss of his wife had caused him to lose everything. Maria had been tossed from her home with no means of supporting herself save one.

Alessandro's hand clenched into a fist, crumpling Lady Catriona's missive.

He was not certain which made him angrier; the delay of his nuptials, which would necessarily mean the addition of more time spent in England, or the reminder of what Maria had endured juxtaposed with the gentle life Lady Catriona enjoyed. Even in her supposed banishment and ruination, she had still lived a life of ease.

"Will there be a reply, my lord?"

The question snatched Alessandro from his grim reveries. His butler was staring at him, expressionless.

"No tengo respuesta," he said.

"Are you certain there shall be no answer, Lord Rayne?" his butler asked, his tone mild.

Dios. What did the man do, sit about in his butler's pantry studying Spanish? Alessandro would sack him, but he had no intention of remaining in England long enough to care. The man would be Lady Catriona's problem.

If she and Alessandro ever managed to wed, that was.

His eyes narrowed on the domestic. *"Estoy seguro."*

The butler bowed. "If you are sure, my lord, I will take my leave."

No, *damn it*, he was not sure. He was not sure of anything any longer. He had believed he had decided upon an excellent solution to the problem of having shot the Duke of Montrose and also keeping his loathsome cousin from inheriting.

Take a bride. Even a ruined one. Even an English one. Even one he wanted to touch.

But he could not seem to wed Lady Catriona, no matter how hard he tried.

He had believed he could stave off his servants by speaking to them solely in his preferred language.

But his butler had learned Spanish.

Said butler was departing the study where Alessandro had been pacing, fretting over the day's nuptials and his inconvenient attraction to his impending bride both.

"Johnstone," he said. "Wait."

His butler paused, then turned to face him, his countenance still as placid as a pond at dawn. "Yes, Lord Rayne?"

"See that a carriage is brought round," he directed, entirely against his will. "I will be paying a call to Hamilton House."

"Of course, my lord."

His butler bowed again and then made a hasty retreat.

Alessandro watched him go, bemused by the situation in which he now found himself. He had a betrothed to worry about now. A *plan*. A plan which had been set in motion by the same man who now seemed hell-bent upon destroying it all with his reckless, insatiable desire for debauchery. Could the duke not have waited one more sodding day to drown himself in drink and race his equally foolhardy friend?

In truth, he wanted nothing more than to let Montrose wallow in pain and learn from his stupidity. But he also wanted his *wife*. He wanted to *make* her his wife. And each day spent without Lady Catriona as his countess, in his bed, was another day he would have to wait.

The longer he tarried, the more time passed. His men in Spain needed him. Though his second in command was capable, a formidable guerrilla soldier in his own right, he was also violent and ruthless. Tomàs had once led their men into a French field hospital and tacked the wounded enemy to trees to bleed to death.

The memory of that day still haunted him, for while battle was in his blood, Alessandro believed in mercy. He needed to return, to retake command. Warfare was what he knew best. Attempting to find his way in the culture which had never embraced him, the culture which had never felt like his own, was not what he was meant to do.

Surely that was the source of the restlessness affecting him now.

Surely that was the source of his anger.

But it was not, and he knew it. Part of the spark igniting his inner fury was his reaction to Lady Catriona. He wanted her. Badly. And it left him riddled with guilt he could not begin to dispel.

Still, he required an heir, but to accomplish such a feat, he also needed to wed.

That much was undeniable.

Johnstone returned, and it was only then that Alessandro realized he had never moved from the spot where he had stood when the butler had taken his leave. Indeed, he still held Lady Catriona's missive clenched in his fist.

Cristo.

"The carriage is awaiting you, my lord," his butler announced.

"Very good," he said, not even having the energy to bait the man any longer. "Thank you, Johnstone."

With that, he stalked toward the front entry, Lady Catriona's note burning into his palm.

CATRIONA'S WEDDING DAY was not going to happen.

She suspected it the moment she woke in the midst of the night to her brother's incoherent hollering. She *realized* it when she found Monty on the staircase, sprawled over the steps, groaning in pain, fortunate he had not broken his foolish neck.

Asking for whisky.

She had not given him the whisky, and neither had Mama, who had also rushed from her chamber in the darkness, fluttering about aimlessly as a moth. In her dudgeon, Mama had almost fallen down the steps herself.

Catriona had caught her by the elbow in time.

And had also subsequently sought their butler, who had rounded up three of the sturdiest footmen to aid in returning Monty to his bed.

But the trouble with Monty was that he was, well, *Monty*.

And he had been out of his mind with laudanum and pain and desperate for what Monty loved second best—liquor. First was women, of course, and in massive quantity but questionable quality.

But Monty had not been appreciative of the efforts being undertaken to restore him to his bed. He had punched one of the footmen in the eye. He had also nearly succeeded in kicking the unsuspecting butler down the stairs. When the phalanx of servants required to restore him to his bed had finally managed to wrangle him to his chamber, he had relieved himself on the carpet.

In front of Catriona and their horrified mother.

She did not think she would ever be able to forget the sound of Monty's stream hitting the carpet. Or the gasp of horror in Mama's throat.

And Monty?

He had merely laughed. Laughed uproariously, as if he had heard the funniest sally in all Christendom. And then he had belched and begun to cry. And then he had fallen over, and all the servants had wrestled him back into bed as he uttered a series of nonsensical curses. *Satan's earbobs. God's fichu. The devil's banyan.*

His splint had been quite ruined by that point.

Poor Dr. Croydon had once more been sent for this morning, and the household was awaiting his arrival whilst attempting to ignore the ghastly hollering emerging from Monty's bedchamber, where he had been tied to the bed posts by their enterprising domestics. The extra laudanum spooned down his throat had worn off about an hour ago, by her estimation. Thankfully, Mama was suffering his tantrum at the moment.

Catriona was tempted to cry about it all now as she tried to consume her breakfast. Torrington was still insensate, and Hattie would probably never speak to her again on account of Monty's reckless ways. She had been forced to write a note to Rayne, informing him she could not marry him. And she had also had to pen a note to Hattie, explaining her brother was…

"My lord, you cannot simply…my lord, this is highly irregular! My lord, I insist you stop!"

The frustrated objections of the butler echoed just beyond the breakfast room. The door opened, flinging against the damask wallcoverings with a thump. And there he stood, the man she had been meant to marry today. The man she had promised, just the night before, she would marry in the morning, regardless of her brother's mayhem.

But that had been before the staircase incident.

And the peeing on the rug incident.

And the earl looked furious.

Beautiful, but furious.

She stood. "My lord. You did not need to come."

"Of course I did," he bit out, striding toward her. "You are to be my wife, and matters concerning you also concern me."

To the butler, who lingered with a look of barely suppressed outrage—perhaps understandable after the evening they had just had—she nodded. "It is well. You may go. I sent a note to Lord Rayne this morning requiring his presence."

The domestic bowed and took his leave.

In truth, she had done nothing of the kind. Rather, she had sent Rayne a note explaining—loosely, of course—the events of the prior evening and begging a delay of their nuptials. Although she had not requested his presence, it stood to reason he would appear, given they had been promised to marry this morning and that he seemed quite intent upon achieving their union.

Clearly, he was here on account of his sense of duty. The same sense of duty which made him promise himself to a woman he then intended to abandon. The same sense of duty which enabled him to believe having an heir would absolve him of all his obligations.

The same sense of duty which told him he could marry her, get her with child, and then leave.

The more thought she devoted to it, the more Rayne's indefatigable sense of duty enraged her.

"You did not have to come here this morning on account of our impending nuptials," she told him. "Waiting one more day ought not to be a problem. Should it?"

His lips tightened into a grim line. "One day does not seem sufficient to tend to the needs of your wastrel brother, my lady. If we are to delay our nuptials based upon Montrose's whims, we shall remain forever unwed."

Rayne was not wrong. Monty was a goodhearted man, and she loved her brother, but even she had grown weary of his antics.

The earl's thinly veiled hostility gave her pause. "Are you not willing to wait one day?"

"After one day, shall it be another, and then another?" he asked. "Lady Catriona, perhaps I have not made it clear before, but allow me to do so now. I need a wife. I need an heir. And then I need to return to my country. All of these tasks must be accomplished as quickly as possible."

He had prowled toward her in the course of their conversation, and he now stood devastatingly near. His scent hit her, along with a wave of yearning she could not shake regardless of how foolish she knew it to be.

The lingering prick of jealousy at his love for Spain and his first wife made her bold. "Is this not your country as well, Lord Rayne?"

His nostrils flared in irritation. "No. It is not. My home is where I make it, and that has never been here. Nor will it ever be."

Of course. It was what she had expected him to say.

"I am sorry, my lord, for requesting a postponement of our nuptials," she forced herself to say rather than pursuing the troubling matter. "You must know, I would not have done so were it not a necessity."

"Montrose," he growled, his loathing of her brother almost palpable.

Ah, Monty. Some days, she despaired of him. Any hopes she had entertained that this incident would curtail his wild ways had been summarily dashed last night.

"This is rather indelicate," she began, not certain how much she ought to reveal to Rayne. What she truly meant was it was mortifying.

Her brother was a disaster, it was true.

Rayne snorted. "I am not a delicate man, *querida*. Tell me everything."

She bit her lip, considering her options. She could either unburden herself entirely, at the risk of humiliating Monty, or she could offer an abridged version.

The earl did not like her hesitation. "Everything," he pressed.

Catriona sighed. "Monty left his bed, strictly against the doctor's orders. In the process, he ruined his splint and upset the bone."

Her brother's indecipherable hollering punctuated her truncated explanation.

"*Cristo*," muttered Rayne. "Is that Montrose?"

"I am afraid so," she admitted hesitantly.

"Is the sawbones already here doing his work?" the earl wanted to know. "Cannot the man do his duty and spoon some laudanum down Montrose's throat?"

She frowned. "Dr. Croydon has yet to arrive, on account of being detained elsewhere. Monty is…distressed because he has been tied to his bed."

"Tied to his…" Rayne's brows furrowed. "An explanation, if you please, madam."

Oh, dear. Where to begin? How much to reveal?

"In the midst of the night, Monty was seeking whisky."

"I knew it," Rayne bit out, the rage emanating from him at his initial entrance, returning.

"He was out of his head, perhaps from the pain, perhaps from the laudanum," Catriona continued. "But whatever the reason, he upset his splint, and he was walking on the leg, which he is not meant to do without a crutch of some sort."

"None of that explains why Montrose has been lashed to his bed like a Bedlamite," the earl pointed out.

Correctly.

"We feared he may make a second attempt," she admitted. "He was not…particularly lucid at the time of the initial incident, and as some of the servants were injured in the effort to return him to his bed, we all deemed it best to remove the temptation. At least until Dr. Croydon arrives."

"And what of Torrington?" Rayne demanded next.

"He has not yet woken," she said sadly. "I have sent for his sister, Hattie, and his mother. I expect they will wish to move him home, whenever it is practicable."

She could only pray the viscount would, indeed, wake. That the damage he had suffered when he had been thrown from his phaeton was not irreversible.

"What of you?" Rayne asked, disturbing her tumultuous musings as he closed the last of the distance between them, then caught her chin in his thumb and forefinger, tilting her face back so he could study her. "You are very pale this morning, my lady, and the darkness beneath your eyes suggests you did not have a proper sleep."

She swallowed, trying not to lose herself in the warm depths of his gaze. Trying to ignore the length of his black lashes, too long for a man's, the aristocratic sweep of his nose, the prominence of his cheekbones.

Trying to forget how handsome he was and how effectively he tied her wits and stomach in knots whenever their paths crossed.

"I am fine," she managed to say, though the words, when they emerged at last, were undeniably breathless. "Thank you for your concern."

"Someone ought to be concerned for your welfare," he bit out. "Where in Hades is your mother?"

"Attending Monty," she answered.

His thumb moved, running along her jaw in a tender caress. "Who is attending you, my lady? Making certain you are eating? Making sure *you* are well? Hmm?"

"No one," she managed shakily. "I can see to myself."

Surely Rayne was not concerned for her. Was he?

"Of course you can, *querida*." His voice had thickened. The sweetness of his baritone licked through her, at once soothing and yet also inciting a flame. "You have had to do so, because everyone else is too busy chasing after Montrose. How many times has he done something as reckless as what he did last night?"

She tried to think, but the earl was caressing her throat, his large hand slipping around to cup her nape. He began massaging the muscles of her neck, easing tension she had not even realized she possessed.

"How many times, Lady Catriona?" he asked again, his voice deceptively soft.

"Not many," she felt compelled to defend, for she was loyal to her brother. Monty was not a villain. He was simply…lost. That was the best way to put it.

"I think you are lying to defend him," Rayne observed, his gaze scouring hers. "I cannot believe the duel and this foolhardy race are the extent of his indiscretions."

She thought about it.

There was the time he had brought an actress to live at Hamilton House until Mama had nearly boxed his ears and chased Mrs. Wilton from the duchess's apartments. There had also been the evening he had gotten so inebriated; he had been attempting to hold a conversation with a potted palm at Lord and Lady Oxley's ball. Later, he claimed he had mistaken the palm for a spinster. He had fallen down the staircase once and tripped into the statuary in the entry hall, shattering a marble bust of the first Duke of Montrose.

She still recalled Monty kicking the poor duke's nose across the polished floor and declaring the bust had been his least favorite anyhow.

Catriona frowned.

And then, there had been the time he had fallen into the lap of one of Mama's friends at a dinner party. The time he had engaged in a heated shouting match with their father's portrait. He had also once decided, in the midst of the night, to paint the second-floor hall. The time she had found him lying prone on the Aubusson in the library in a drying puddle of his own vomit...

"Your face is expressive, my lady," Rayne said grimly. "You need not speak a word, for I already have my answer."

She did not like the judgmental tone in the earl's voice. "Monty is a good man."

"He is more child than man, if you ask me." Though Rayne was curt and his expression rigid, he continued to knead the tightness in her neck. "I have a proposition for you, Lady Catriona. Montrose has done enough damage. We will wait until the doctor returns to set his bone. I will even aid him in his task. And then, this afternoon, we will wed. The special license enables us to marry whenever we wish, after all."

Something inside her thrilled to the notion at the same time as something else within her balked. "But Dr. Croydon will likely need to give Monty more laudanum to set the bone, which will render him incoherent. I wished for Monty to be present at our nuptials."

He was her beloved brother, after all.

Even if he was a scapegrace.

"We can speak our vows here rather than in the church," Rayne suggested soothingly. "In the drawing room, the library, wherever you prefer. We will have Montrose brought down for the occasion. He will miss nothing."

"But what of Torrington?" she asked next. "How can we carry on when he may be…"

Dying, was the word she had been about to say.

She would not speak it.

It was far too daunting, far too frightening.

"Torrington is not your brother," the earl pointed out calmly as he continued his ministrations. "He is not even your family. We will pray for a complete recovery from him, but he, like Montrose, is a man grown. He, too, made the decision which led him to where he now lies."

Once more, Rayne was not wrong. But her heart ached when she thought of Torrington's injuries, his very life in question, and her dear friend.

"Hattie will be beside herself with upset," she protested. "I only just sent her a missive this morning informing her of what has occurred."

"Miss Lethbridge strikes me as a very strong sort, and I have no doubt she will carry on as she must. If she is your friend, she will not wish you to delay your future on account of the uncertainty of her brother's fate."

Was it Rayne's nearness or the dexterity of his long fingers working every ache from her tensed muscles, or was it the decadent scent of him invading her senses? Whatever the cause, she was beginning to see the reason in his suggestions. They should not have to wait to marry because of Monty and Torrington.

She thought then of how many excuses she had made for her brother, how often she had raced to his defense, how many occasions upon which his lack of control had left her scrambling to cover up his foibles or somehow diminish or excuse them.

"It is time for you to live your own life, Lady Catriona," Rayne urged. "We will see your brother's bone set, and by that time, Lord Torrington will likely be awake. Our marriage will take place this afternoon, and by this evening, we will be on our way to Riverford House."

Catriona bit her lip.

"Do not fret, *querida*." The earl did the oddest thing then, the one gesture she could not resist.

He pressed his lips to her forehead in a chaste kiss. Like a benediction.

"All will be well," he whispered against her skin. "You shall see."

And she believed him.

She exhaled slowly. "Yes. You are right, Lord Rayne. We will marry this afternoon, here at Hamilton House. But first, I would like a chance to speak to my brother, if you please."

"It will be done." She felt him smile against her skin. "Thank you, Lady Catriona. You will not regret it, I promise."

She closed her eyes and breathed him in, wondering how he had already become such a familiar, important part of her life.

Catriona hoped he was right.

Chapter Nine

Alessandro stared down at the Duke of Montrose, who was pale, sweating, and clearly uncomfortable. He was no longer tied to his bed, but he was in a great deal of pain. As he should be.

The foolish drunkard had managed to unleash all manner of havoc upon not only his own household, but his friend's and, most importantly, Alessandro's. He was fortunate Alessandro had allowed him two hours of laudanum-induced sleep before seeking an audience.

"Why does it reek of piss in here, Montrose?" he asked the duke.

They were alone now, so he could speak plainly. The bone had been reset. The much-suffering doctor had left. Alessandro had decided a moment alone with his future brother-in-law was imperative. They needed to come to an understanding.

Today was the very last day the duke would cause him or his future countess any grief. He was determined.

Montrose looked shame-faced despite the laudanum he had been administered to aid the setting of the bone, which had rendered him droop-eyed. "I think I may have inadvertently used the carpet as a piss pot."

Cristo. He had been hoping there was a poorly trained canine about, but it had seemed exceedingly unlikely since he had seen no hint of such a creature.

"*Maldición*, Montrose," he bit out. "You are worse than a mongrel."

"Yes," the duke agreed. He closed his eyes. "I am a worthless bastard, and I know it."

No point in arguing against such a statement. From where Alessandro sat, it certainly looked like truth.

"I am marrying your sister this afternoon," he said.

"The wedding. Christ." Montrose shifted as if he were about to rise from the bed, but then winced. "Beelzebub's ballocks. I forgot about the ankle for a moment. And the wedding. And my ankle. Fucking laudanum."

"Lady Catriona loves you," he said, unmoved by the duke's sickbed garble. "She wants you to be present for the nuptials. I want to be certain you are amenable."

"Hell, yes. Marry her." Montrose grimaced. "I am more than amenable. As you know."

"Perhaps I should be more specific." He paused. "I want to be certain you will not embarrass her."

"Jesus! Do I look like I will embarrass her?" Montrose asked angrily, before closing his eyes. "Do not answer. Damn it to hell. The room is spinning."

"Yes," Alessandro answered, not bothering to heed the duke. "You do."

"I will not," Montrose said on a groan. "Christ, my leg hurts."

"You have your own stupidity to thank for that," he observed. "Twice over."

"Yes. And countless other non-blessings as well," Montrose agreed. One could only suppose.

Alessandro's imagination was wicked, populated by the ghastliness he had seen and partaken in over the last few years of war. But somehow, the Duke of Montrose's foibles seemed equally dangerous.

"You do not have to live as you do, Montrose," he pointed out. "If you stopped drowning yourself in spirits—"

"Then I could not live with myself." Montrose passed a hand over his face, looking ashen and weary. "Believe me, Rayne, I am far better gin-soaked."

"I doubt that." He sniffed, for he was not going to argue the duke's future with him. If Montrose wished to poison himself and continue living a reckless life of debauchery, that was his choice. "If your maids do not soon attempt to clean the carpet, you will have to replace it."

"What are you, my bloody housekeeper?" Montrose growled, unappreciative of his advice.

"Thankfully not," he clipped, "else I should be concerning myself with such affairs as how to most readily remove the scent of a drunken fool's piss from the Aubusson."

Montrose's eyes were closed, but he scowled. "Go to hell, Rayne. You may be marrying m'sister, but that does not give you the right to pontificate."

"I am not pontificating," he denied. "I am merely tired of holding you down for your bone to be set. After today, all such duties will be someone else's problem. Not, I suspect, Torrington's, however."

"Satan's breeches, do not remind me," the duke said. "How is Torrie?"

"He will live, though apparently, he has no recollection of anything." Not even his own name. Alessandro had seen such a case once before, on the battlefield. A man had fallen from his mount and could not remember anything for days. "It is a case of amnesia, I believe."

"Oh, Christ. Are you certain, Rayne?"

Dr. Croydon had gone to Lord Torrington after resetting Montrose's broken leg. His face had been grim upon his exit of the chamber. But Alessandro had been relieved the viscount had awoken at last. The final impediment to his nuptials with Lady Catriona had been removed.

He sighed, irritated with Montrose anew for the mayhem he had inflicted upon his plans. "As certain as I am tired of playing your nursemaid, let me be clear on the reason I am here, Montrose. You are a ne'er-do-well scapegrace, and you have been worrying your sister for far too long."

Montrose's eyes opened, the pupils dilated and large. "I know. Ought to have sent m'self to Scotland instead of her. My fault she was ruined. I should have challenged Shrewsbury to a duel and gutted him like a fish, too."

Alessandro had not ruled out such a possibility himself.

The mere reminder of the foppish lord who had dared to ruin Lady Catriona was enough to make a sinister bolt of murderous rage slice straight through him. But today was not a day for violence. Today was a day of new beginnings.

His. With Lady Catriona.

Today, she would be his, in spite of all the obstacles blocking their path. In spite of the duke lying so pathetically before him.

"Forget about that spineless maggot," he directed Montrose with a bite he could not temper. "I am looking for a promise from you."

"A promise from me?" Montrose raised a brow. "Look here, Rayne. You are wedding my sister today, not me."

When he was not being a drunken fool, Montrose was almost a likeable fellow.

Almost.

"I am aware of who I am about to marry, thank you." He fixed the duke with a determined glare, the likes of which had made many a man crumble before him. "The promise I would ask of you is that you attempt, for Lady Catriona's sake, to tame your ways. If I am to be leaving her behind to raise my heir, nothing would aggrieve me more than to learn she was forced to chase after you, fretting over you, playing your nursemaid, and keeping you from kicking your butler down the stairs."

"Cat does not need to worry over me." Montrose frowned. "I am perfectly fine without her interference. I already have one mother, and I do not really care for her interference either, if you must know."

"Montrose," he pressed. "Your promise. Lady Catriona loves your sorry hide. You owe it to her and your mother both—*Dios*, to yourself, too—to pull yourself together. You cannot spend the rest of your life drinking and fucking and crashing."

"Any more than you can spend the rest of your life running?" Montrose returned.

Alessandro stilled, shocked by the duke's rare moment of insight. Perhaps he had been running. Running from the past, from England, from the memories of Maria and Francisco and everything he had lost.

"What I do is none of your concern," he bit out. "I will see your sister is well-cared for, as is my duty. She will want for nothing. All you have to do is promise not to mire her down with your foolishness. Try to be better. For her. For your mother. For yourself. Starting today, Montrose."

Montrose's eyes closed. "For Cat's sake, I will try."

"Good." He would believe Montrose's promise like he believed pigs would stop living in their own shit. But it was neither here nor there. The duke's future was in his own, incapable hands. All Alessandro cared about was securing his wife at long last so he could begin his quest for an heir.

But there was one more thing that would have to happen first. He had promised his betrothed an audience with her brother, and an audience she would have.

Montrose had begun to snore.

Alessandro flicked his nose.

The duke snorted, his eyes flying open, a scowl on his face. "I say, Rayne. That was uncalled for. I am an invalid."

Alessandro sighed. "Your sister wants to speak with you. No pissing on the rug."

Montrose grumbled something that sounded suspiciously like *bastard Spaniard* beneath his breath. "Send her to me, then. I have grown weary of your presence."

He sketched an ironic bow. "Likewise, Montrose."

Catriona settled herself at her brother's side, relieved he seemed much more lucid this afternoon. His jaw was clenched and his countenance set with the grim evidence of pain, but he had calmed considerably.

"How are you, Monty?" she asked softly.

"How do I look?" her brother countered, a trace of his ordinary good humor coming to life.

She tilted her head, considering him. "Truth?"

His eyes narrowed. "Truth."

"Awful," she admitted. "Though much improved over the last time I saw you."

His eyes fluttered shut and remained thus. "Apologies, Cat, for what you witnessed."

He sounded tired, and she knew a prick of guilt at having forced him into seeing her. "You were not yourself," she told him quietly.

His eyes opened once more. "I was myself, and that is the trouble. I am a monster, and I know it."

"You are a good man," she defended, much as she had to Rayne earlier. "But I am worried for you, Monty. Your…incidents are growing more frequent and drastic in nature. This time, you have suffered a broken bone. What shall it be next time?"

"It depends on whether or not I drink blue ruin," he joked.

"Monty."

She was decidedly not in the mood for his banter. He had given her quite a fright, and she feared for him. Feared what the devils in him would lead him to do. Feared what would become of him.

He grimaced. "A broken head if I am fortunate enough. Or perhaps amnesia. It is not fair only Torrie is allowed to forget."

The reminder of Lord Torrington's injuries was sobering indeed. Hattie and her mother had rushed to Hamilton House and to his bedside. Seeing her dear friend awash in tears had hurt her heart.

"You must not make light of it, Monty," she chided. "Torrington suffered a severe head injury. The doctor is not yet certain if he will recover fully…if he will remember."

Monty closed his eyes again. "I wish to God I did not remember."

"Will you not confide in me, Monty?" How she wished he would unburden himself.

"There is nothing to confide," he said grimly. "I am a scoundrel, Cat. But there may be hope for me yet. I have decided there is only one way in which I can rectify the wrongs I have done. I will marry Miss Lethbridge."

Catriona could not have been more surprised had her brother started clucking like a chicken. She stared at him. "You? Marry Hattie?"

"Yes. Torrie is always moaning about her being a spinster, no proper lords wanting her and all that," Monty said. "I will wed the chit. That ought to make amends for the damage I have done."

She could not be certain if his horrible idea had been predicated by the laudanum, or if he was merely that oblivious. "There is one problem, I fear, and it is rather an insurmountable one."

He raised an imperious brow. "Oh?"

"Hattie despised you before you decided to race Torrington whilst you were both heavily in your cups." She paused, frowning. "Now that he has been so grievously injured on account of your foolishness—"

"On account of *our* foolishness," Monty interrupted indignantly. "Torrie was a part of it, you will recall. Racing was his idea."

She compressed her lips. "As you say."

"Because it is true, by Satan's chemise," Monty insisted.

"Lord Torrington cannot recall," she pointed out. "He did not even recall his own name when he awoke. Given the circumstances, I hardly think you are in a position to ask Hattie to wed you. Or to expect her to accept your proposal if you have the daring to make one."

"Of course she will accept me." He scowled at her. "I am a duke."

Catriona sighed. "Dukes do not impress Hattie."

"I am also the Marquess of Ashby," he countered. "And the Viscount Lisle. She may take her pick of any of my other titles if a duke will not do."

"Hattie is not impressed by *titles*," Catriona elaborated, taking pity on her brother, who seemed genuinely perplexed by the notion Hattie would not leap into his arms immediately upon the delivery of his proposal. "She has had her choice of suitors, but none of them have suited her."

"Fops, all of them," Monty growled. "Lord Hayes has a beak of a nose, and the Earl of Rearden is a scoundrel."

Monty knew the names of Hattie's most recent suitors? *Interesting. Very interesting indeed.*

"*You* are a scoundrel," she pointed out.

"One who owes her brother a debt of honor, having been the man who did not stop him from drinking the last of the blue ruin and who raced him instead," Monty countered.

"You truly believe you can somehow rectify the events of yesterday by wedding Hattie?" Catriona knew without a shred of a doubt that her friend would never have him.

"I do not merely believe it," her brother said with complete confidence. "I know it."

"You were also once convinced you could make a flying machine," she could not help reminding him. "I will never forget the sight of you on the turrets at Castle Clare, with those wings fastened to your back."

"It was an excellent idea," he argued. "I have simply never had the opportunity to test subsequent models. If the wind had not caught the wings prior to fastening them to me, they would not have flown down to the courtyard and become hopelessly mangled. Marrying Miss Lethbridge will be a far easier achievement to accomplish than flight."

She well recalled the sight of the wings crashing to the ground. Their father had been furious when he had learned what Monty had been about.

"Hattie will not have you, Monty," she felt compelled to tell her brother. She knew her friend. There was simply no means through which Hattie would ever agree to marry Monty, who she regularly dismissed as a scandalous jackanapes.

"Of course she will," he argued with complete confidence. "She harbors a secret *tendre* for me. Has for some time, I daresay."

Surely it was the laudanum and not Monty speaking now?

She studied him. "Has someone given you whisky?"

"No."

"Gin?"

"No."

She thought for a moment. "Brandy?"

"Damnation, Cat," he roared. "It is just the bloody laudanum. And it is time for me to have more, I am certain of it. My pain grows worse by the second."

"You may have more after the wedding," she said, quite certain Monty had received his dosage already and that he was not due another for several hours.

"Would you have me in severe pain when I give my only sister to the black-hearted, half-Spaniard who shot me?" Monty demanded.

"How is your wound?" she asked.

Though a few weeks had passed since the ill-fated duel which had set in motion the events of today, the accident may well have caused him to reinjure himself.

"Painful. I require more laudanum."

She sighed. "Monty, I want you to promise me something."

"First Rayne, now you," he grumbled. "Cannot a man swill laudanum and lie about in his sickbed like a proper invalid?"

"Monty."

"Cat."

Her brother was the only person who called her Cat. The only person she would allow to call her by the diminutive. He had teased her with it in their youth, but as they had matured, the name had rather stuck. They stared at each other now. Suddenly, the enormity of what was about to happen—the tremendous change her life was going to undertake—hit her.

Tears pricked her eyes. Tears of worry, sentimental tears, tears for the Monty and Cat they had once been, for the people they had become, for the uncertain futures awaiting them both.

"I want you to be happy, Monty," she said softly. "That is all."

"I want the same for you." His smile was slow and lopsided. "I am sorry I banished you to Scotland, sorry I did not do something more about that blighter Shrewsbury."

She shook her head. "I did not want you to. The fault was mine for being so reckless."

"I suppose recklessness is in our blood," Monty said.

"Yes, I suppose it is." She paused. "You will be comfortable, being moved to the drawing room for the ceremony? I do not want you to suffer on my account."

"I will be fine, Cat." His eyes closed for a beat, as if he found them too heavy to keep open. "As fine as I can be."

It was her fervent wish that one day, her brother would not simply be fine.

That he would be *well*.

But for now, she would settle for him being present at her wedding. For the half-smile he flashed her as his eyes opened once more. For the color that had come to life in his previously pallid complexion.

"You need not worry on my account," he said then. "I promise I will not take a piss on the drawing room carpet."

She sighed. "Oh, Monty. I love you."

"I love you, too, Cat."

Chapter Ten

For the second time in his five-and-thirty years, Alessandro had a wife.

She was seated across from him in his carriage, en route to Riverford House, looking as if she were about to be shepherded to the gallows before a jeering throng. Or perhaps led to the guillotine. Her gloved hands bit into her pelisse, her fists clenched. Her neat, even teeth had caught the fullness of her lower lip, and though her face was averted to the window, her countenance was undeniably grim.

Quite a drastic contrast to his first marriage. He and Maria had been drunk, in love, and smiling foolishly at each other. And then they had been drunk, in love, and in each other's arms soon thereafter.

But Catriona and Maria were two different people. The past could not be resurrected. Nor could the joy he had lost. The present was…London, a city he abhorred. A cold rain had begun to fall as they exited Montrose's townhome, the weather as forbidding as the mood.

The ceremony had not taken long. The duke had been aided to the drawing room by a team of footmen. To his credit, he had neither fallen asleep and begun to snore nor committed some other sin of similar proportion to the violation of his bedchamber carpet. Catriona's friend, Miss Lethbridge, sister to the unfortunate Lord Torrington, had been present as well, her expression stricken. Lady Catriona's mother had not seemed any more hopeful.

Suddenly, the quiet of the carriage ride, interrupted only by the normal street sounds of fellow carriages plodding by and the rustling of tack, seemed untenable.

"You are fretting, *querida*," he said simply, breaking the silence. "What is the reason for your unhappiness?"

Her attention jerked toward him, her gaze clinging to his. "I am not fretting, my lord."

She could not fool him. "Honesty, if you please."

Catriona sighed. "Do not all new brides experience some trepidation on the day they wed?"

He supposed they may, but he had only one comparison. He said nothing, struggling to find the right words to say, now that he had initiated a conversation.

But she was perceptive. "Ah, I see. Your last bride did not."

His last bride.

How haunting it sounded. How final. For it was. Death was life's end, and no one understood that fact better than a man who had wept into the freshly turned earth over the graves of his wife and son.

The abrupt pain slicing through him was almost palpable. As always, he forced it down through sheer will.

"No," he was able to answer simply. "She did not."

"Yours was a love match from the beginning?" his new wife ventured to ask.

He swallowed against a rising tide of grief. "It was."

"I am sorry." Her countenance was open. Kind.

Too kind.

Alessandro flinched. "I do not want your sympathy or your pity. Both are meaningless to me."

She paled. "Of course, my lord."

Cristo, what a bastard he was. He had not meant to lash out at her. She was not at fault for the pain he had been dealt in his life. His aim was to put her at ease. Tonight, he would come to her bed. Their marriage would begin in truth.

He passed a hand over his face and sighed. "Forgive me. I am not accustomed to having a wife."

Not for the last few years, anyway.

Though he had known being a husband once more would feel strange, he had not been prepared for the enormity of his emotions. Ordinarily, he kept his emotions at bay. He had been a machine of war for so long, he had forgotten what it felt like to be a man.

To *feel*.

"I understand, my lord," she told him.

No, you do not.

But he did not care to go down that road. Not with her. Not today. Not ever.

"The past is where it belongs," he said dismissively. "We shall leave it there, as it has no bearing upon our union."

She looked as if she wanted to argue. Instead, she nodded. "If that is what you wish, my lord."

"It is the way it must be." For he did not *want* to feel. He did not want to speak about Maria and Francisco. He did not want to relive the pain of losing them, the agony of his darkest days when the despair had been enough to drown him.

"Of course," she said quietly, returning her gaze to the window.

The carriage was not large, and the distance separating them was small. He could extend his arm and settle his palm upon her knee without exerting any effort. But they may as well have been an ocean apart.

His fault, and he knew it.

He cleared his throat. "We will leave for Wiltshire tomorrow morning. Given the lateness of our nuptials, it seemed best to wait."

She frowned, her attention returning to him once more. "I was hoping we might postpone the honeymoon, my lord."

He studied her, attempting to measure her mood. "Why?"

If her hesitance was being caused by more Montrose-related nonsense...

"Hattie may need me," she said. "And Monty, too."

What if I need you?

Where had that stupid thought emerged from? Ridiculous. He did not need anyone. Not any longer.

"Miss Lethbridge has a family of her own to look after her," he pointed out firmly. "And Montrose has caused you enough trouble to last a lifetime."

Catriona's grip on her skirts tightened, her frown deepening. "But what if Lord Torrington does not regain his memory? And what if Monty should do something foolish?"

He raised a brow. "Lord Torrington will regain his memory or not, regardless of where you are in the world, *querida*. And it is high time Montrose had to clean up his own messes."

"Please, my lord. I would prefer to remain in town for a few days at least," she pressed.

Irritation twisted through him. This entire affair was meant to have been simple. Marry Lady Catriona, travel to Wiltshire to check upon the management of his estate, fuck her until she was breeding. Feel nothing.

"Is it me you object to, or is it Wiltshire?" he bit out, having a suspicion he already knew the answer—both.

"I..." She stared at him, eyes wide, her words trailing off. "Pray do not be angry, my lord. It is merely that you are still very much a stranger to me, and I would prefer some time for us to become acquainted before traveling so far from my family."

Precisely as he had thought.

"*I* am your family now."

"How can I consider you my family when you intend to leave as soon as possible?" she asked.

He had no answer for that question. At least, not one she would wish to hear. Not one which would mollify her misgiving.

"I am your husband," he said, and though the word felt strange upon his tongue, it also held a significance. A rightness he could not deny. This woman was *his*. At last.

The knowledge chased some of the grief crowding his mind.

"Of course you are my husband. That has never been in dispute. Family is a different matter, Lord Rayne."

For some reason, her formality irked him, seeming to underscore her insistence. "Call me Alessandro, if you please. I *am* your family, whether you like it or not, *querida*. You are going to bear my son."

"Or daughter," she reminded.

Alessandro clenched his jaw. "Preferably the heir first, which is all I require."

"An heir you have no intention of seeing." She did not bother to hide the sadness from her voice or her countenance.

"This discussion grows tired, Catriona," he snapped. "We have already endured it once. I do not like children. You will raise the child. Perhaps, when he is grown, I will be more inclined to meet him, but I make no promises in that regard."

"No, you make no promises at all, do you, save that you will leave?" she flung back at him, bitterness in her voice.

More anger, the only emotion he welcomed, surged. "The time to air concerns for my stipulations was well before now. You know what I want of you, and you must accept it. My return to Spain has no bearing upon our honeymoon to Wiltshire. Nor does it have any effect upon us here and now."

"How wrong you are, Alessandro," she said softly. Sadly.

Warmth settled over him at her use of his given name. For so long, he had been known by either his title or *El Corazón Oscuro*. His half-sister Leonora was the only other living person who called him Alessandro. Hearing it again, this time in Catriona's dulcet voice, affected him. He could not deny it.

The carriage came to a halt.

"We have arrived at your new home," he said, for continuing to argue with her would be fruitless.

He was returning to Spain as soon as she was with child, and that was that.

The introduction to Rayne's domestics proved lengthy and awkward.

Settling herself in her new chamber had been strange indeed. Her trunks were still arriving from Hamilton House by the time dinner began.

After dinner concluded, Catriona was dazed and exhausted. She expected to retire to her chamber and await the wedding night her mother had warned her she would face.

You must lie still, Catriona.

Distract yourself as best you can. Think of the weather. Perhaps recite your favorite psalm.

There will be pain.

Pray your husband is quick and merciful with his attentions.

None of which had sounded particularly promising to Catriona, who had already been harboring an endless font of foreboding in regard to becoming Rayne's wife.

And all of which was why her new husband's suggestion took her by surprise.

"Shall we retire to the library, my lady?" he asked formally as he offered her his arm to escort her from the dining room.

"My lord?" she looked at him askance. "I was given to understand you would expect…"

A muscle in his jaw clenched. He was so darkly beautiful in that moment she could almost forget what was to come. She could almost, in fact, welcome it in spite of her misgivings.

"I am not a beast, Catriona," he said in a low voice so the servants attending them could not overhear.

Once again, her husband left her an odd combination of flustered and confused. "I had not believed you to be one," she returned, even though she was not entirely certain it was the truth.

But just the same, she allowed him to escort her to the library. Once inside the book-lined chamber, she settled herself upon a striped divan and watched as he strode to a sideboard. She could not deny he cut a fine figure in his well-fitted breeches, which clung to his long, muscled legs like a second skin.

As she watched, he poured two snifters of brandy before returning to her side and extending one to her in offering. When she accepted it, their fingers brushed. A jolt of awareness shot through her. Their gazes met and held.

"Thank you," she forced herself to say.

He inclined his head. "You are most welcome, *querida*."

Dear.

There he went again, calling her by an endearment with such effortless ease, making her feel things she did not want to feel, things she had only ever felt once before…wicked things. Things that had led to her ruination.

Only, this time, they were far stronger than they had ever been before.

And then, he settled upon the divan at her side.

Devastatingly near.

He flashed her a rare smile. "Take a sip, Catriona."

She did as he suggested, taking just a tentative taste of the stuff. It was potent and bold on her tongue, with a hint of floral sweetness. "Are you attempting to get me in my cups, my lord?" she could not resist asking.

"Alessandro," he reminded her, raising his own snifter to his lips and taking a long, slow drag.

With his head tilted back, his cravat tied in an understated knot, she caught a glimpse of his throat. His Adam's apple bobbed as he swallowed. A fiery rush of heat washed over her, and she could not be certain if the reaction was owed to the brandy or to him.

"Alessandro," she repeated.

How strangely intimate it felt to call him by his given name.

An intimacy which was only heightened by his nearness.

"What do you wish to know?" he asked.

Her ears went hot. Surely, he did not mean concerning the consummation of their marriage. Breathing became suddenly difficult. Her heart wanted to leap from her chest.

"About me," he added, his lips quirking. "In the carriage earlier, you said I am a stranger to you. Ask me a question, and I shall do my best to answer."

There were so many things she longed to ask. She took another slow sip of her brandy, considering which she ought to pose first. And startled, too, by his show of concern for her, so at odds with the dispassionate man who intended to abandon her after he achieved what he wanted.

"How old are you?" she asked first. A safe question, she reasoned. A place to begin.

"Five-and-thirty." He, too, took another slow and steady pull of brandy. "My turn. We shall trade a question for a question. What do you say?"

He was older than she was, but younger than his somberness had seemed to indicate.

She swallowed. "That seems fair enough. What would you like to know about me?"

"Why do you truly wish to postpone our honeymoon?"

Had she thought him fair? She instantly suspected his game of questions had been a ruse all along. "I already told you, my lord."

"No *my lord*," he said. "Alessandro, if you please. And what you told me was not the truth. At least, not the full truth. I wish to know

now."

"I..." She paused, uncertain of how to answer. Not wishing to reveal too much of herself to this enigmatic man, who had shared so little of himself with her.

"Come, Catriona," he prodded. "I answered your question without hesitation."

"The answer was not nearly as complicated as mine," she argued.

His regard intensified. "Why?"

"I fear being alone with you in Wiltshire," she admitted.

He stiffened. "I will not hurt you."

"That is not my fear," she admitted, her cheeks going hot now. "At least, not in the way you mean. I..."

How to say she feared she may grow to like him too much?

How to say a part of her already liked him?

"Say it," he bit out.

"I am afraid of liking you." There. She had made her confession even though she now felt as if she were drowning in mortification.

She raised the snifter to her lips and took a healthy sip.

It singed a path to her belly.

"Liking me," he repeated in his velvet-smooth baritone.

More brandy seemed just the thing. She took another swallow, then decided to change the subject.

"It is my turn for a question." Only, she could not think of what else to ask him. She thought for a moment before finding a suitable topic. "If you do not plan to live in England, why do you want to have an heir? Is it truly because of our cousin?"

"*Sì*." He was still staring at her in a way that seemed to suck all the air from the chamber. "My cousin is a despicable, empty-headed wastrel who insulted my mother. I would sooner see the title bestowed upon a chicken than upon his worthless hide."

Well, that rather answered the question, did it not?

"Indeed," she said, thinking of nothing better to offer. What *could* she say to such a response, really?

"My turn for a question," he said. "What did you mean when you said you are afraid of liking me? Am I to infer you *dis*like me now?"

"That is two questions," she said weakly, before drinking the remnants of her brandy snifter. "And no, I do not dislike you now."

Not at all.

Which was the problem.

A problem that did not seem nearly as troubling with the brandy beginning to take an effect upon her. Her entire body felt flushed. Almost feverish. And concerns which had been multiplying in her mind on the carriage ride to Riverford House dimmed inside her. In their place was an undeniable surge of yearning.

For what, she could not say.

For *him*, perhaps.

Oh, dear.

His gaze had never left her, and he studied her now, almost as if he were seeing her for the first time. "But what of the rest of my question, *querida*? Why do you not want to like me? What is it you fear, precisely?"

"That I will like you too much," she confessed and then promptly clapped a hand over her mouth. "And then you will leave me."

Drat. She had not meant to say that.

He startled her by caressing her jaw. Slowly, almost tenderly. "I am no good for you, Catriona. I am a broken man."

"Let me try to heal you," she blurted.

Where had that thought come from? The brandy? *Yes, surely.*

He shook his head. "Some wounds cannot be healed. They run far too deep."

For a moment, his mask fell away, and she saw him clearly. Saw his misery, his anger, his pain. And she wanted to soothe it. To chase all the darkness inside him away and replace it with the unending light of a thousand summer suns.

She pressed her hand over his, absorbing his warmth, his vitality. "Perhaps you have not wanted to allow them to heal. Or perhaps no one before me ever tried."

"Or perhaps I am not worth healing."

"I do not believe that, Alessandro." With her thumb, she stroked the top of his hand. She felt somehow more connected to him than she ever had, even as he held her at arm's length.

"More brandy?" he asked.

She was sure she ought to say no. But she wanted more of the languid, molten heat roaring through her. She wanted to forget her husband was so in love with his first wife he would never love another. She wanted to forget her jealousy, her fears, her disappointments.

"Yes, please," she said, and mourned the loss of his touch when he took her snifter and rose to his feet.

She watched as he prowled back to the sideboard, refilling her glass. He returned to her, more somber than ever, and also more handsome. She took the snifter and raised it to her lips at once, drinking.

"Easy," he said. "You are a novice to brandy, no?"

Of course she was. "Yes."

But she had never before married the Earl of Rayne, a man who made her heart pound and her stomach flutter. A man who was going to come to her bed later tonight. A man who touched her with such tenderness and showed her more consideration than any gentleman ever had, and yet planned to get her with child so he could go back to his life in Spain.

If she were the sort of lady who easily turned into a watering pot, she would have resorted to tears then and there. But she was not. She was Lady Catriona Hamilton, and she was made of far sterner stuff. Strike that, she was now the Countess of Rayne.

The mantle seemed oddly fitting somehow.

Right.

"It is your turn to ask me a question," he prompted her, interrupting her troubled musings.

"Why have you never kissed me?"

Her face went hot all over again. She had not meant to ask such a bold query. Truly, she had not. This, too, she blamed upon the brandy.

His expression had not changed. He lifted his own snifter to his lips, taking a hearty sip of the spirits, before responding. "I do not kiss on the lips."

"Why not?" she asked.

"No, *querida*," he said. "That is two questions."

The glow the brandy had filled her with dissipated at the coldness of his tone. And she instantly knew the reason for his refusal to kiss had something to do with his first wife.

"What is your question for me, then?" she snapped, irritation replacing the warmth.

"I believe that is enough brandy and more than enough questions for the evening," he said softly, plucking the snifter from her fingers and rising to his feet once more. "We should retire before the hour grows too late. Tomorrow morning, we will need to rise early to prepare for our journey."

Ah, yes, of course. Wiltshire. Their honeymoon. The pretense they had something more than a marriage of convenience was to continue, it seemed. *Blast it all.*

She rose to her feet as well, but the room tilted. Or she did.

All she knew was that one moment, she was standing with perfect grace and dignity—or so she thought—and the next, she was toppling to the floor.

Chapter Eleven

*C*RISTO.

His bride was drunk.

And on the floor of his library, shaking.

Had she injured herself? Alessandro rushed to her and dropped to his knees at her side. He had understood that, as a lady, she had likely never consumed brandy. But he had believed he had not given her too much. That he had given her just enough to soothe the edge off the nervousness which had held her in its iron grip since their vows had been spoken earlier that day.

Clearly, he had been wrong.

He supposed he ought to be thankful she did not possess the constitution of her drunkard brother, but it seemed a small mercy at the moment. She had been felled like a tree in a wind storm.

With ginger care, he rolled her over to her back.

She was *laughing*.

And sotted.

"Catriona," he said, brushing a few stray curls from her face. "Have you hurt yourself?"

She giggled.

His chest seized. Her giggle was adorable. There was no other way to describe it. Her smile was infectious. And she was lovely. So lovely, she made him ache.

Longing struck him. For the first time since Maria's death, he did not just want another woman physically. The desire he felt for Catriona, it was something more. It was something *different*. He felt…connected to her somehow. He wanted her smile. He wanted her joy.

Her lips were pink and lush and full, and the temptation to cover them with his own was as strong as it was undeniable. He yearned to claim her laughter, to swallow it, to inhale it, to take it inside himself.

"Catriona," he said again, this time thickly.

Instead of helping her up, his fingers—cursed fingers, with minds of their own—sank into her hair. He cradled her head.

"Oh, Alessandro," she said on a sigh. "Only my pride is injured. What must you think of me?"

He thought rather a lot of her. But his emotions were too complex, too confusing.

"Are you certain you did not injure something?" he asked.

She seemed fine, but he had spent the last few years of his life with a band of guerrilla soldiers. He had seen inebriation before. Many times. And he knew from experience she may not even notice if she had been hurt.

"I am fine," she assured him, still smiling. Another giggle escaped her lips. "I am sorry. I cannot seem to stop laughing."

He did not mind. He liked the way she laughed. Indeed, he liked the way Catriona did a lot of things. He also liked the silken strands of her hair in his hands. He had not noticed before the sheen of copper glinting in the warm depths of brown. The urge to pluck the pins from her luxurious tresses, to let them fall down around her shoulders, was strong.

"I fear I allowed you too much brandy," he told her.

As for his excuse? He had none, other than he had been too long without a woman. Perhaps the combination of once more having a wife and his self-imposed celibacy in England had taken their toll upon him. Perhaps it was merely the reaction he had to Catriona.

"I should not have drank so much." She giggled up at him, then startled him by catching his face in her hands, pressing her palms to his cheeks as if she were admiring him. "You are beautiful, even when you frown at me."

"I do not frown at you," he denied. "I frown at the world."

"Then perhaps you will smile with me," she murmured, her thumbs tracing over his cheekbones. "Whilst you are here. Whilst I have you."

She was not laughing now.

And he was not frowning either. *Perhaps you will smile with me. Cristo,* such innocence. Such goodness. He was staring at her, bemused. She was his *wife.*

He wanted to say it.

So he did, but in the language he preferred. *"Mi bella esposa."* But he could not find it within him to smile. "Come. We must get you to bed so you may rest. A long day of travel awaits us tomorrow."

Her fingers traveled to his lips then, stilling over them. Her touch was a brand. An uncontrollable bolt of desire licked down his spine, settling in his groin. The effect she had on him was almost damning.

"Will you smile for me first?" she asked, her voice little more than a hushed whisper. "Please, Alessandro."

Inside him roiled a foreign concoction of want, of desire, of frenzied need, of unwise affection. But of guilt, too. Of pain. He could not separate the anguish from the joy, the grief from the hope. All he knew was this fierce woman was making him feel things he had no longer believed he was capable of feeling.

"Please," she said again. "I know it is foolish. I know you do not like me."

And then she issued a half-laugh, half-snort that was somehow even more endearing than all the others preceding it.

The strange urge built to a crescendo within him. He smiled.

And then he kissed the fingers lingering over his lips. Kissed them because this was all he dared. "I like you too much, *querida*," he confessed against her gentle touch.

One more kiss was all he dared, lest he start making love to her here on the library floor. For there would be no lovemaking tonight, and he understood that. She had over-imbibed and was not herself. And he... He was not himself either. Their nuptials had left him shaken.

But not just their marriage.

Something had shifted this evening. They had crossed boundaries he had not believed could be trespassed against. He understood that as he gazed down upon her, her fingertips still pressed over his lips in a parody of the kiss he was determined to deny them both.

"I have been *dear* for some time," she observed.

He noticed how long her lashes were.

"Yes, you have." Only he had not realized it himself until now. Until she had pointed it out to him.

Dios.

"I need something to call you," Catriona murmured, her gaze searching his.

"Alessandro," he supplied, grim.

She shook her head. "If I am your dear, you shall be my darling."

She said it with such conviction, he could not deny her. He kissed her fingers again, and then reluctantly withdrew his fingers from her hair, leaving her coiffure largely intact.

Instead, he took her hands in his, removing her touch from his mouth at last. "As it suits you, *querida*. Now come, if you please. Let us get some slumber. The morning will come all too soon."

<hr />

THE MORNING ALWAYS seemed to come far too soon.

On a yawn, Catriona stretched her arms high above her head, her toes pointed. Dawn was beginning to lighten London, seeping through the heavy window dressings of her new chamber. Her bed was comfortable, the linens soft and expensive and scented delightfully of lavender.

And that was when the full realization hit her.

She was no longer at Hamilton House.

She was in the countess's chamber at Riverford House. Because she was now the Countess of Rayne. Yesterday, her life had been forever altered. She had married Alessandro, and he had brought her here. Still stretching, she blinked as fuzzy remembrance returned to her.

He had brought her here. Introduced her to the domestics. Dined with her. He had taken her to the library, and...*oh dear heavens.*

The brandy.

Her entire body tensed at the same moment she realized she was not alone in her bed. A deep sound of contentment cut through the stillness of the air, and then a strong arm snaked about her waist, pulling her into a hard, hot, undeniably male body.

Her bottom was lodged soundly against something thick and long. Lips nuzzled her ear. A scorching wall of masculine chest pressed into her shoulders, searing her through the fine fabric of her night rail.

"Mmm," he murmured contentedly.

Was he asleep?

What had happened last night?

She could recall nothing beyond brandy in the library, followed by pitching to the floor. *Yes*, she remembered that much. She had fallen, and he had rushed to her aid, dropping to his knees at her side. Had she dreamt his concern? Had she made a complete ninny of herself? Had she truly touched his mouth? And called him *darling*?

A low groan of misery emerged from her.

Her husband had married her for the express purpose of securing an heir. And she had unburdened her foolish heart to him, just before falling face first into his Aubusson. She was never drinking brandy again.

What else had happened? Alessandro had dismissed her lady's maid. Had he helped her to disrobe? Had he seen her naked? *Good heavens*, had she slept through the consummation? Had she lain still? Thought of the weather?

His hand moved, staying further thoughts, and suddenly, he was cupping her breast.

The mortification inside her dissipated. In its place was warmth. And sensation. A glorious, delicious sensation. His thumb grazed over her nipple, making it tighten and sending an answering pulse of something wicked between her thighs. His lips grazed her ear.

More of that, please.

He worked his thumb over her nipple again. The pulse turned into an ache. She forgot about her embarrassment, forgot to wonder what had happened the last night, forgot everything but him. He had touched her before, of course, but never so intimately. Her entire body felt as if it were aflame.

"*Querida*," he murmured, his voice gruff and low from sleep. "You are awake?"

Would he stop touching her if she answered in the affirmative?

"I know you are not sleeping," he pressed, then answered her silent question by giving her breast a gentle squeeze.

She liked his hands on her. "How did you know I was awake?" she forced herself to ask.

"You snore." He kissed behind her ear.

Her breath caught. "I do not."

"Yes, you do." He caught her nipple between his thumb and forefinger, then tugged. "Though perhaps it was the brandy."

"I ought not to have imbibed." Shame wanted to return to her, but then he plucked at her nipple again and fresh sensation blossomed. "It was dreadfully...*oh*."

She closed her eyes and arched her back, wanting more of that delicious contact. Never before had she realized how sensitive her breasts were, how eager for touch. His teasing caresses were a revelation. Her bottom was pressed more snugly to him, his rigid length more pronounced.

His manhood, she realized, her mouth going dry. Instinctively, she wiggled her rump, trying to get closer, aching for him in places she had not realized could ache.

He made a low sound, half-growl, half-groan. "Stop moving like that *querida*, or I will not rest until I am inside you."

She *wanted* him inside her. She wanted him near to her, a part of her. She wanted more than just his hand on her breast and his body pressed to her back.

She wanted *everything*.

Surely Mama was wrong about the wedding night. What woman could think of rain or wind when Alessandro Forsythe touched her thus?

She moved against him slowly. "Stop moving how?"

"Like that." His hand left her breast, gliding down her belly to grip her waist. He undulated against her. "I do not want to take you now. The day will be a long one, and I have no wish to be the source of discomfort for you."

She moved again, allowing her instinct to guide her rather than his warning words. There again was the suggestion she would not like the marriage bed. That it would cause her pain. But thus far, it was difficult indeed to believe Alessandro could bring her anything more than pleasure.

"Did we… last night," she began softly, "I do not recall…"

"If I made love to you, *querida*, you would remember," he said, the promise in his words heating her blood even more.

"Oh."

His lips settled upon her neck, and this kiss was slow and hot, followed by another, then another. "*Dios*, I want you." His hand traveled from her waist, gliding over her hip. "I want you too much."

That hardly sounded like a problem to Catriona.

"I want you, too," she confessed on a sigh of bliss as his hand fisted in the skirt of her night rail, dragging the hem over her knees.

Desperately, she could have added, but refrained.

Higher still, he pulled the hem, all the way to her waist. He explored her thigh in slow, tender caresses. And then he kissed the place where her shoulder and neck met before sinking his teeth into her flesh and delivering a light nip.

Dear heavens. That was… He was…

His touch drifted over her inner thigh before settling between her legs. His fingers delved into the sensitive flesh there, parting her folds, nimbly working over a part of her that made her jolt and cry out. The pleasure was intense. Unlike anything she had ever felt.

Terrifying and thrilling all at once.

"Has anyone ever touched you here, *querida*?" he asked against her skin.

His wicked fingers continued to tease her, stroking, stoking the fire within her. "No," she said on a gasp.

"You are so wet." He groaned into her shoulder, kissing her over the fabric of her night rail. "All for me."

The raw desire in his voice heightened her awareness. She was more than desperate now. She was voracious. Mindless and greedy. Beneath the bedclothes, her hand found his arm. She clutched him, urging him on.

He bit her shoulder. Not hard enough to hurt, but with more pressure than the last little nip. It was a sign, she knew, he too was losing control. He was just as helpless to resist the undeniable connection between them as she was.

With his other hand, he urged her onto her back. Though she instantly missed the heat and strength of him behind her, she recognized the benefit of her new position instantly when he nudged her thighs apart. Their gazes connected in the early morning light as his fingers worked over her faster, rubbing her into a frenzy.

Watching him as he touched her so intimately heightened the sensations already threatening to overwhelm her. She felt as if she were going to come apart. As if something inside her was about to break open.

"*Sí*," he rumbled with approval, his free hand tunneling into her hair. "Take your pleasure, *querida*."

Nothing mattered but his touch. Her hips were moving, thrusting. He increased the pressure, knowing what she needed before she did.

Suddenly, everything changed. The desire inside her peaked. Her body bowed from the bed, surrendering to a burst of bliss so powerful, she could do nothing but cry out. He lowered his face to her throat, kissing her there, his fingers continuing to play over her as quivers of pleasure licked down her spine.

And then his touch moved lower, slipping through her slick folds to teasingly rub over her. When the tip of one finger dipped inside her, she gasped at the intrusion. His mouth opened over her neck, his tongue tasting her skin.

"Are you still a virgin?" he asked softly.

Her ruination had been nothing more than a series of foolish kisses. "Yes."

He muttered a Spanish curse into her neck. "I cannot take you now."

Most gentlemen would have been relieved, she thought. And well-pleased. Her husband seemed disappointed.

"You can," she argued, for she was chasing more of the pleasure he had introduced her to. "Please, Alessandro. I want you to."

His finger worked in and out of her in shallow thrusts. The desire that had never fled increased. Her heart was pounding, her body filled with the same languor the brandy had imbued the night before, only better.

He lifted his head, staring down at her with an expression she could not decipher. Her gaze caught on his mouth. How she wished he would kiss her in truth. She wanted to feel his lips against hers. But he did not.

"No, *querida*," he denied. "There will be a time for lovemaking later."

But he had not removed his touch. And her body was still singing with bliss.

"Now," she said. "The time is now."

She pushed back the sleeve of his nightshirt to access bare skin. She relished the strength, the way he felt, so strong and masculine. Even the hairs on his skin intrigued her. But she supposed that was hardly surprising. Everything about him did.

"Catriona," he protested. "We must travel."

"Not yet." She lifted her left hand to his jaw, tracing it with her fingertips. The prickle of his whiskers was a delightful surprise. "I want to touch you."

He inhaled sharply at her confession. "*Maldición*."

"Show me how," she said.

He was not as impenetrable as he liked to pretend.

She affected him every bit as much as he affected her, and the realization filled her with a newfound sense of power.

"This is foolish," he said, withdrawing his hand at last.

She ached where he had touched her, the stirrings of a fresh rush of pleasure already kindling into more unquenchable flames. "It does not feel foolish to me."

Indeed, it felt incredible.

He had spent the night in her bed. He had brought her to the pinnacle of pleasure. And he wanted her. The walls he had erected around himself were beginning to lower, but she wanted to tear every last one of them down. She wanted *him*.

"It is unwise," he repeated, staring down at her.

She decided to be bold. She reached for him, and her fingers skimmed over his taut belly. Though he wore a nightshirt, his heat tantalized her through the unwanted barrier.

He hissed out a breath. "Catriona."

"Alessandro." She moved lower, seeking the prominent thickness she had felt against her rump earlier.

She was curious, but she also wanted to bring him pleasure as he had done for her. She wanted to make him lose the tight rein he kept upon his control. To undo him. She wanted to consume him.

She found his length and skimmed over it hesitantly.

His hips jerked. She hummed her approval, a bolt of desire piercing her all over again.

"Fine. You want to touch me?" His jaw was clenched. He reached between them, jerking up the hem of his nightshirt. He gripped her wrist and guided her hand to his flesh. "Like this, *querida*. Stroke me."

Her fingers closed around him, with his atop. Nothing could have prepared her for the feeling of him, firm and smooth, velvety soft, thick and long. He moved her hand up and down, showing her what he liked.

She wished for the bedclothes to be gone so she could see all of him. But she would settle for this, his hardness filling her hand, the groan he could not suppress falling from his beautiful lips.

Yes.

This.

More.

"Catriona." Her name was low and guttural.

He was losing himself. She was making him.

She wanted to kiss him, but she would not push him that far. Before he left her, his lips would be hers to claim, she vowed it to herself. For now, she closed the distance between them instead and pressed her lips to his neck. She found his pulse. It was fast, as fast as her own.

And then she licked him. Tasted his flesh as he had tasted hers.

Delicious.

"*Mierda*," he bit out before grasping her wrist and pulling her away from him. "I warned you, but you would not listen."

As she watched, he hauled back the bedclothes in one swift motion, and then, in the next, his big body was atop hers, her legs naturally spread to accommodate him. Her night rail was still bunched around her waist, and his shirt had flipped up in his movement. His manhood rested against her center without any separation between them.

She had won this battle, she thought.

And victory, when it came to the man she had married, was so very sweet.

Chapter Twelve

Consummating his marriage with Catriona had not been Alessandro's intention when he had decided to spend the night in her bed. After he had aided his drunken bride in slipping into her night rail—all whilst carefully averting his gaze lest he be tempted by the sight of a breast or even a hint of nipple—he had gone to his own chamber to prepare for bed.

It had only been when he had ventured next door once more to check on her and she had complained of being cold that he had reluctantly joined her beneath the bedclothes. He had meant to offer her warmth, but instead he had fallen asleep at her side, oddly comforted by her presence.

Bedding her had not been his initial intention that morning either when he had awoken to her body close to his and her breast in his hand. But as lucidity had gradually restored itself to him, he had been reluctant to stop touching her.

And now, he had to be inside her.

He had almost come in her hand.

That would not do. He could only spend inside her.

To get her with child, he reasoned with himself. But reason had nothing to do with yanking his night shirt over his head and discarding it. Nor did it have anything to do with removing her night rail with equally swift measures. It had precious little to do with lowering his head to her beautifully upturned breasts and sucking a nipple into his mouth.

No, that had everything to do with passion. With the yearning that had been building inside him from the first moment he had crossed paths with her. He could not deny he wanted her. Had to have her.

The lusty sound of satisfaction she made when he suckled her pleased him. So did her hands upon him, soft and small and eager, traveling everywhere and leaving hunger in their wakes. He sucked her other nipple, then flicked his tongue teasingly over it.

Her moan rewarded him. Her nails dug into his shoulders. His cat had claws, and he liked it. He liked it far too much. *Slowly*, he reminded himself. *Go slowly. Cuidado.*

She was a virgin, and he must proceed with caution. He had never before taken a woman's maidenhead, for Maria had lain with others before him out of necessity, and the women he had bedded before her had been well-experienced. He did not know what to expect. That he must take Catriona's innocence at once filled him with a potent combination of reverence, trepidation, and lust.

His. She would be his. Forever.

Until you return to Spain, taunted a voice inside him.

Here and now, the notion of her ever taking another lover was unthinkable. He cast it from his mind and delivered a gentle kiss to her stiff nipple. She made a throaty sound of feminine pleasure, and it was so unbearably erotic, he could not stop the bolt of lust that shot straight to his ballocks.

It had been so long since he had last been inside a woman.

Too long.

But this woman, being inside her would be different, and it was something he knew instinctively. Not just because she was his wife. Because she was Catriona. Somehow, they had connected in a visceral way. He felt it in the way their bodies moved together, in the urgency rolling through him.

He wanted to make this good for her. As painless as possible. As pleasurable as he could.

Alessandro kissed a path down her belly, marveling at the smoothness of her skin, the heat of it against his lips. Then lower still. He caressed her hips first, then her inner thighs, spreading her legs wider.

He kissed to her mound, and then he parted her with his tongue, running it along her slick folds. When she cried out again, her hips jolting from the bed, he hummed his approval. She tasted sweet and musky, and he wanted more.

He fluttered his tongue over her pearl, then took her into his mouth and sucked. Here, she was as responsive as ever. Her fingers were in his hair now, not gently sifting but grabbing. She was wild in her pleasure. He had not expected that from a gently bred young lady.

But he was grateful for it.

Grateful for the way she pumped her hips against him with unrestrained abandon. For the strangled sound of his name on her lips, along with a plea for more.

"Please."

She begged so prettily, he could do nothing but attempt to appease her. He licked down her slit, then delved deeper. He sank his tongue inside her wet heat, where he would soon slide his cock. The thought made him even harder.

But first, he wanted to make her come again. This time, on his tongue. As he licked her, he worked his thumb over her clitoris. She thrust against him, making the most delicious sounds, rather like a purring feline.

Sí.

This was good. So very good. Her body tensed beneath him, and he knew she was close. One more gentle surge of his tongue, a swirl of his thumb, and she was gone. She cried out as her release quaked through her. He pleasured her until he could not wait another moment to take her.

He rose, before settling more firmly between her legs. Poised to enter her, he stopped first, drinking in the sight before him. Her eyes were half-closed, her lustrous hair fanned out over the pillow. Her breasts were full and ripe, waist perfectly curved, and even her arms were things of beauty, elegant and pale, her hands clutching the bedclothes at her sides now instead of his hair.

"You are ready, *querida*?" he asked, rubbing the head of his cock over her.

Dios knew *he* was ready.

"Ready," she repeated. "Yes. Oh, yes."

He guided himself to her entrance. Without another word, he pushed inside her, slowly. Wet heat engulfed him. Sensation flooded him. He could not suppress a groan at the feel of her. She was so tight, almost squeezing him out. So good.

He moved again, a deliberate thrust, sinking deeper. His ability to think fled. He was mindless now, lust roaring through his veins, need holding him in its possessive grip. He had to have more. All of her. Another shallow thrust until he reached the barrier of her maidenhead.

His body took on a life of its own. He pumped deeper, gripping her lush bottom in his hands and angling her to slide all the way home. They both cried out when he was fully seated inside her. Heat flooded him.

But he remembered she was a virgin. He lowered himself over her, leveraging himself so he did not crush her with his weight, but so they were flush against each other, her hard, little nipples poking into his chest. He kissed her cheek.

"Shall I go on, or do you want me to stop, *querida*?"

Her brilliant eyes burned into his gaze. "There is more?"

A pained laugh emerged from him. *Cristo*, this woman he had wed...

"*Sí*, there is more. Much more." He paused. "Are you in pain? I do not want to hurt you."

"No pain." Her hands glided over his forearms before settling on his shoulders once more. "There was a pinch, an ache. Now I feel only…restless."

Restless.

Her admission burned through him. Not plunging into her over and over again like a savage beast was growing more difficult by the moment.

"You must tell me to stop if it hurts," he forced out.

And then he moved again, withdrawing almost completely before sinking home. The breath hissed from his lungs. His heart pounded. The relentless ache inside him, the need to empty himself in her, grew. He reached between their enjoined bodies to pleasure her pearl as he thrust in and out of her. His rhythm grew faster. His body was needier.

So, too, was Catriona's. She was moving, her breath coming in gasps. They found their pace together. Faster. Deeper. Harder. He staved off his climax for as long as he could, savoring the feeling of her silken depths clenching on him.

He rode her harder, relishing the tremors of her pleasure until he could not wait another moment. He came with a roar, filling her with his seed as white-hot desire exploded through him with such tremendous force, his vision went black.

His release was so potent, he collapsed onto her for a moment, burying his face in her throat, breathing in her sweet scent of jasmine. Feeling her heart pound in tandem with his.

He had not expected bedding his wife to feel so right.

To take his breath and drive every other thought but her from his mind.

As his wits slowly restored themselves, he forced himself to withdraw from Catriona. The undeniable smear of her blood on his cock seemed a recrimination. He had just consummated his marriage. Had taken his wife's innocence.

And deep inside him, where his love for Maria hid, he felt at once only a grim sense of hollowness. The sooner he got Catriona with child, the sooner he could return to Spain, he reminded himself. This was duty. Obligation.

As natural as breathing.

But it did not feel natural. Instead, it felt like a betrayal.

HER HUSBAND REGRETTED making love to her.

Catriona understood it the moment he flung himself to his back as if she were a flame that had just burned him. In a way, she probably was. He was still in love with his first wife, and the reminder, in the form of his harsh countenance and the distance he had placed between them, was visceral.

Sobering.

He had made her body come to life.

And then he had withdrawn.

She lay there, acutely aware of her nudity. Should she retrieve the bedclothes? Should she excuse herself? What was the protocol for experiencing the most passionate encounter of her life, only to become the object of her husband's guilt?

Not bursting into tears, as she longed to do, surely.

Her body still hummed with the pleasure he had given her. They had just become one, engaged in the deepest form of intimacy, and yet he was quiet at her side. Close enough to touch, but emotionally, he may as well have been an ocean away from her. He may as well have already returned to Spain.

Where his heart was.

Misery descended, warring with the bliss that had rendered her body so pleasantly sated. She swallowed against a rush of emotion she did not want. Emotion she could not face. Not yet. Perhaps, not ever.

She longed to say something, anything, to fill the silence with her words. But none would form upon her tongue. At least, not any she ought to speak.

"Are you well?" he asked, breaking the quiet with his question, so oddly stilted for a man who had just displayed a grand capacity for passion.

"No," she replied, staring at the ceiling. For the first time since her arrival the day before, she took note of the elaborate Grecian plasterwork of the cornice. It was lovely. If only she could truly admire it.

"I am sorry, *querida*."

The low rumble of his voice was her undoing. She turned her head toward him, and he looked so torn, so confused. Vulnerable, almost. He undid her, as always.

"What do you apologize for?" she asked.

"Hurting you." He reached toward her in a gesture of surprising tenderness, cupping her jaw.

He had hurt her, but not in the way he supposed. The discomfort she had experienced—a pinch, then a dull throb, some soreness as he had stretched and filled her with his length—had been soon replaced by pleasure. The sensation of him lodged deep within her, sliding inside, then withdrawing, only to thrust home once more, had been nothing short of exquisite.

What hurt the most was the distance he created. The way he kept himself from her. His *true* self—his heart and soul—not just his physical body.

"Do you regret it?" she asked.

The moment she posed the question, she wished she could rescind it. For it was not an answer she wanted, she feared.

"Hurting you?" He frowned. "Of course. If there was some other way, I would have gladly... It is not my intention to cause you pain. Nor has it ever been."

How strange it was, she realized, for the two of them to be alone, in a bed, engaging in a conversation. No chaperone. No trappings of civility. They were only woman and man, husband and wife, alone. Stripped of every artifice.

Her newfound freedom made her suddenly bold. More daring than she had ever been. She met his deep, brown gaze, unflinching. "I did not refer to hurting me physically. I referred to the consummation. Do you regret that?"

He clenched his jaw, staring at her with his customary intensity. "No, *querida*. It needed to be done if you are to bear my heir. There is no escaping that."

Ah, yes. Necessity. His heir.

All the reasons why he had married her.

Catriona did not know why his lack of emotions for her left her so aggrieved.

"Of course," she said, feigning a smile.

For his benefit. And for hers—for her *pride*, that was.

"Are you in much pain?" Still frowning, he ran his thumb over her cheek in soothing strokes.

She wondered how he could show her such tenderness and yet eviscerate her at the same time? The question she had been tamping down within her, withholding at all costs, rose, strident and demanding. She could not hold it in another minute more.

"Yes," she answered him honestly. "It pains me to believe you were thinking of *her* before. That you are thinking of her now."

He tensed, a muscle in his jaw beginning to twitch. "The heart wants what it wants."

Dear heavens. That confirmed it. The pleasure her husband had seemed to take in bedding her had belonged to another. Just as his heart did.

She swallowed. "Of course."

Catriona understood he had loved his first wife. He had suffered her loss. And she could not fault him for either his grief or the circumstances in which she now found herself. He had entered their marriage with brutal honesty; he had no use for her but one. It was only her own failing that made her heart ache.

Without another word to her, he rolled from the bed. Without a care for his own nudity, he stalked across the chamber. She watched his progression, her stare undeniably drawn to him. He was lean and spare and powerful. Every part of him, from the thick, wavy dark locks atop his head, to the chiseled muscles of his buttocks, was perfect. His back was strong, a plane of sinews and strength. His stomach was lean. His calves, never a part of a gentleman which had previously attracted her interest, captured her attention now.

And his feet.

Heavens, even his feet—large and masculine—seemed regrettably perfect.

Perfection as he left her. He did not bother to close the door, however. Exhaling on a deep sigh filled with her own regrets, she reached for the discarded bedclothes at last, drawing them to her chin. Never in her life had she been entirely nude, lying in her bed.

It seemed blasphemous.

Dangerous.

Wicked.

Wonderful.

She could not deny the way her newfound freedom left her feeling. If she were not so confused by her reaction to her husband and his reaction to her, she was sure she would be pleased by the state in which she currently found herself. Thoroughly wedded, and even more thoroughly bedded.

But before she had too long to dwell upon her tumultuous thoughts, he reappeared at the threshold, bearing a cloth and a basin.

Still naked.

And even though she had so recently experienced every part of his tall, masculine form pressed against her body, she could not help but to allow her gaze to travel over every inch of him. He made her heart beat faster, and he made an ache begin between her thighs anew.

Even as she recalled he did not want her. That he had been pretending she was someone else as he had made her body come to life.

The heart wants what it wants.

If only his heart wanted *her*.

She struck the thought away at once. For it was foolish. Unworthy. And she was doomed for disappointment if she continued in such a reckless vein.

He joined her on the bed, his expression solemn as ever. He looked like a man who had just received his sentence rather than a man who was newly married. And though it was small of her, and though she was ashamed of her instinctive reaction, Catriona knew a burst of fierce jealousy toward the woman who had come before her.

"Will you allow me to tend you?" he asked.

She stared at him, uncertain. "What do you mean, my lord?"

His nostrils flared, his expression hardening, almost as if her formality had caused him a great offense. "Alessandro."

"What do you mean, *Alessandro*?" she asked, emphasizing his name.

Irritated with him. He had taken her to the heights of ecstasy, and then he had allowed her to plummet, like a star burning through the night sky.

"You are bleeding," he bit out, looking distinctively uncomfortable. "I have never before taken a virgin, and I am trying to aid your discomfort as best as I know how."

Little did he know, her discomfort was not caused by what he had done to her physically.

Not at all.

And then the rest of what he had said occurred to her. He had revealed much in his simple statement, perhaps more than he had realized. His first wife had not been a virgin. Had she been a widow? Something else? Questions multiplied within her, clamoring to be answered.

Catriona was reminded, once more, of how little she knew of her husband. And of how little he knew of her in return.

"Catriona," he said again. "Will you let me?"

Ah, yes. He had claimed she was bleeding, and perhaps she was. A different sort of blood than her monthly courses. Her mother had been informative, but not descriptive. Indeed, her mother had led her to believe her sharing the marriage bed with her husband would be a chore, when it had been nothing of the sort.

But she did not want any more of her husband's attentions today. She was confused, her heart a hodgepodge of emotion, her mind stubborn as ever.

Catriona sat up in bed, careful to keep the bedclothes pinned to her chest, resting just beneath her chin, held there firmly by a clenched fist. With her free hand, she reached for the cloth and basin. "I can tend to myself, my lord. You need not concern yourself with me."

He allowed her to take both from his hands. But still, he made no move to leave. And still, he showed no evidence of recalling his nudity.

So blatant.

So arresting.

She inhaled slowly, then exhaled. The cloth and basin were in her hands. She settled the basin in her lap and rested the cloth over its lip.

"Catriona," he prodded, lingering when she wished he would just go.

That he would just take his endless love for his first wife and leave, for she had so little to offer him. Nothing but her body, really. She was the house for his heir. She was offering him freedom in the same way he offered hers. An even exchange.

If only she could think of their arrangement in such cool, passionless terms.

"Do we not have a long day of travel ahead of us, Lord Rayne?"

she asked him, making certain to refer to her husband by his title.

If he wanted distance between them, *by God*, she would give him precisely that.

"*Sí*," he clipped, his countenance turning stony once more. "We do."

"I will prepare myself," she told him. "You may go."

Chapter Thirteen

They passed most of the first leg of the journey in stilted silence.

His bride kept her nose in a book.

He pretended to doze.

But Alessandro was not tired. He was aware. All too aware of each movement she made. Every rustle of her skirts. Every soft sigh. The turns of the page. Her scent. *Dios*, her scent. It filled the carriage.

It filled *him* with lust.

Base lust. Surely that was all he felt. A natural urge to bury his prick in her sweet, tight sheath.

She shifted again. Her slipper-shod foot caught his boot for the second time. He had to wonder if she was not intentionally jostling him. The traveling coach was well-appointed. Large enough. There was no need for her to crowd him, blast her. His legs were long, but hers were not.

He opened his eyes at last to find her looking at him. The force of her stare pierced him all the way to the darkness simmering deep within him. Her beauty hit him just as it always did, as a teeming wallop of remorse laden with desire.

"You wanted something, my lady?" he asked her formally.

Far better, he had decided since that morning's folly, to keep her at a distance. Far safer and easier.

"Yes," she said, her chin tipping up. The defiant spark he had noted in her eyes from the moment their paths had first crossed was back.

"You snore."

His eyes narrowed. "You are lying."

He did not snore unless he over-imbibed, and he was reasonably certain of that fact. Moreover, he had not been truly sleeping.

She shrugged, and even the act of apathy was somehow elegant when performed by her. "I am not. You were snoring, and it was ruining my ability to concentrate upon my book."

"*The Silent Duke*," he read the title aloud, raising a brow. Feminine nonsense, he was sure of it. "Perhaps your concentration was ruined by the tripe within the pages you are attempting to read."

"Perhaps the issue instead is with my company rather than the book itself," she suggested, unsmiling.

He wondered if she had tapped his boot so she could have a row with him.

"Playing nursemaid to your brother has made me tired, *querida*," he said dryly.

The devil was already tempting him today. His intention to keep her at bay had been broken like the waves upon the shore. His bid to maintain formality had been failed by his own inability to think of her as he must.

He ought to have continued to feign sleep.

But his wife was no fool, and he suspected she knew he had not been napping at all.

At his mention of Montrose, her shoulders stiffened. "If we are to be husband and wife, you might try to like my brother. He will be the uncle to your heir."

He shuddered at the reminder. "I forbid my heir from associating with such a blighter. You will raise my son to be an impeccable gentleman, to do his duty to the succession."

"Monty is a gentleman as well," she defended.

In addition to having the loveliest pair of breasts this side of the English Channel, his new countess also apparently had a heart the size of London. When it came to her scapegrace brother, that was.

"Nevertheless, I do not wish for my heir to become a drunkard," he said coolly. For it was true. "I am not enduring this marriage and getting an heir on you so the future Earl of Rayne is a reckless wastrel no better than my idiot cousin."

His words were harsh, and he recognized it the moment they escaped him. They were dripping with bitterness caused by the untenable position in which he now found himself, a man with a wife he had never wished to take. A man who had enjoyed bedding said wife far too much this morning.

A man who was drowning in guilt.

Catriona flinched as if he had struck her, her already creamy skin going paler. "I had not realized marriage to me was so abhorrent to you, my lord, that you must *endure* it. I know I am an unwanted duty, just as you are to me, but did it never occur to you that you might make the best of the time we will be forced to share?"

"Marriage to you is not abhorrent," he corrected, a new stone of regret lodging inside his chest, this one a pebble to join the boulders already residing there. "It is, however, not what I would choose, had I the freedom of decision."

Her lips thinned, and he understood though he had attempted to ameliorate her concerns, he had only served to heighten them.

"And pray, my lord, tell me what you *would* choose. Mourning your first wife forever until you join her in the grave?" she asked.

It was his turn to recoil, for her words cut deep. Too deep.

Was that what he was doing? Living for the dead, dead to the living?

"I have never made a secret of my past," he forced out. "I loved my wife. If I had the freedom to choose, she would never have died. My son never would have died. I would not have held him lifeless in my arms only to watch his mother slowly fade away."

He had said more than he had intended. Revealed far more than he wanted to reveal. And now, he was once more firmly trapped in the past. The agony of that long-ago day revisited him in the form of a fiery ache in his heart. A bayonet to the gut would not hurt as badly. Would not wound him as deeply.

The juxtaposition of his former life with his current life was not lost on him.

He was in a carriage, hurtling onward to the estate he had not bothered to visit since he had been a lad. From the time he had reached his majority, he had spent as much of his time as possible abroad. Away from the father who had never truly accepted him. From the land that had never felt like home. From the obligations he had never wanted.

"Your son," Catriona repeated softly, the word on her tongue as effective as a lance to his heart.

Somehow, hearing someone else acknowledge Francisco was more difficult than keeping his son's memory to himself had been.

He wanted to look away from her, from the compassion in her eyes, the softness in her countenance, which had replaced the anger. Somehow, he could not. But neither could he speak. The carriage swayed over the road, and the sudden silence which had fallen between them seemed loud enough to reveal the furious thumps of his heart.

"Alessandro," she said.

The tenderness in her voice cut him like a blade, for it was undeserved, and yet precisely what he craved.

He gripped his thighs with bruising force. "Enough, my lady. I have grown weary of this discussion."

"I have not." Her expression was determined. Fierce.

Cristo.

"I do not speak of it," he bit out. "Not to anyone."

This was the truth. Speaking of Maria, of Francisco, of what he had lost, was far too painful. Far too difficult. Their deaths had left an unspeakable hole in his life, in his heart. And so, he had thrown himself headlong into war instead. He had become a machine of death and destruction. It was all he knew how to be, for it was the only way the pain had become bearable.

It had been the only way his life had been worth a damn.

"Perhaps you should speak of it," Catriona pressed. "You lost a wife and child, Alessandro. You cannot endure such pain alone."

"I am not alone," he lied.

"You did not tell your sister," his wife stated.

Correctly.

Mierda.

"How do you know?" he bit out.

A flush colored Catriona's cheeks. "I asked Lady Searle. I was curious about you, about your past. I wanted to know more. But I discovered your sister knows less about you than I do. I cannot help but to wonder why."

He looked away from her, his entire body feeling as if it were wound as tightly as the coil of a pocket watch spring. He gazed out the window, wondering if they were near the inn where they would have a respite and a change of horses. It had been so long since he had last made this journey to Wiltshire, he could not recall the landmarks of his youth.

"Alessandro," she prodded, ever persistent.

And then, there was a rustle of skirts. Jasmine fluttered over him in the same moment the soft, feminine weight of her filled his lap. He turned back to her, and her face was close. So close, their noses almost brushed.

The carriage hit an untimely bump in the road, making the entire conveyance sway. Catriona was jostled. He caught her waist in his hands, steadying her. What else was he to do, allow her to go sprawling to the floor?

"What are you doing in my lap?" he growled.

"Making you look at me." Her hands fluttered to his shoulders.

At this proximity, he could once more see the vivid striations in her irises. The freckles decorating the dainty bridge of her nose. Still as alluring as ever. A rush of longing he could not contain hit him. Not just primal desire, but something far stronger.

Something far more dangerous.

Something he must avoid at all costs.

"I have already looked," he gritted. "Return to your seat."

"You have been looking *through* me," she argued. "Ever since this morning. We were closer than we have ever been, only for you to withdraw and place this icy, unscalable wall between us. I will not have it. If we are husband and wife, you must look me in the eyes. You must speak to me, confide in me. Seek comfort in me."

Seek comfort in me.

What a strange thing for her to say.

No woman before her had ever uttered such an invitation. But they had been different. Camp trulls, women who followed armies and soldiers and offered a different sort of consolation than the one Catriona did.

"I do not need comfort," he told her. He had been living these last few years without it. Nothing would change just because he had married her. Nothing *could*, for he was irreversibly broken. "I am leaving you as soon as you are with child. You do understand that, do you not, *querida*? There is no point in this madness you would foist upon me."

He felt her stiffen beneath his touch, but still she did not retreat. "You *do* need comfort, Alessandro. You lost the woman you loved. You lost your son."

Yes, he had, and curse her, the kindness in her voice drove him near the point of breaking. A point he had not descended to in some time.

"I have been comforting myself as I see fit," he told her coolly. "I am fighting for the land Maria loved, the land where she and our son are buried."

"What happened?" Catriona searched his gaze, her right hand going to his cheek, cupping his jaw tenderly.

Part of him wanted to haul her back to her side of the carriage. Part of him wanted to keep her here. To bask in her solace.

His hands tightened on her waist, and yet he did not remove her from his lap. "He never took a breath."

He had not meant to make the revelation. But saying it aloud somehow lightened the burden of the weight upon his chest. Catriona said nothing. Instead, she drew his head to her shoulder. Her arms came around him, holding him tightly to her.

And though he told himself to push her away, Alessandro embraced her back. He buried his face in her throat, stifling the sob rising within him only through sheer force of will. He had not cried in years. He told himself he would not do so now.

Her skin was soft, her pulse a throbbing affirmation of life against his lips. She stroked his hair. Slow, soothing ministrations. Another realization nudged him, no one had touched him thus since he had been a lad. Since his mother. Not even Maria had dared.

He had been a young buck when he had met her, angry at the world. She had always told him he reminded her of a wild horse. She approached him with caution, never knowing what to expect. *Peligroso*, she had called him teasingly.

Dangerous.

And he had been. He still was.

But this foolish woman he had married, who had settled herself upon his lap as if it were where she belonged, seemed unconcerned. She did not know half the things he had done. The violence he had committed with his bare hands, the men he had killed in the name of war.

He was a monster.

He did not feel like one now, however.

He felt like a man.

Like a husband.

Like *her* husband. Catriona's.

"The birthing was difficult," he said against her throat. "Maria labored for hours."

He would never forget her screams. The relief of the doctor's pronouncement the babe was arriving at last. The silence that came after. A shuddering sob fled him before he could control it.

"You can tell me, Alessandro," Catriona murmured, still stroking his hair. "Let me share your burden."

No one could share his burden. But he did not say that.

He inhaled jasmine and sweet, warm woman. "The cord was wrapped around my son's throat. He was an angel when he came into this world."

"Oh, Alessandro," she crooned, kissing the crown of his head. "I am so sorry."

"It was too much for Maria. She was weak and bleeding." He stopped himself from saying more.

But he would never forget the sight of Maria, ashen and wan. Of their son, perfectly formed yet lifeless. Within hours, he had been sobbing into the bedclothes covering his dead wife.

"She died soon after?" Catriona guessed softly.

To his eternal shame, he realized her throat was wet with tears. His tears.

"Yes," he found himself answering. "Not long after, Murat occupied Madrid, and all hell broke loose."

Dos de Mayo had come and gone, innocents slain in the streets by Murat's French soldiers. Alessandro had decided he must do something. And so, he had been swept up in the gathering storm of the conflict, eventually leading a band of guerrilla soldiers in an effort to inflict as much damage as possible upon enemy troops. To stop

Bonaparte.

He had been fighting ever since.

Until he had returned to England, driven by the Marquess of Searle's campaign of vengeance against him. And though his post as a spy for the English troops had come to an end, he still had his men to lead. There was still a war to be fought.

To be won.

He must not lose sight of that now.

He jerked his head back. His wife watched him with an expression of such tenderness, he wanted to slam his fist into the squab. He did nothing. Instead, he stared back at her.

"You were a soldier in Spain, were you not?" she asked then, her gaze searching his.

Seeing too much. "Yes," he bit out. "But I have said enough. We are due to arrive at the coaching inn any minute now."

At least, he prayed they were. He could not withstand much more of this torture.

Alessandro Diego Christopher Forsythe did not weep.

He did not feel anything.

Damn Catriona for making him.

"What do you fear?" Still, her hands were upon him, holding him captive, touching him with such feminine care, it reminded him of a time when he would have reveled in it.

"I fear nothing," he told her. "Not even death. I have nothing left to lose."

"Why do you close yourself off," she continued, undeterred. "I am your wife now, Alessandro. You must trust me. If I am to be the mother of your heir, it stands to reason we should have a bond, some understanding between us."

"Our bond is what happened between us this morning," he told her cruelly. The need to inflict some of his own inner torment upon her, to chase her away, could not be denied. "I am bedding you to get you with child. I will never love you. Spare us both and stop trying to make me feel that which I cannot feel."

His words were harsh, and he recognized it the moment her lips tightened. She had only shown him kindness and compassion, and he had devoured both like a starving man laid before a table laden with delicacies.

But still, she made no move of retreating. He was beginning to realize his bride was stubborn. Strong and relentless, and determined, too.

"I am aware of the reason for our marriage," she said, her voice going quiet. "I do not require you to love me. As for trying to make you feel... I believe you are wrong about yourself."

He almost laughed at her pronouncement. Would have had he been capable of levity, but the desolation of mourning was still enshrouding him, and he could not smile. Could not laugh.

"Indeed, *querida*? Pray, tell me how you might know me better than I know myself."

She framed his face in both her hands now. "You think you cannot feel, but in truth, you are terrified of acknowledging just how much you do. I still have your tears on my skin, Alessandro, proof you have a heart."

But she was wrong about that. He had spent years proving it.

"My heart is dead," he denied, "and the sooner you realize that, the better off you shall be. Ours is a marriage of convenience and nothing more."

And having her examine him was decidedly inconvenient.

How easy it had been to hide from the pain when he had been at war. When his every move had been made for the sake of survival and vengeance against the enemy. When it had been either kill or be killed.

"Hearts do not die," Catriona insisted. "We are all capable of healing and loving again. Will you not try, at least for this time we have together, if not for your own sake, then for mine?"

He thought of all he had seen, all he had done. The bloated corpses of dead soldiers, the screams of dying men. Death had become commonplace, but he was not as numb as he had imagined. He was beginning to realize that now.

Something inside him froze. "Precisely what is it you want from me, madam?"

"I want to feel as if you do not resent me," she said.

"I do not resent you." That much was truth, for he did not.

"I want to feel as if what I feel for you is returned, at least a modicum," she pressed.

"What is it you feel for me? Hmm? You do not even know me."

If she knew him, the real him, *El Corazón Oscuro*, she would flee. She would not be on his lap. She would not be holding his face in her hands with such indefinable gentleness. If she had seen the sins he had committed, if she had walked in his boots, she would run screaming, recognizing him for the soulless devil he was.

But still, she did not go. Nor did she allow him to retreat. She remained where she was, a weight in his lap he liked far too much. Her thumbs traveled gently over the ridges of his cheekbones. Twin, silken caresses.

"What would you do if I kissed you now?" she asked.

Kiss you back.

He was saved from folly by the carriage rocking to a halt.

They had arrived at the coaching inn at last, and not a breath too soon.

With more force of will than he had recently been able to evince, he clasped her wrists, loosening her hold upon him. Then he deposited her on the opposite bench.

"We have arrived at the inn," he told her. "Perhaps you wish for a respite whilst the horses are changed."

Without waiting for her response, he threw open the carriage door and leapt to the ground as if the fires of Hades were upon him.

Perhaps, in a sense, they were.

Chapter Fourteen

She had pushed Alessandro too far.

Catriona knew it when, after the first change of horses, he had chosen to sit on the box rather than share the carriage with her. Subsequent stops had maintained the same distance. And his imposition of space had not improved by the time they reached the inn where they would be staying for the evening.

She had dined in a private room alone.

She was now in the room where she would be staying for the evening, also alone.

And her patience for him had reached an end.

Although her lady's maid had already arrived to help her prepare for the evening, Catriona had sent her away. She had harbored a suspicion her husband's attempts to keep her at bay were not at an end. Their time alone in the carriage had left him shaken.

It had left her hopeful. Hopeful she may be capable of scaling his walls. Of battering down his defenses. Or forcing him to let her in.

Instead, he had withdrawn at once.

She should have known.

Catriona left the room, gathering her courage and her pride both, and made her way to the public rooms. Alessandro was seated, a tankard of ale before him, a pretty, young serving wench not far from his side. Catriona knew a pang of jealousy at the sight. Of course, he would have ladies fawning over him wherever he went. He was not just handsome but compelling in a way few men possessed.

But she was his wife, even if he was determined to treat her as if she were nothing more than a duty, he had not been able to escape. She reached the table, giving the serving wench a pointed stare.

"Husband," she greeted brightly. "I have been awaiting you."

The girl took her cue to leave, fading into the background in a pretense of seeing to the needs of another customer. Catriona turned her attention to Alessandro. He exuded a different energy this evening. He was cagey and raw, his eyes heavy-lidded and dark as they assessed her.

His sullen lips were drawn into a frown. "*Cristo*, what are you doing wandering about alone, Catriona? Do you not know any better? Something could have happened to you."

She seated herself even though he had not bothered to stand or invite her to join him. "Perhaps you should have concerned yourself with such matters before you abandoned me."

He clenched his jaw. "I did not abandon you."

"I have been alone since this morning," she countered.

"I wished for solitude," he said, unrepentant.

He could have his solitude when he returned to Spain.

She stared him down, equally unmoved. "You ought not to have married me, in that case."

"Return to the chamber and get some rest." His tone was curt, his brooding expression even more forbidding than it had been upon his initial sight of her. "Tomorrow is another long day of travel before we reach Marchmont."

"No."

She had allowed him to hide from her for long enough.

"Lady Rayne." His voice was low, a warning growl.

She was not afraid of him. Rather, it seemed clear to her he was afraid of her, which was why he had devoted the day to avoiding her and wallowing in ale.

"Lord Rayne," she returned, unflinching. "Will you order me an ale, or shall I have to procure one myself?"

His lip curled. "You are not sitting in a common room swilling ale."

"Not yet. If you will not oblige me, I will seek out your friend. Or perhaps an obliging fellow."

But when she made to stand, his hand closed over her wrist. "Stay."

Catriona sent him an inquiring glance. "Have you changed your mind, husband?"

The urge to find her way beneath his façade, to rattle him, was strong.

"If you are half as intelligent as I believe you to be, *querida*, you will return from whence you came," he warned as firm in his resolve as she was in hers.

"Ah, but I am foolish," she dared to tell him, her tone conspiratorial, "for I married a man who is determined to leave me. You may say I traded one banishment for another, of a sort. Hardly the action of a wise woman. Nor was it wise to ruin myself and cause my exile in the first place. And it is most certainly vastly unwise to find my heart softening for a man who has told me in no uncertain terms he cannot feel the same."

There.

She had revealed to him what she had only come to grasp herself in the hours alone, silent, in a carriage rocking toward an uncertain destination.

"*Verdad*," he said at last. "That is all truth. There is nothing more foolish than fancying I will ever feel anything for you beyond obligation and lust."

His words found their way beneath her armor, as sharp as spikes, digging into her tender flesh where she was most vulnerable. *Obligation and lust*, he said so dismissively, but she reminded herself of the way he had touched her this morning, what seemed a lifetime ago.

She recalled the kisses he had placed over her body even though he had denied her lips. She remembered every moment of his tongue on her flesh. Of his fingers working their magic, his mouth on her breasts. Of him, deep inside her. The pleasure he had introduced her to had been the likes of which she had never imagined existed. No man who had merely been slaking his needs, bedding her to get an heir on her, would have gone to such lengths.

He was struggling, fighting to keep his ties to the past and the encumbrance of all his guilt. But she had always been strong. She had needed to be, for her mother, for Monty, for herself. She could be strong for Alessandro. She could fight him back.

What remained to be seen was whether or not she could win him.

She leaned toward him, across the scarred table, as if she were about to impart a great secret. "Was I just an obligation this morning?"

A muscle in his jaw ticked. "Catriona."

She was pushing him again, and she knew it. "It is a fair question, is it not?"

Mouth tightening, he signaled for the wench who had been eying him in much the same manner a stray dog watches scraps of meat thrown into an alleyway. The woman returned, casting a dismissive gaze over Catriona before turning all her attention to Alessandro.

"How may I help you, milord?" she asked.

The suggestive tone in her voice was not unnoticed by Catriona.

You may help me by finding the nearest chamber pot and emptying it over your head, she thought disagreeably.

It was small of her, she knew. But it could not be helped.

Her husband brought out the worst in her. Also, she hoped, the best.

"Ale for my companion, if you please," he said, his gaze still hot and hard upon Catriona.

"Yes, milord." The serving girl dipped into a curtsy that allowed a view straight down the front of her bodice.

Catriona barely suppressed the fiery need to trip her.

Fortunately, her husband's eyes remained trained to her. Unfortunately, the warm, brown depths simmered with anger.

She decided to prod him more. "You never did answer my question."

He took his time responding, lifting his glass to his lips for a lengthy draught. "Your question was impertinent."

"Or necessary," she said.

"Impudent," he returned.

"What manner of woman did you imagine you had wedded?" she asked. "I am the scapegrace sister of a scapegrace."

He drank more of his ale, his eyes never leaving hers. The way his tongue flicked over his upper lip when he had finished—a slow, torturous half-revolution—was not lost upon her. "I imagined I married the sort of lady who would not shamelessly sit in my lap. The sort of lady who was intelligent enough to understand the manner of union I offered her. A lady who would go to sleep rather than wandering through a public house. The sort of lady who would not wish to place her already tenuous reputation in jeopardy by once more acting in a manner most scandalous."

"And I imagined I married the sort of gentleman who was not afraid of kissing me on the mouth," she retorted.

Then instantly wished she could recall her hasty words when she saw the way his mien changed, growing grave and harsh where before he had been coolly engaging.

"Oh, *querida*. I am not afraid of kissing you," he said with deceptive softness. "It is merely a distinction I reserve for another."

His first wife.

How crushing.

Unsurprising, for he had never intimated he had tender feelings for her. Their every interaction thus far had centered on how very unfeeling he was. Which, as it happened, was a blatant lie, and she knew it.

Even so, though she did her best to remain stoic, she could not deny the effect his words had upon her. They were akin to a dagger in the heart. For every forward step she thought she had taken with him, she found herself forced back three.

She was saved from responding by the return of the serving wench.

Catriona held her tongue until the girl had gone, throwing longing looks toward Alessandro and swaying her hips as she went. The dreadful female. She envisioned casting the entire content of her tankard in the other woman's direction. Oh, how glorious it would be to soak her enemy in the bitter-scented brew which had been grudgingly placed before her.

"I have always been honest with you," Alessandro added before tipping back his head and quaffing more of his ale.

The sudden craving for the scent of his skin hit her. Unwanted. Powerful. How she longed for this man, even more so after this morning. More so after their carriage ride. She felt more for him than she ever had another man, including Shrewsbury.

"You have been honest with me in some regards," she told him, though hardly all.

Not that she would compare the two men. Alessandro and Shrewsbury were nothing alike. One had upended her world, the other had righted it. One had been a tiny spark on dry kindling. The other had been ravaging, unquenchable flames. One had made her feel safe, and the other made her feel shockingly vulnerable.

But alive, so very *alive*.

"I have been honest with you in all regards, *querida*," he returned. "You merely do not wish to hear the bitter truth. *La vida es fea, mi esposa*. Life is ugly."

Catriona would prove him wrong. She was more convinced than

ever that she could. That she must.

She shook her head, disturbed by his succinct view of the world, for it was not so clear and concise, nor so dark and bleak as he would have it. "Life is night and day. It is summer and winter, warmth and ice, blossoming flowers and frozen ground. Life is spring and fall, new beginnings, and withered deaths. It is pain and pleasure. But you are wrong to think it ugly, Alessandro. The disparities of life are where its beauty hides."

He said nothing, and she could not be certain if it was for the best or for the worst that he maintained his silence. She felt, all at once, as if she had said too much. Revealed too much. And yet, she also felt as if she had not said enough.

Catriona busied herself by taking a tentative sip of her ale. Bitterness coated her tongue. Why had she imagined it would be sweet and delicious, like an elixir of the gods?

In truth, the stuff was awful. It required all the self-control she possessed to keep from spitting it out.

"You do not enjoy your ale, *querida?*" her husband asked, and for the first time that evening—nay, for the first time that day—there was laughter in his voice.

She liked the laughter, even if it was at her expense, for she reasoned he was a man who deserved levity. Who had earned it. Who did not exercise it nearly enough.

She also liked her pride. Too much, in fact. Which was why she raised her own tankard to her lips for another sip. This time, she held her breath as she swallowed the swill down.

Catriona settled the drinking vessel upon the battered table with a thud. Some of it sloshed over the brim. "I do not just enjoy it. I adore it."

"Indeed?"

Was it her imagination, or had her husband's lips twitched?

"I can see why it is called the nectar of the gods," she lied.

He raised an inky brow. "Has it ever been called that? I confess, I do not recall."

Perhaps it had not.

"Oh, yes," she insisted. "It has."

She held her breath and took another sip. Then another. The taste on her tongue when she exhaled was worse than dreadful. It was despicable.

"*Ambrosia*," he said.

Catriona took two more healthy draughts. "Precisely." The urge to belch clamored up her throat, and she pressed the back of her hand over her mouth.

How ungainly.

She could not expel air in such fashion before her husband. Not before anyone. She swallowed the belch and promptly let out a hiccup in its stead.

Drat it all.

"Ah, I understand now." He drained the remnants of his tankard and gestured for the wench. "Another," he told the awful woman when she reappeared. He flicked a glance toward Catriona, a glint entering his gaze. "Rather, two more, if you please. My companion and I are thirsty."

Catriona hiccupped.

She pressed three fingers over her lips, staying future, unladylike interruptions from barreling forth. The awful woman cast a disapproving look over her before turning back to Alessandro.

"Are ye certain, milord?" she asked. "Yer lady friend seems to have had plenty already."

Catriona threw back her head and drained the awful, bitter dregs of her tankard. The good thing about such an action was that it served to kill her hiccups. The bad thing about it was that as the fermented beverage swirled through her stomach, she felt as if she were on the verge of casting up her accounts.

But she would do everything in her power to keep from showing her weaknesses, both to the man seated across from her and the hovering woman. She slammed the tankard down. "I do thank you for your concern, but I am well and quite ready for another."

―――

For the second night in a row, Alessandro had gotten his bride inebriated. He kept his arm around her waist, all the better to steady her, as they made their way to the chamber they would be sharing for the night. She clung to him as unabashedly as an ivy vine.

The first night had been unintentional.

The second night? Utterly deliberate.

He was not ashamed of his admittedly underhanded tactics, either. Nor was he sober either. He had just managed to drown himself in enough ale to dim the ferocious hunger threatening to consume him whenever he was in the presence of his wife.

His wife, whom he had been doing his damnedest to avoid since she had settled herself upon his lap and shaken him to his very core.

He wanted her too much. He liked her too much.

Everything was all wrong, and he needed some time to sort through the disastrous thicket his mind had become. But not tonight. Tonight, he merely needed quiet. And sleep. And no temptations.

Catriona hiccupped. "Forgive me, husband. I do think perhaps I should not have had the second tankard."

Maldición. Her hiccup, like her giggle, was adorable. As was the way she called him *husband*. He did not like it. He liked it far too much.

He needed to get her into bed so she could go to sleep and leave him in peace. They reached their lodgings for the night at just the right moment.

"Or the third," he told her wryly as they crossed the threshold together.

She stumbled over her hem and nearly fell. Another hiccup punctuated her awkward movements. Alessandro swept her in his arms. He kicked the door closed behind them, then cast a glance about the chamber, in search of her lady's maid.

His wife's face was upturned, laughter flirting with her lips and the flashing blue of her eyes. "Was it three? Why did you not advise me better, husband?"

Because I wanted you too silly to present a danger to me.

But he would not say that. "Where is your woman?"

"Sadler?" She smiled up at him and waved a flippant hand. "I dismissed her hours ago."

He stalked across the chamber, aware he was left with two options: either go in search of the domestic or play lady's maid to his wife. Whilst getting Catriona with child was his primary aim, he had already determined it would be in his best interest to maintain the distance between them for the night. Some slumber ought to grant him the clarity he needed.

Because what he needed more than anything was to remember his country awaited him. He did not belong here in England. He never had, and he never would. As long as the French occupied Spain, he could not rest.

For Maria's sake. For Francisco's.

He settled Catriona gently on her feet. Her hands remained on his shoulders, clutching him. *Step away,* he cautioned himself. *Create distance.*

But the scent of jasmine hit him, and he was instantly reminded of the tenderness she had shown him in the carriage. "You ought to get some rest, *querida*," he told her.

His cock was already hard.

She leaned into him, her smile fading. "I do not want rest."

He frowned. "Yes, you do. Today was long. Tomorrow will be just as arduous, and I am not certain what awaits us at Marchmont."

He had been neglectful of the earldom, and this he knew. But he had entrusted matters to his stewards and his step-mother. He had never asked to bear the burden of estates and the livelihoods of so many people.

"Very well," she said, whirling about and presenting him with her back. "Will you help me to open my carriage dress? I fear I cannot manage it alone."

More temptation.

He ought to have drunk more ale.

It had been some time since he had aided a woman in the act of undressing. Presented with the elegant swath of her neck revealed by the upsweep of her hair, he could not resist skimming the backs of his fingers over her skin. She was so soft here. And warm.

He swallowed.

She shivered.

All the tension he had been so determined to avoid had settled upon him. The very air of the chamber had shifted, growing thick and heavy. Anticipation pulsed through him, settling in his groin. Need licked down his spine, fiery and undeniable.

Alessandro forced himself to find the closures of her gown, hidden cleverly within the fine muslin. One by one, they opened. He plucked at a bow which had been tied to emphasize her waist until it, too, came undone.

"Thank you," she told him when the twain ends of her bodice gaped.

She stepped forward, severing the contact, and turned back to face him before stripping the sleeves from her arms and shimmying to allow the gown to fall. And then she stood before him in nothing more than her chemise, petticoats, and stockings. Her gown billowed to the floor.

"*De nada*," he said, forcing himself to walk away from her before he gave in to the mad urge to seize her, take her to the bed, and make love to her all night long.

Instead, he loosened his cravat, stalked to the wash basin, and splashed water on his face, relieved to find it cold. He would need a veritable waterfall of it to cool his ardor.

Behind him, the unmistakable sounds of his wife disrobing could be heard. Soft rustles. Half boots being toed off. A sigh of contentment as the bed creaked and she settled within it. More rustling of bedclothes.

Each noise sent a tiny arrow of lust bolting straight through him.

"I am settled now, husband," she called.

He did not bother to reply, merely splashed more water on his face. Alessandro took his time, removing his garments with care. Slowly. Until the steady sound of his wife's breathing in sleep reached him. Only then, did he move silently toward the bed.

She had succumbed, at long last, to the arduous journey and the ale. Her hair was unbound, a dark halo fanned on her pillow. Grimly, he pulled back the bedclothes and joined her.

And promptly realized his wife was not wearing a stitch.

Cristo, this was going to be a long night.

He blew out the brace of candles he had carried to the bed, pitching the room into darkness, and willed himself to go to sleep.

Chapter Fifteen

For the final leg of their journey through Wiltshire to Marchmont, Alessandro deigned, at last, to join her within the carriage once more. Catriona did not bother to hide her displeasure with him as he settled himself on the squab opposite her.

Her head had only just begun to cease aching, which was his fault.

She had risen to a dry mouth, a swirling stomach, and her lady's maid hovering over her, telling her Lord Rayne had implored her to get her ladyship dressed. They needed to depart. Her breakfast had been small and unforgiving. The haste with which she had been prepared had been most displeasing.

But her greatest frustration had not been in the sad state she had found herself by morning's grim, disapproving light. Rather, it was because of her husband. He had been avoiding her, sidestepping her, and ignoring her for nearly two days straight.

And she had reached her limit.

"Why such a frown, *querida*?" he asked, as if he had not an inkling.

"You know why, my lord," she returned, keeping her voice cool.

As she had ridden alone in the carriage for most of the day, her nose in a book she had not possessed the heart to read, a plan had begun formulating in her mind. A bold plan. A change of tactics.

Perhaps just what she needed.

If he wanted distance, she would give it to him.

And hope it would draw him nearer.

"You are displeased," he observed. "With me?"

"Who else?" She pursed her lips, raking him with a cold stare. "If you do not mind, I would prefer to continue the rest of the way on my own in the carriage. Surely the box is more than suitable for your needs?"

"No." His dark brows drew together. "The box does not suit for our arrival. My need for fresh air is at an end, and I want to spend the journey's close right here in this carriage. With my wife."

"Perhaps your wife does not wish for you to belatedly join her now," she suggested.

He inclined his head, gazing back at her intently. She was losing her heart to him. Another small piece each day. Soon, there would be nothing left for herself. He would own it all.

But she would be damned before she would allow him to crush it beneath his boot or to simply cast it aside as he returned to Spain. Over the lonely course of her journey, she had made a vow to herself. She would not allow her husband to abandon her and their child. He may be winning the battle between them, but she had every intention of emerging the victor in the war.

"You seemed to have no problem sharing the carriage with me yesterday," he said at length as the carriage rocked into motion and they began swaying down the road. "I do not see what should have changed betwixt then and now."

What had changed was her realization she was falling in love with him. That the more she learned about him, the more determined she was to help him heal. To allow him to grieve his wife and son so he could move on from the past and into a future.

A future they could share together.

"What has changed is the way I have been looking at our marriage," she said, putting the wheels of her plan into motion.

He raised a brow. "Oh?"

"I discovered I have been troubling myself over the task of making our marriage work until you achieve your goal and return to Spain," Catriona explained. "In truth, I need to be concerned far more with what I shall be doing afterward. The time it takes for your objective to be achieved will be small. However, the rest of my life looms before me, and I hope it shall be long and full."

He drummed his fingers on his thigh. "I see. And?"

She wished she did not notice how long and elegant they were. She also wished she was not recalling how they felt upon her. Touching her.

Do not think of that now, Catriona, she cautioned herself. *You will stray from your course.*

"It will be easier if we are to have a distance between us," she said. "From this point forward, I think it for the best that we spend as little time together as possible. Aside from the carrying out of our marital obligations, that is. To that end, I really do think you ought to continue on the box."

"No," he bit out. "I will not."

She feigned disappointment. "Very well. If you must remain, then perhaps you might make our shared confinement worth my time."

He looked at her. "Confinement, madam?"

"Yes. What else would you call being forced to suffer your presence in this carriage?"

A stuttered sound of outrage emerged from him. "I beg your pardon."

"I would far prefer to beg yours," she said. "You have made your position to me quite clear. I do apologize for not seeing the wisdom in it before now. But all the hours I have had to while away on my own have proved a boon."

"I thought you were reading a book. *The Malodorous Duke* or some such rot."

She bit her cheek to refrain from chuckling at what had to be his intentional confusing of the title of the book she had been attempting to read. The Earl of Rayne was not always as forbidding and grim as he had been yesterday. Indeed, she was treated to fleeting glimpses of lightness, a boyish air he must have once possessed. This gave her hope she could brighten his heart. Change his mind.

Mend his broken parts.

"*The Silent Duke*," she corrected at length, "and I set it aside for now, giving me ample time to make discoveries of my own."

He quirked a brow. "Such as?"

"How many questions I have for you." She paused, studying him before she continued. "Questions I should have asked before now. For instance, I have been thinking about the time after I bear your heir, when you have already returned to Spain. How long will I be required to wait?"

"How long will you be required to wait?" His jaw clenched. "For what, *querida*? I am afraid I do not follow."

"Yes, Lord Rayne. That is exactly what I said. Your hearing is commendable," she drawled. "You mustn't be so silly. Now, then, have you a length of time in mind, or may I carry on with my life immediately?"

"Carry on in what capacity?" he growled.

She was certain he already knew. His reaction boded well for her plan. "Taking a lover. Or perhaps *lovers*, I should say. I do imagine there shall be more than one."

His countenance turned thunderous. "More than one, madam?"

Catriona tore her gaze from his and settled the drapery of her pelisse and skirts to distract herself. She had always been bold, but blithely informing her husband she intended to acquire a string of lovers was the sort of daring she had never yet attempted.

"Oh, yes." She sighed. "I should hardly think one shall suffice. At least a dozen or so, perhaps more. Since I will be allotted so much freedom, it stands to reason I may as well take advantage of it. Does it not? I expect you to do the same when you are in Spain, of course. I will be most understanding."

She stole a glance at him from beneath lowered lashes, pleased to note he was no longer drumming his fingers against his thickly muscled thigh but gripping it. In the absence of gloves, the ridges of his knuckles rose in stark contrast.

His reaction boded very well indeed.

"You will conduct yourself with circumspection, as befits a countess," he said.

"Of course." She paused. "I will be discreet."

"Prudence is, of course, to be expected. I do not wish for my heir to witness a parade of lovers entering his mother's bedchamber as if she were no better than a broodmare."

"A broodmare, you say?" Compressing her lips, she held his gaze. "What a ludicrous thing for a woman to be reduced to. My future lovers will be well reminded I am a woman, with a woman's heart. That I have feelings. I will choose my lovers wisely."

His lip curled. "Perhaps this is a dialogue best reserved for another day."

"This day seems remarkably suited to it."

"*Mierda!* It does not."

"Yes," she insisted. "It does. Was this not what you intended when you interrupted my solitude?"

He was glaring at her.

She was just beginning to enjoy herself. Here, she thought, was a faint sheen of hope.

"What I intended when I joined *my* wife in *my* carriage was that we should together draw up the drive to Marchmont Hall for the first time."

"Mayhap you should have thought of that before encouraging me to drink enough ale to satisfy an infantry brigade last night and then abandoning me before I woke for all the hours up until this one," she could not resist pointing out bitterly.

"Ah, *querida*." A small smile flitted over his sensual lips. "I begin to see. You are *celosa*, jealous. Was it the serving wench?"

Yes. And his endless attempts to create a divide between them. And his fierce love for his dead, first wife. And his determination to leave her.

To say nothing of her stupid, careless heart. What she had before her was more proof she was abysmal at finding a man who was capable of caring for her in the same way she cared for him.

But she offered him a smile just the same, determined to remain impervious. "Of course not. I am merely realizing I must plan for my future. Our situation will, of necessity, be concise."

The thought made her heart ache. Never again seeing him, conversing only through letters... In a short span of time, Alessandro had become important to her. The connection they had developed was real, and she knew it. Only his own stubborn refusal to let go of the past was keeping them from a true marriage. Now that she had him, she did not want to give him up.

Not ever.

"You have not even given me an heir yet," he said, his accented baritone cutting through the carriage with the force of a whip. "Plan for that first. Before you share anyone else's bed, you must share mine alone."

She almost shivered at the way he said *mine*, somehow making it laden with sensual promise. Still, she knew she could not relent. "I think a month should be sufficient. After I am increasing, you will go to Spain, will you not?"

He clenched his jaw. "That is my plan, *sí*."

"When the babe is born, what if I bear you a daughter?" she asked next.

"Then I shall return," he muttered. "This marriage does me no good without an heir to show for it."

It required every bit of strength she had not to flinch. "But after the heir, I am free to do as I wish, when I wish, and with whom, just as you promised me. Yes?"

His eyes had darkened, becoming almost as black as his hair. "We will discuss this later, Catriona."

"Why not now?" she asked.

"Because I find it distasteful to agree upon the terms of my wife's future lovers when I have only tupped her once myself," he snapped. "Does that satisfy you?"

Yes, she rather thought it did.

The sheen turned into a flicker.

Her hope would not be deterred.

"I suppose it must satisfy me," she allowed, careful to infuse her every word with the greatest reluctance she could manage. "For now."

He muttered something under his breath in Spanish.

Oh, how she wished she could understand it.

BY THE TIME the carriage rolled to a stop before Marchmont House, numerous realizations had become apparent to Alessandro.

One, his wife was trouble.

Two, the urge to thrash her unseen future lovers was as wide as a flooded river and every bit as dangerous.

Three, despite his best intentions, he was becoming increasingly obsessed with her mouth. Specifically, with the way it would feel beneath his. Four, he wanted to kiss her. And not just behind her ear or on the delectable bit of skin where her creamy throat met her shoulder, not over her throbbing pulse, and not even just on the sweet mound between her thighs.

Five, he was going to kiss her, unless he could rein himself in properly.

Six, his wife was trouble. And *sí*, that one was apparent enough and important enough, it required repetition.

Seven, Marchmont was no longer a reflection of splendor. When he had left it behind years ago, it had been a testament to his father's architectural dreams and the prosperity of the Forsythe family over the centuries. But as their carriage had meandered through the familiar drive flanked by laurel and pines, he could not deny both the grounds and grand Palladian façade of Marchmont itself evidenced blatant signs of neglect.

And eight, he was going to hunt down his steward and beat him to oblivion.

But he could do nothing about any of these realizations now as he leapt down from the carriage he had spent the last few hours in lusting over his wife. The gravel drive was the same, though perhaps dustier. The castle-like arch through which they had traversed was covered in ivy. The hedges flanking the wings of the edifice were overgrown. The lawns of the park too were lumpy and unkempt.

A feeling of foreboding settled over him as he offered Catriona his arm and assisted her in alighting from the carriage. His legs were stiff. He was tired as much from his journey as from the marked changes his life had experienced in the last few months, and he could not shake the feeling that something was dreadfully wrong here, in the one place he had been reassured, repeatedly and most vociferously, that everything was so very right.

Catriona clasped his arm, cutting a lovely figure in her fawn pelisse and sprigged muslin carriage gown peeping beneath it. Marchmont's imposing front stole her attention, and he eyed it now along with her. Somehow smaller than he remembered from his youth, the house was nevertheless sprawling and huge.

"This is Marchmont?" she asked.

"*Sí*, it is." His gaze swept over the familiar details, which returned to him now as if he had merely blinked and then found himself standing in the same place, almost as if he had never left.

In truth, so much time had passed. A veritable lifetime. And he was not the same man returning now as the hopeful youth he had been when he had left.

Four massive Corinthian columns framed the front portico. Grecian deities were in abundance, statues standing watch from above. The entire edifice was a magnificent sight to behold. Except for the east wing.

The east wing looked as if it had been ravaged. The windows had been planked over, and the roof looked, even from below, as if it were in ill repair. Black stains marred the limestone.

And though he had sent word ahead, notifying the permanent staff of domestics which remained at Marchmont—the steward, the gardener, the gamekeeper, the parkkeeper, the small group of servants the steward had promised Alessandro he had hired from the nearby village to assist in the airing of rooms—no one seemed to be about. Indeed, for a building so immense and august, the quiet was undeniably eerie.

More carriages were arriving in the lane, bearing the servants he had brought from London.

That was when he realized there was no groomsman.

The stables appeared deserted. Not a horse or a human to be found.

Alessandro had a sinking, desperate feeling he would not even find his steward to deliver upon him the beating he so soundly deserved. It would appear the bastard had not just deceived him but also robbed him with the proficiency of a cutthroat pirate.

"Alessandro."

Somehow, Catriona's dulcet voice cut through his wild musings. He jerked his attention back to her.

"Lady Rayne," he said formally, for there were servants all about them. "Welcome to Marchmont."

And what a welcome it was. Thank *Cristo* he had been cautious enough to bring a good number of domestics from Town. It had been some time since he had been forced to think of households, servants, and travel. His every day had been concerned with warfare, troop movements, and attacks on invading enemy soldiers. Strange how easily his old life returned to him.

Even though it had never felt right, and even though he had never felt as if he belonged here, it was still what he knew. Still in his blood. He carried the obligation of his birth. His mother had adored Marchmont. So had he, as a lad. Before his mother had died.

Before everything had changed.

"Marchmont is beautiful," his new wife said then. "But it seems to be rather closed up. Did you not send word, Rayne?"

"Oh, I sent word," he gritted. And he suspected that was the reason Marchmont had been vacated. "Await me here, if you please."

Without waiting for her response, he strode away from her, his boots crunching on the gravel of the drive, then echoing on the limestone stairs flanking the double doors beneath the portico. He took them two at a time, reached the front portal, and rapped angrily.

Predictably, no one answered.

He rapped again.

Sound reached him. Footsteps on the marble in the entry hall. So small they were almost soundless. The door opened a crack. One eye appeared, situated somehow within the face of what appeared to be a grimy urchin.

"Who goes there?" the creature rasped.

Dios.

"The Earl of Rayne," he bit out. "The owner of this home."

The eye scowled. "The mad earl be abroad."

"The earl is standing before you, *diablillo*, and he is not mad. Now let me pass." He said the last with as much kindness as he could muster.

"No."

The door slammed shut.

Alessandro stared at it, disbelief coursing through him, along with impotent fury. He had spent the past two days hauling his wife and a small army of servants through the countryside, only to arrive in Wiltshire, weary and prepared for his dinner, to find he had a miniature squatter.

He knocked again.

Once more, the portal opened. This time, two eyes and a scowl on a distinctly dirty, childlike face greeted him. "Oh, devil. You *isn't* the mad earl is you?"

"Yes, I am," he growled. "And if you know what is best for you, you will open the door and let me pass. Where are the domestics? Where is Bramwell?"

"Bramwell is gone. Left with Mrs. Fitzpatrick and half the paintings. I don't expect either of them to return any time soon." The urchin stepped back, pulling the portal with him. "I am the only one here, m'lord."

Half the paintings. Though he had few fond remembrances of his sire, the portrait galleries he had cultivated at Marchmont had been tremendous.

He stared down at the grimy child before him. "Precisely who are you?"

The lad, who could be no more than eight or nine years of age, squinted. "Olly's the name."

"Well, Olly," he said grimly, "I believe you and I have a great deal to chat about."

Nothing about this trip to his ancestral home was turning out as he had thought it would. But then again, nothing about his marriage to Catriona was either.

Chapter Sixteen

To say Catriona had settled into her apartment at Marchmont would have been a prevarication of the first order. There was no settling to be done. The house and grounds were nothing short of a disaster. She and the servants who had traveled with them from London had taken an inventory while Alessandro went to the village in search of more servants.

A quick tour of the interior had revealed a fire had ravaged one of the wings and yet no attempt to repair the damages had been made. Furniture was in a state of disarray, some bearing no dust covers, chairs haphazardly stacked in the gallery, bedchambers laden with dust, the slate roof leaking, plasterwork ruined. The walls of the gallery were distressingly bare, having been relieved of their treasures by Alessandro's scheming steward.

A man who, if the dirty little scamp inhabiting the home was to be believed, had fled three days ago with his mistress and as much loot as he could carry, fearing the impending arrival of his master. Leaving behind the scamp, who was his ward.

"What a dreadful rotter, abandoning an innocent child whose wellbeing had been entrusted to him, stealing from a man who trusted him," Catriona muttered to herself as she stood on a chair and hung a freshly aired set of window dressings.

"Who is a dreadful rotter?"

The sudden voice of her husband at her back gave Catriona such a start, she jumped, lost her balance, and fell from her tenuous perch on the chair. Backwards she went, until a pair of strong arms enfolded her, dragging her into his hard chest before she could land.

She clutched at his hands where they rested upon her waist, delighted to find them bare. "Oh, Alessandro," she said, breathless. "You gave me a fright."

He buried his face in her hair, inhaling, still holding her. "Apologies, *querida*. Why are you doing a maid's labor, toppling from chairs?"

"I am helping where needed," she said simply.

Was it wrong of her to take comfort in the warm presence of him at her back? To revel in the way he seemed to take joy in breathing in her scent?

"You are the mistress of this house," he returned, pressing a kiss to her crown. "It is not your duty to be climbing upon furniture and hanging window dressings."

She eyed her handiwork, trying not to think too much of his small show of affection. Likely, he did not even realize what he was doing. "I do not mind. The house is in dreadful need of as many spare hands as it can get. All the better if some of them shall be mine."

"I have hired a gaggle of servants to sweep in and help to repair the worst of it." He sighed into her hair, ruffling the tendrils which had come loose from her chignon in her efforts. "And not a moment too soon, it would seem. I am afraid to leave your side for fear when I return, you shall be playing the part of chimney sweep."

For a moment, she could almost believe they were an ordinary husband and wife, melting into each other after an arduous day of travel. "I dare say I would not fit, or I would try," she teased, spinning about in his arms to face him.

Her palms lay flat against his chest, her right hand over the steady thumps of his heart. A frisson of awareness seared a path straight through her, in spite of her weariness and in spite of the unusual circumstances in which they now found themselves mired.

"I have no doubt you would." His countenance was serious, his gaze penetrating. "I am sorry to have brought you here. If I had possessed an inkling of just how treacherous that lying worm was…"

His words trailed off.

"What would you have done, Alessandro?" she asked. "Returned from Spain?"

"*Cristo.*" His arms were still draped loosely around her waist, holding her to him. "I do not know."

"I am amazed your sister and step-mother did not visit here whilst you were gone and discover the depth of your steward's deceptions," she said.

He shook his head. "My sister suffered an accident here in her youth, falling from the bannister. It is the reason for her limp, and it is also the reason why she did not wish to visit. The memories were too painful. Bramwell knew it, and he knew he could go unchecked by me, the *bastardo.*"

"What will you do now?" That was the more pressing question, as far as she was concerned. They had only just skimmed the surface of the damage which had been done at Marchmont over the past few years of Alessandro's absence.

"Fix it, as I must. I am not a man who takes his duties lightly, Catriona." He shocked her then by caressing her cheek so tenderly, her heart gave a pang. "The eastern wing will need rebuilding. I must comb over what ledgers I can find, speak with my tenants, the farmers. There is much to be done."

"Yes, there is," she agreed, her mind instantly flitting to her own obligations as the mistress of the household. "Thank heavens we have the best of the London staff with us. The beds have been treated to fresh linen. Every surface is being scoured and wiped clean as I suspect has not been done for some years."

"*Gracias, querida,*" he said, kissing her forehead with a reverence that stole her breath.

In the aftermath of their arrival, the tension between them in the carriage had dissipated. They had come together. And that same odd closeness lingered now. Not a pax, precisely. But an understanding of sorts. They needed each other.

She knew she must not allow it to undermine her plan.

And yet, in his arms, extricating herself seemed almost impossible.

"You need not thank me," she said softly. Sincerely. "I am your wife now, Alessandro. And neither am I a woman who takes her duties lightly. We will have Marchmont returned to its glory in no time."

They stared at each other.

She became acutely aware of his heat searing her, his height, the muscled strength of his lean body, his scent enveloping her. Was it her imagination, or was his heart beating faster beneath her touch? Her lips parted, longing overwhelming her.

She wanted his kiss.

On her mouth.

Oh, how she wanted it.

A knock came at the chamber door. They pulled apart as if they were two unwed lovers being caught in a clandestine embrace. Reality returned to her in a swift, bitter rush, reminding her they were not lovers helplessly in each other's thrall. They were husband and wife out of necessity.

Her husband did not love her.

He could not even bring himself to kiss her lips.

Straightening her skirts and brushing a stray tendril of hair from her face, she turned to the door. "You may enter."

The door opened to reveal her lady's maid, Sadler. Her gaze instantly darted back and forth between Catriona and Alessandro. "Oh, I do beg your pardon, my lady, my lord. I did not mean to intrude. I was going to see about unpacking the rest of your trunks, my lady."

There is nothing to intrude upon, Catriona thought grimly.

Instead, she smiled at the domestic. "No need to beg anyone's pardon, Sadler. His lordship was just informing me of all the wondrous help we shall have invading these halls tomorrow."

"That will be most excellent, my lady, my lord." Sadler smiled back, her expression still hesitant.

She could not blame her lady's maid, for Catriona was not accustomed to her husband's presence in her chamber either. She hoped he planned to visit frequently, embraces included. She flicked a glance back at her husband, who showed no indication of leaving. He was yet gazing upon her, his countenance unreadable.

When he looked at her like that, she forgot to breathe.

How vexing he was, hot and then cold, pulling her in and then pushing her away.

"Will you walk with me, my lady?" he asked suddenly, startling her when he offered her his arm.

She eyed him, not trusting her resolve. Not trusting *him*.

"Where do you intend to go this late in the evening?" she asked.

"To the gardens," he answered enigmatically. "You will not regret it. I promise."

She was sure she would.

But she took his arm, casting a glance back at her maid. "Sadler, I—"

"Do not wait up for her ladyship," Alessandro interrupted. "When you finish your unpacking, you may settle yourself for the evening."

"Of course, my lord." Sadler dipped into a curtsy.

Catriona allowed him to whisk her from the chamber, wondering precisely what her husband was about. But then, she realized it did not matter.

For she would follow him anywhere.

※

ALESSANDRO LED CATRIONA through an overgrown gravel path. The late summer sun had long since settled, leaving the moon high overhead to bathe the landscape in a silver glow.

His abbreviated inspection of the immediate grounds of Marchmont earlier had revealed once pristine gardens dreadfully overrun. Even the path on which they traversed now was in desperate need of attention. Laurels and trees crowded them on either side, in some places narrowing the pathway enough so it was almost closed entirely.

"You do realize it is dark, do you not?" his wife grumbled at his side.

"Is it?" He feigned shock. "I thought the sun was a trifle dim this evening."

His lightheartedness appeared to surprise her, for she was silent. It surprised him as well, in truth. He had believed returning to Marchmont at long last would bring with it the bitterness that infected him whenever he thought of England. He had thought it would be strange and unfamiliar, that it would leave him with the same unwanted sense of obligation that weighed down his chest whenever he thought of the earldom and the entail.

But strangely, it had not. His initial discovery of his steward's duplicity and the ravages the home and grounds had suffered had infuriated him. Gradually, however, the rage had been replaced with something else.

As he rode into the village in search of decent men and women to employ, a barrage of reminiscences had settled over him. His mother had been happy here, and so, too, had he, a lifetime ago. He recalled the old mossed oak he had climbed in his youth. Fishing in the river. Hiding from his governess in the temple of Artemis, which overlooked the rolling park grounds and lake.

"Where are you taking me?" Catriona demanded now.

"It is a surprise," he said easily, breathing in deeply the lush scent of the countryside. London, with its soot and fog and its crowded streets, was a far cry from where they were now. He had not known how much he had missed this rich smell of summer, of grasses and flowers in bloom, of life at its fullest blossom.

She huffed a little sigh he was certain had more to do with his refusal to reveal to her their destination than it had to do with aught else. "I am tired after a long day of travel and attempting to restore Marchmont into some semblance of a home once more. And that is to say nothing of the battle I waged with our resident ragamuffin."

"I know the day has been long, and I appreciate your efforts and patience." As they continued their stroll, he rested his hand over hers where it lay in the crook of his arm. "I am grateful. But what is this about the squatter? I ought to have taken the little devil back to the village with me. Was he giving you trouble?"

What a strange creature. Scarcely more than a grimy face, two bright, blue eyes, and greasy brown hair stuffed beneath a cap. Short legs encased in dirty breeches. After losing Francisco, children had oft filled him with a sense of dread, as if the sight of them alone would cause him to be swallowed by the voracious maw of grief perpetually waiting to claim him.

Strangely, this one did not. This one filled him with consternation.

"Oh, you must not send him back to the village," his wife said then in her sweet, dulcet voice that never failed to make his cock twitch to attention. "He has already been abandoned by his greedy villain of a guardian. I shudder to think what will become of him if he does not stay at Marchmont with us."

The way she said *us* should not affect him.

But it did.

Even so, he would not allow the beggar to remain. "He must go to the village. He is not our burden to bear."

"He is a child," Catriona admonished. "And a hungry one at that. We are fortunate indeed Monsieur Olivier brought plentiful stores with him. The lad initially refused to eat a bite, clinging to his pride. He was destined to lose any battle of stubbornness against me, however."

The notion of his wife battling with the dirty imp touched a place inside him he had not known existed. He wished he could have seen it. "How did you defeat him?"

"I told him his pet mouse would be fed to my cat if he did not eat," she said, her tone ringing with pride.

What the devil?

"Do you mean to tell me the squatter is keeping a rodent as his pet? And still you wish for this squalid little ragamuffin to remain?" He paused, warming to his cause before something else occurred to him. "You do not have a cat."

She laughed softly, and the sound sent heat licking through him, settling in his groin. Why must he like every part of her so much? Too much?

"Olly has not yet discovered I do not have a cat," she confided. "Do not tell him, if you please. I cannot imagine how I shall convince the rascal to break his fast and have a bath without the threat that Ashes will meet a bloody end by my feline's ravenous jaws."

"Why should we care if the rascal eats his kippers and eggs or not?" Alessandro returned. "And what sort of creature names a mouse Ashes?"

"A child who has been mistreated and ignored. A child who was so desperately in need of companionship, he befriended a rodent," she said softly, breathlessly. "I am quite resolute in my determination to keep Olly with us for the time being. And you must cease calling him the squatter. He has a name."

"Yes," he said peevishly. "Olly. But I have already told you, madam, I do not like children."

"I will make sure Olly stays out of your way. Since your time here will be short, we need not fear doing so should prove unusually onerous." There was a hint of censure in her voice.

He took note. He also could not fail to notice the manner in which she continued to harp upon his future plans. And for that matter, her plans after she had given him the requisite heir.

Alessandro told himself none of this should be his concern. None of it should bother him. He would set matters to right here at Marchmont, make certain an able and honest steward was in place, task Catriona with looking after the house and grounds in his absence, so that the line carried on after him and that the tenth Earl of Rayne was his son and not his loathsome cousin.

And he would walk away. Damn this return to Wiltshire and the sudden maudlin sentiments attacking him. They did not belong. He had neither the time nor the inclination to entertain them.

"Let us forget about all this for now, *querida*." By the light of the moon, he could see they had almost reached his intended destination on the winding path from the main house. The glow overhead seemed to suggest the view would be good enough, in spite of the darkness.

"I cannot forget it, Alessandro. This is to be my life now, but it will not be yours. If you insist upon leaving me, the least you can do is to allow me to choose my own path. I will not allow you to simply cast poor Olly out and leave him without a home."

His wife's impassioned speech trailed off as they stopped in the clearing on the path overlooking the lake. Even in the darkness, the lake his father had created by damming the river running through the valley below glistened and reflected the light of the moon beautifully. On the hill opposite them, the Temple of Artemis stood in stark relief against the dark woods and grasses. The limestone of the columns took on an ethereal glow, the statues of deities standing proudly.

"Good heavens," she breathed. "What is that?"

The night could not hide the splendor of the view. And even if Bramwell had pillaged the contents of the temple as Alessandro suspected he had, nothing could diminish the tranquil beauty of the scene before them. Overhead, the night sky was clear, an endless blanket of inky velvet laden with twinkling stars. Before them, the lake, the temple.

How had he forgotten how glorious, how calming Marchmont was? Or perhaps it was that distance, years, grief, and loss had somehow rendered him able to see what he had not seen before.

"That is the lake, and on the hill above it, the Temple of Artemis," he said. "The last earl used the river to his advantage by forcing the water to collect. There are four temples here on the grounds. Artemis is the largest and the most stunning."

"The last earl," she repeated. "Your father."

As always, she heard too much. Both the spoken and the unspoken. "*Sí.*"

His sire had married his mother, a free-spirited courtesan who was as loving as she had been beautiful. And he had resented her. He also resented Alessandro for not bearing the proper pale skin of an Englishman. For not looking like the son of an earl.

"Oh, Alessandro," she said softly. "It is beautiful."

"Yes," he agreed. "It is."

But he was no longer looking at the sheen of the moon on the lake or the beacon of the temple and its proud Corinthian columns and elaborate statuary.

He was looking at his wife.

She must have felt his regard, for she turned to him. She was still clutching his arm, which made drawing her nearer all the more natural. So very right. And *sí*, it was. After so many years of grief and torment, here, in the silver-kissed darkness, he found solace for the first time.

Because of *her*. What an astonishing discovery to make. Catriona gave him comfort.

Her hands settled upon his shoulders. Her head tipped back. The brokenness inside him shifted. Fused together, fracture by fracture. He cupped her face in his hands. The contact of her silken skin on his was a revelation.

An absolution.

The time for thinking was done.

Her mouth was his.

And he took it. *Dios*, how he took those lips. They were full and plump and soft, slicked with a hint of dew. Whether from the night air or from her tongue, he could not be certain. She made a sweet sound of surrender, and then she was kissing him back.

Having denied himself for so long, he was ravenous. His tongue demanded entrance, and she gave it, opening for him. He plundered. There was no other way to describe it. This was not the kiss of a man wooing his bride.

Rather, this was the savage claiming of a man who had not felt this deeply in…

Since…

Years.

Cristo, it had been years since he had been so moved. Since he had hungered for a woman's kiss the way he did Catriona's. He had already been inside her, and yet this was the greatest intimacy he had experienced with her.

Her tongue moved against his, and the last thread of his restraint broke.

One kiss was not enough.

One kiss would never be enough.

Mierda.

Chapter Seventeen

H ER HUSBAND WAS kissing her.
Kissing.
Her.
On the lips.
And it was splendid. Not just splendid. *Magnificent.* Yes, that was the word. That was the most apt description.

Catriona kissed him back with all the ardor within her. She kissed him in spite of her plan to keep him at a distance. Kissed him though the day had been long and tiring and arduous. Kissed him even as her mind attempted to make her recall all the reasons why she should not.

How could she not twine her arms around his neck, lick into his mouth as he had done to hers? How could she not want every part of him he was willing to give? And all the parts he was unwilling to give her, too?

Surely, however, this was a victory of sorts. She recognized the significance of this kiss.

I do not kiss on the lips, he had told her. And he had held true to that assertion, never wavering. Indeed, he had consummated their marriage without ever once touching his lips to hers.

Something had changed. Everything had changed. She did not know. She did not care. All she could do in this moment was feel.

Somehow, her back found the trunk of a tree. Her fingers found her husband's hair. They had not stopped for gloves or hats in their mad dash into the gardens. The upheaval of the day, combined with the informality of their arrival at Marchmont, had stripped them of the pretense of civility.

And she was grateful for it now, because she wanted nothing between them. She wanted to be wild, unpredictable. There was no place she would rather be than in her husband's arms, in the moonlight, surrounding by eerie beauty and overwhelmed by the way his lips moved over hers.

Witchcraft, surely.

Shrewsbury had not kissed thus.

No man had.

Alessandro's kiss was slow and languorous, as if he were savoring her taste, her response, the sensation of her mouth beneath his.

One of his hands was on her waist. The other clenched her skirts, dragging it higher. His touch glanced over her knee, up her outer thigh where there was not the barrier of stockings to keep his flesh from hers.

And then, as quickly as the kiss had begun, it was over.

His lips were gone.

The hem of her gown fell into place at her ankles.

His long, wicked fingers had fled from her thigh.

He was staring down at her, his breath furious bursts fanning her lips in a phantom kiss. She wished she could see his expression. But perhaps it was best she did not. Knowing him as she did, she suspected his lapse had aggrieved him.

Mightily.

Her own instinct kicked into action then. She could not allow him to withdraw. To retreat. He had crossed the divide, and she was not about to let him seek to erase it.

Catriona stepped forward, straight into his hard, lean form. A wall of masculine muscle embraced her, emanating heat and his scent.

She grasped a fistful of his shirt and hauled him to her until her breasts and his chest crushed together. Her other arm hooked around his neck, and then she drew his mouth back to hers.

This time, Catriona kissed *him*.

It was a kiss to banish her past. A kiss to banish *his* past. It was a kiss to expel anything that would come between them. It was a kiss of passion and plunder.

Suddenly, her back was thrust once more against the accommodating trunk of an ancient tree. Her husband's tongue was in her mouth, his lips moving over hers. This was not just a kiss but a claiming.

An affirmation she was his.

And he, too, was hers.

Her fingers sank into the thick strands of his hair. Every part of him seemed a miracle. And she wanted to revel in him, to rejoice.

The man she had believed would never kiss her had broken. Or perhaps, he had healed. Whatever the case, she would not question it. She would only accept it. Take it.

Take *him*.

His tongue was in her mouth again. And she was braver than before. This time, one of her hands left his hair. She slipped it between them and found his hip and then traveled across his thigh. Her hand connected with the rigid length of him, his breeches the only impediment to what she wanted.

He made a low sound, his tongue licking deeper into her mouth, the pressure of his lips increasing over hers. Encouraged, she cupped his staff. He was thick and rigid and long, and now that she had experienced her wedding night…wedding morning…she understood what it meant. So too, she understood what her body's reaction indicated. She wanted him inside her, filling her, bringing her to pleasure.

Everything else had fallen away. There was only hunger, raw and pure and primitive. There was only need and want, and along with it the undeniable sensation of rightness. The knowledge nothing between them would ever be the same after this night.

But he had brought her to this spot for a reason.

He had married her for a reason.

Duty and obligation had a place. But tonight, for the first time, he had shown her he regarded her as more than a mere marriage of convenience. He had shown her he respected her. That he cared enough to bring her here. To kiss her, at long last giving her the last intimacy he had withheld from her.

But she wanted more from him.

"Take me here," she whispered against his lips.

"No," he denied, but he did not withdraw his mouth. Nor did he make any effort to extract himself from her embrace.

She realized something else. He was trembling. The strong, menacing Earl of Rayne was trembling in her arms. Emotion vibrated in the space separating their lips. Their eyes were locked. In the darkness, everything seemed heightened. Her heart thumped so loudly, she wondered if he could hear it. Their breaths mingled. The night air around them was heavy and thick, sweetened with the scent of late-summer blossoms.

"You do not want me?" she asked, though the evidence of his desire for her grew beneath her hand. She dared to curl her fingers around him, to stroke.

"Catriona." His voice was harsh. "I am not going to take you in the dirt."

None of this had been part of her plan. But she could not shake the feeling that if she did not push him, he would retreat and withdraw from her for good. That her chance to keep him would vanish.

His anguish still seeped into her as if it were a tangible thing. Was it guilt which trapped him, or was it love? Or was it a combination of the two, weighed down by a heaping portion of fear?

Whatever the answer, she wanted it gone.

"We are not in the dirt. We are in the trees." Gently, she pressed her lips to his.

She was a novice, it was true, but surely they could find an accommodating patch of grass? They need not lie on the gravel path. Perhaps lying was not a requirement at all. Perhaps the massive trunk against her back would do.

He kissed her back for a moment before tearing his mouth away. "No, *querida*. This is not right."

"Yes, it is." She caressed and kissed him again, gratified when his hips jerked, thrusting himself into her hand.

On a growl, he caught her wrist and moved her hand away. His breathing was harsh. Ragged. In the paleness of the moonlight, his eyes were almost onyx, burning into her.

But he did not break free of her as she feared he might. Instead, he gazed down at her, as if she were a cipher he desperately sought to comprehend. "*Cristo.* What do you do to me?"

If it was even a hint of what he did to her, she could well understand his plight.

Before she could form a suitable response, he laced his fingers through hers, tugging her as he moved down the path. "Come."

"It is dark," she protested, even though the moon was large and high in the sky, shining brightly enough to illuminate their progress.

"Stay close to me." He tugged her into his side, keeping her near. "I know the way."

They were not headed back in the direction of the main house. Her fingers tightened on his as she matched his long strides. "Where are you taking me?"

She knew she ought not to protest. That he was holding her hand in his and hauling her along for his impromptu journey was in itself as miraculous as his kisses had been. But she was so uncertain of where she stood with him. Her lips still tingled with the knowledge of his. Her body yet thrummed with desire.

"To the temple," he said calmly, as if he had not just upended her world with his kisses. "I thought you might like to have a look inside."

Such a thing could have waited for daylight. For a day when she had not spent hours traveling and frantically attempting to make Marchmont inhabitable. The Earl of Rayne escorting her, however, was a rarity indeed.

"That would be lovely, thank you." She held her tongue about the rest, shivering at the realization of how different he was here. He was almost at home.

There was no doubt Alessandro did not find London to his liking. In Town, he had been a caged, wild animal. Here, he belonged. The land changed him. The home changed him. Even with the unexpected tumult and devastation they had arrived to, he seemed lighter somehow. More intense, though less unhappy.

Still a man at war with himself. But mayhap a man who could win the war rather than allow it to defeat him.

"You are shivering," he observed into the silence, stopping on the path to shrug his jacket from his shoulders. "I am a beast to haul you all over Marchmont like this. Forgive me?"

She would have told him she was not cold at all, that rather it was her reaction to him and the subtle changes she noticed within him that made her shiver. But he was behind her, draping his coat over her shoulders, running his hands over her in soothing strokes to settle the garment into place. The jacket was warm from his body, and his scent drifted to her. Even had she been suddenly thrust into the midst of a sweltering desert, she would not have denied his coat.

"I will forgive you anything," she told him.

"Ah, *querida*," he said softly. "Do not make promises you cannot keep."

She could not argue the point. "Very well. I shall forgive you *most* things. That is, perhaps, far more accurate."

His hand was in hers again, and they were walking once more down the path.

"I am not even certain you should forgive me most things," Alessandro told her, maneuvering them around a fallen branch obstructing the path.

One more sign of the lack of care the massive estate had been receiving in his absence.

"Half the things?" she suggested, seizing the sudden nonchalance of the moment, for she sensed it was what her husband needed.

"Which half?" he quipped, his tone rueful. "What would you not forgive me for?"

"I would not forgive you if you sent Olly away," she said, returning to the cause which had so concerned her until he had distracted her on the path with the glistening lake and the looming temple and his soul-stealing kisses.

"What has the miscreant to do with either of us, hmm?" he asked, leading them to the left when the path before them diverged into two separate routes.

"He is a child," she said, holding her breath after the words emerged from her. For Alessandro had told her he did not like children, just as he had told her he did not kiss on the mouth.

But he had kissed her tonight.

A child may be more than he could handle.

Particularly when the child in question was a rude, dirty little scamp with a pet mouse named Ashes.

"You want to keep the little *pícaro*?" he asked.

They wound around a bend. "What is a *pícaro*?"

"A rascal, a rogue."

She frowned at him. "Olly is none of those things. He is a child. An innocent child, who cannot help the situation in which he has found himself."

"A squatter with a pet rodent? You will have a child of your own soon. You would be better served to concern yourself with your future son." His tone was cool, but his fingers had tightened on hers as he spoke.

Though something inside her melted at the mention of a child of her own, she was not about to give up her fight for Olly. There was something about the lad that tugged at her heart. "Surely you would not be so unfeeling as to send away a child in desperate need of a home."

"I do not trust the little beggar." Her husband's tone was grim.

"Let it be my worry, not yours."

"Enough talk of the scamp for tonight," he bit out, leading her through a cove of trees and into a clearing.

Before them, the Temple of Artemis loomed larger than it had appeared from a distance, imposing in its grandeur. Breathtaking really, but not as breathtaking as the man holding her hand. The man whose jacket was draped over her shoulders.

Her husband.

"It is beautiful, Alessandro," she said in awe.

Even through the darkness, she could discern the attention to detail. Corinthian columns, exquisitely carved statues, the entire temple rounded with a domed roof. She had never seen the like.

"I have not been within it since our arrival," he said. "Judging from Marchmont, the interior may well be ruined."

The most beautiful exterior could hide a damaged interior.

Alessandro was living proof of that.

"If it is, we will restore it to its former glory," she told him, giving his fingers a gentle squeeze.

She was talking about far more than the temple. But she held her tongue as they made their way to the entrance. In the spell of the moonlight, the temple was even more beautiful at such proximity. They stopped before a closed door flanked with statues on either side. In the ethereal glow, she could see enough details to discern one was Apollo and the other was Artemis.

"Wait here for me," he said as the door swung open. "I will see if there are candles within, or if that *bastardo* has robbed them as well."

She did as he asked, remaining on the threshold. Moonbeams cut through the darkness of the interior, casting circular patterns of light on the stone floor. A series of windows lined the domed roof, allowing the illumination.

Alessandro's shadowy figure was at the far end of the room. The familiar sound of him striking a flame echoed, and then, one by one, he lit the candles in a candelabra. Warm light glowed, flickering through the cavernous temple. But she only had eyes for her husband. He was handsome, so very handsome. The intensity in his gaze stole her breath.

He extended a hand to her. "You may enter, *querida*. Watch your step over the threshold."

She moved inside, as inescapably drawn to him as ever. The interior of the building was circular, studded with alcoves bearing statuary. The effect of the moonbeams, the soft candle light, and the Greek gods and goddesses standing as silent sentinels, Alessandro in the middle of it all, was nothing short of magical. She placed her hand in his.

As always, the touch of his bare skin upon hers sent a jolt of desire straight through her. He emanated heat. His dark eyes devoured her.

"Thank you for bringing me here," she said softly.

"When I was a lad, I would hide from my nurse here. It was one of my favorite places. The view of the lake is unparalleled."

The notion of a young Alessandro touched her heart. "Why did you hide from your nurse?" She wanted to know.

"She was a miserable crone," he said. "Chosen for me by the earl. She refused to allow me to speak *en español*, which was my mother's preferred tongue. If I did not speak English, she rapped my knuckles with a wooden rod."

Her fingers tightened over his, and the protective urge to hunt down his horrid nurse and break a wooden rod over her head could not be stymied. "How awful, Alessandro. Why would your father employ such a creature?"

"He was looking after the best interest of the earldom." He flashed her a self-deprecating smile. "He was taken with my mother's beauty, but he had always hoped his son would be born pale-skinned and fair-haired. I had my mother's dark skin, hair, and eyes. He reasoned if he could not change the way I looked, he could at least control the rest."

"I am sorry." How awful it must have been for him not to be accepted as he was by his own father. Little wonder he had fled England. "I cannot believe he would allow that wretched woman to abuse you."

"It was a long time ago now, *querida*." He placed the candelabra on a ledge, at the base of a statue of Zeus. "I am a far cry from the helpless lad who needed to seek concealment here."

Of course he was. He was all male, undeniably. Tall and strong, lean and harsh, masculine and muscled. But that did not mean he did not still bear the scars of his past. She could not shake the feeling that slowly, bit by bit, she was beginning to understand the man she had married.

There was nothing helpless about him now, and yet she still saw the boy he must have been. She stepped closer to him. "Alessandro—"

"No," he bit out, interrupting what she had been about to say. "Do not. Do not look at me with your heart in your eyes. Do not look at me as if I am anything more than the man who married you to get an heir on you and then leave you. Because that is all this is. That is all we are to each other, Catriona."

He was pushing back. Trying to create distance between them.

But he had *kissed* her. On the lips.

It was too late for the pretense he was not attracted to her or affected by her, and she was not about to allow him to get away with the suggestion theirs was nothing more than a marriage of convenience.

Her every plan previously constructed on the carriage ride to Marchmont flitted away. Feigning disinterest was impossible. Because she was not just losing her heart to the man who had led her here, she had already lost it.

She was in love with the Earl of Rayne.

"If that is all we are, then kiss me again," she dared him, trembling. Emotion as vast as the seas overcame her. She had never felt anything like it. "Kiss me again and walk away."

"*Maldición*," he said. "You know I cannot."

And then, his lips were once more on hers.

Chapter Eighteen

He did not know what his original intention had been in bringing his wife to the Temple of Artemis. All he did know was that she was too kind, too caring, too good. *Far too good.*

Just like her lips.

Cristo, this woman's mouth.

Kissing Catriona was a revelation, lighting him up from the inside, just as the candelabra had illuminated the temple. His body was aflame. His cock was rigid, straining against the fall of his breeches.

He was awash in contradiction, too. His heart was confused. Coming here to Marchmont with Catriona had been a mistake. It stripped him raw. Memories, always memories. Of his sire, his mother, of the child he had been, of the injustices he had experienced.

Being here reminded him he had never had the chance to bring Maria.

But it also reminded him he was alive.

The same way kissing his wife did.

And she was responsive. So damned responsive. Her full lips opened exquisitely to the pressure of his. His tongue was in her mouth, claiming her, tasting her again. Sweetness and tea, mysteries and woman, and pure *Catriona*.

Nothing else mattered but her in his arms, her sweet mewls of pleasure, the way her fingers tightened on his hair. Nothing mattered but kissing her, having her, taking her.

For she was his, was she not?

He could take her, could he not?

He told himself doing so would be duty. He could not have an heir if he did not bed her. There it was. A reason. The guilt which ordinarily assailed him whenever he was in her presence was muffled now beneath the crushing tide of the inevitable. If he wanted to return to Spain and the war effort, he had to get a child on her. Kissing her with this in mind did not feel like treachery so much as it felt like duty. Delicious duty, to be sure. He had never been tempted to take another woman's mouth. Not until *her*. In the years since Maria's death, he had gradually found the ability to slake his needs. He had bedded women, much to his shame. But he had never kissed them on the mouth.

Catriona's lips had been the first. And as if he were a dying man in the desert, newly led to water, he could not slake his thirst fast enough. He kissed her with bruising force, one of his hands grabbing her chignon and angling her to just the right position. His other hand was on her waist, anchoring her to him.

Her breasts were crushed against his chest. Her tongue met his, kissing with a fervor to match his. It proved his undoing. If she had stood still, allowing him to ravish her mouth, he could have controlled himself.

But she was as eager for him as he was for her.

Blood thundered through him.

His cock was so hard, he feared he would spend in his breeches if she cupped him once more as she had earlier on the path.

He told himself he was performing a duty as he moved them to the wall, kissing her as they went. But every part of him knew it for the lie it was. Catriona affected him in a way he had not anticipated. In a way he had not believed possible. And now that his lips had owned hers, he could not seem to stop. His mouth on hers was as natural as breathing.

He did not cease moving until her back was against the wall. His hand slid from her hair to her neck, cupping the base of her head as he deepened the kiss. But it was not enough. Never enough. He had to be inside her.

Both his hands found her waist, and he withdrew his lips from hers with the greatest of self-restraint. Her breaths were as ragged as his. He stared down at her in the warm flicker of the candles. She was so beautiful, she made him ache.

He did not deserve this woman, and he knew it. He was battle-scarred and life-scarred. He was broken. Imperfect. Flawed. He would never be the proper lord his father had intended for him to be. He would never be the husband Catriona deserved.

But he was selfish. She was his.

And he had lost the reins of his control.

He spun her around. Dipping his head, he pressed a fervent kiss to the nape of her neck as his hands sought hers. Clasping her wrists in a gentle hold, he guided her hands to the wall.

"Brace yourself," he told her. For a moment, his hands settled over hers.

To their left, the statue of Zeus towered, immense and forbidding. To their right, a marble of Venus proudly watched over their folly. The moment was perfect. The woman was perfect. He was imperfect.

Cristo, how very flawed he was.

But she was his, and he was ready to worship her. He released his hold on her and sank to his knees. With one hand, he pinned the hem of her gown to her waist. With the other, he found the delicate curve of her calf, following it all the way to the sensitive dip behind her knee. Over stockings and garters. Finding bare skin above it, her thigh, then higher still.

Mierda, her hips were luscious and beautiful. She was a miracle of femininity, her body a study in softness and ferocity, in supple grace and reluctant surrender. He could not resist memorizing every part of her with his lips and tongue.

First, his mouth.

A kiss on the back of her right thigh, just above the tie of her garter. Bare skin, warm and feminine and silken. Then her left thigh next. *Gloriosa.* His fist tightening on her trapped hem, he kissed his way to the treasure he sought, her sex.

He guided her thighs apart, kissing her center. He licked along her slit, parting her with his tongue. She tasted good. Musky, life-affirming, and sweet. His cock swelled as his tongue dipped inside her.

She made a soft sound of surprise, then a low moan. He stimulated the needy bud at the same time until she was arching her back, her knees buckling as she came on a wild cry of release.

With the taste of her sweeter than honey on his tongue, he stood. Alessandro undid the fall of his breeches, and his cock sprang free, rigid and ready. He held his breath as he guided himself to her entrance. She was slick and hot, kissing his tip with wetness and pure temptation.

"Are you ready, *querida?*" he asked against her ear.

She nodded, her breaths emerging as short little pants.

He bit her earlobe gently, tormenting them both by sliding home just a bit deeper. "I did not hear you. Tell me you want me."

"*Oh.*" The word sounded torn from her, half-moan, half-sob. She pressed her bottom into his groin, seeking more.

He kissed her throat. "Say it."

"I want you." The admission was a plea now.

"*Sí,*" he growled, all he could manage.

In the next instant, he plunged inside her to the hilt. *Cristo*, she was all tight, slick heat. Gripping him with so much force he almost came after one pump. Reining in his rampaging lust, he withdrew from her almost entirely before rocking back into her.

Their rhythm was easy and tinged with desperation. They moved together in the semi-darkness, their ragged breaths and low sounds of need echoing in the stone walls of the temple. The pleasure bursting down his spine was so forceful, he could not resist. Pumping in and out of her, her silken depths welcoming him, he knew he would not last long. He wanted her too much. She felt too good.

His ballocks tightened. He moved faster, driven by the need to claim. He wanted to bury himself inside her so deep, to plant his seed in her womb. *Duty*, he told himself. *El deber.* Nothing more.

But she did not feel like a duty in his arms. Her cunny did not feel like an obligation. She felt like perfection. Like desire. Like raw need. He pumped harder, repositioning her so he could drive into her at a better angle. Even deeper.

Dios, it was so good. *She* felt so good. Too good.

She tightened around him, convulsing as she spent once more.

And he was lost.

On a roar, he thrust, filling her with the torrent of his release. He came so hard he thought his heart would pound out of his chest. So hard, a blinding flash of light exploded across his vision.

Struggling to catch his breath, he leaned against her back, holding both of them upright against the wall of the temple. One of the tapers on the candelabra burned itself out. Then another.

He withdrew from her body at last, using a handkerchief to clean first her, and then himself. The sight of her pale, rounded arse and legs in the moonlight were unbearably erotic. She said nothing as he tended to her. With a muttered curse, he flipped her gown back down, then restored his breeches to proper order.

Artemis mocked him from across the chamber.

El deber, he reminded himself pointedly.

"The hour grows late," he told Catriona as yet another candle burned itself down to a nub. An omen, perhaps. "We should return."

She spun around to face him at last, and even in the dim light, he could see the faint rose in her cheeks. "Alessandro?"

"*Sí, querida?*" he bit out, angry with himself for his lack of control.

"*Gracias*," she told him with a tender smile, and then she threaded her fingers through his once more.

And with that lone word and gesture, the anger burning inside him sputtered out just like the next candle.

Mierda.

<hr />

HOURS AFTER HE had taken his wife, Alessandro was prowling the dark halls of Marchmont. He had escorted Catriona back to the main house, seeing her to her chamber before doing the cowardly thing and leaving her to settle for the evening alone.

Though he was beyond weary, exhausted from travel and the trials of finding his home pillaged and abandoned, and sated from the heights of pleasure he had reached with his wife, sleep eluded him. His mind was a jumbled confusion of past and present, of regret and guilt, of need and desire. His chest was heavy with the weight of knowledge.

Tonight, he had crossed boundaries with Catriona he could not uncross.

Biting back a curse, Alessandro stalked to the study that had belonged to his father. Like every other part of Marchmont, he recognized each creaky floorboard, every last stick of furniture, even though it had been years since he had last been within these walls. This chamber was no different as he settled the brace of candles he had been carrying with him upon his father's desk.

He skirted the mahogany, Grecian-inspired monstrosity. The heads of the gods were carved on each of the four legs supporting it. His father had requested his own likeness carved into the chair. Alessandro slid his fingers over the familiar dips and planes, the fleshy pad of his forefinger finding the almost indiscernible crack in his father's prominent nose.

Once, when he had been angry at the former earl as a child, he had lopped the nose right off with one of his knives. In a fit of panic, he had later returned and glued the nose into place without his sire ever being the wiser. Indeed, his father had died without ever knowing the nose upon his prized chair had once been savaged by his only son.

Alessandro lowered himself to the chair, staring into the flickering play of light and shadow before him. The art in this room remained hung upon the walls, he noted now. There had not been time to investigate earlier, pressed as he had been to attempt to find some suitable staff to work Marchmont back into its former state of elegance and grace.

But how ironic it was that his thieving steward had only stolen the portraits from the gallery, where he had clearly presumed the most valuable paintings hung. The last Earl of Rayne had kept his most treasured paintings within this very chamber, and thank *Dios* they had not been the victim of water damage, flame, or outright thievery. The Titian and Caravaggio still ornamented the wall in the same place of honor he remembered from his youth.

Sitting in his sire's chair felt damned odd.

Wrong.

As wrong as kissing Catriona on the mouth should have felt. But kissing her had not felt wrong at all. Rather, it had felt necessary. It had felt like the beginning and the end, all at once. It had felt as if he had always been meant to feel her lips move beneath his, as if he would perish of hunger without the chance.

Hell.

He stood as if the chair had been fashioned of flame, and in a sense, it was. The burning pain of his past. The boy he had once been confronting the man he was. If he recalled correctly, his father had always kept brandy on his sideboard. Years had passed, but it was possible, he reasoned, his *bastardo* of a steward had not stolen the liquor stores as well.

Raking his fingers through his hair, he reached the sideboard and plucked up a decanter.

"I would not, were I you."

The voice, unexpected and small, coming from somewhere within the shadows at the opposite end of the room, had a sudden and intense effect upon him.

"*Cristo!*" he bit out, slamming the decanter back atop the sideboard with so much force he was surprised it had not shattered. "Who is there?"

"Bramwell was fond of blue ruin," added the voice, unrepentant. "But his swill is sure enough to make you ill. I drank some of it myself one night, and I spent the evening casting up my accounts in the gardens."

Gritting his teeth, he searched through the darkness for the source of the voice, for he already instinctively knew its owner.

The little beggar.

Olly.

The dirty, unkempt creature his wife was determined to take under her wing. The same dirty, unkempt creature he was determined to send to the village.

"And what were you doing, drinking gin, *pícaro?*" he asked. "You can have no more than eight years of age."

"Twelve," said the lad from a far corner of the room.

"Twelve?" he raised a brow, scanning the darkness for signs of the imp. "Surely not. When I was twelve, my voice was becoming a man's, and I had already begun to grow whiskers."

He had spotted nothing of the sort in the lad earlier, which was why he had guessed him to be a good deal younger, and he likewise heard nothing of it now.

"My voice is changing." The lad made an obvious effort to convince him, lowering his voice an octave. "And I am fair-haired. Golden whiskers require more time."

His eyes narrowed. He stalked deeper into the darkness covering the front half of the chamber, determined to discover where the usurper was hiding. "I remain unconvinced, despite your excuses."

"What is a *pícaro?*" the lad asked.

"Why are you not abed as a child ought to be at this time of the night?" he countered.

"I don't like the darkness," came Olly's response.

For the first time, Alessandro believed the squatter was telling the truth. "Why not?"

But he was sure he knew already. The darkness always held its terrors. Memories. Pain. The unknown. After he had lost Maria and Francisco, he had spent untold nights staring into the murky blackness of the night, questioning his place on terra firma, the fragility of life, his belief in heaven and even *Dios* Himself. He had stared into the inky gloom, alone in his bed, his heart feeling as if it had been severed in two, wondering what death was like. Begging for death to claim him as well and put him out of his misery.

"I aren't afraid of it, if that's what you think," Olly said.

"I am not afraid of it," he corrected gently, as some instinct within him, previously dormant, awoke and wondered what education this child had received in his short life, if any.

"I didn't say you was."

"You were," he said. "*I didn't say you were.* That is the correct way of saying it, *pícaro*."

The imp made a rude sound of disgust. "How do you know? You don't even talk like the rest of us."

"I was educated here," he clipped, irritated with the runt as much for the disruption as he was for the ease with which the miscreant hid himself. "I am an Englishman by birth."

How strange it felt to acknowledge. He had not considered England his home since his mother had died here. But he was now surrounded by all the reminders, the little chains tying him irrevocably to this land, to these people. He wondered how his mother must have felt, torn between her family and everyone she knew at home in Spain and becoming the wife of a wealthy and important English earl.

"You doesn't sound like one," said the squatter, his tone dubious.

"And yet, I am." He stalked toward a chair, convinced that must be where the little devil was hiding. "And the proper way of saying it is *you do not sound like one*. How much schooling have you had, *pícaro*?"

"More than I need," claimed the little voice in the night. "You never did say, what is *pícaro*? For all I know, you be calling me horse dung or donkey piss."

A reluctant laugh burst from him even as he discovered the chair where he had believed the miscreant was hiding was empty. "And why should I call you horse dung or donkey piss?"

"I've been called worse." The child's voice seemed to have moved. "I'm a bastard, after all. No one wants me, least of all Bramwell. But my mother died and left me with her sister. And then she died along with her husband. A lung infection, it were. They was both gone in one sennight."

Frowning, Alessandro stalked next to a settee, but it, too, was empty. "How did you come to be with Bramwell? What is his relation to you, and what do you know of him?"

These were questions he would have asked earlier—should have asked earlier—but he had been too preoccupied with Marchmont's state of abandonment. And, too, he had known he would need servants. Badly. Those had been his first concerns.

"Bramwell be a cousin of my uncle's. He be's a rotter and I do not like him."

He quirked a brow. "That makes two of us, *pícaro*. Why do you not tell me where you are hiding so I can cease searching the chamber for you like an imbecile?"

"What is an imbecile?" asked the impudent creature.

He clenched his jaw. "I will give you all the answers you seek if you emerge from your hiding place."

"What makes you so certain I am hiding?" he asked, his query accompanied by the rustling sound of a small body sliding across the carpet.

Cristo, the beggar had been secreting himself beneath the settee. Alessandro should have known. "Because you were lying on the floor beneath a piece of furniture," he said dryly.

"Very well."

Alessandro detected a flurry of movement in the darkness as the lad emerged from his hiding place. He stood to his full height, then offered a bow.

Upon second glance, the lad was taller than he had recalled, but his frame was wiry and slight. His face, too, was soft and almost feminine. Bright eyes. Rounded cheeks. The lad was almost pretty, in fact.

Suspicion crept over him.

What if the lad was not a lad at all?

He resembled a female of twelve years far more than he resembled a male.

"There you are, *picaro*," Alessandro said slowly, feeling as if he were seeing a great many things now for the very first time. "It means rogue, child. And an imbecile is—"

"A man who were swindled by another?" the cheeky miscreant interrupted.

"No," he bit out.

"A man who be's wandering about in the darkness when he could have as much light as he wished?"

"A fool," he said. "A dolt. A halfwit. That is what it means."

"Same difference," said the squatter with a sniff.

"See here, imp," he said. "If I had my way, you would already be back in the village where you belong. Lady Rayne has taken pity on you, and to your great fortune, my wife possesses a heart of utter gold."

In that sense, she reminded him of his sister Leonora.

The sister who felt too much, who loved with her heart upon her sleeve. The sister he had very much feared would have her heart broken. But who was looking after the heart of Catriona? Her drunkard brother? He nearly scoffed aloud at the notion.

"Are you certain it don't mean donkey piss?" the lad dared to inquire.

To his utter shame, Alessandro felt his lips twitch involuntarily. The boy had daring, he had to admit and admire.

But he was not about to acknowledge either of those facts. "I am certain," he said, stoic. "Just as certain as I am you must find the bed assigned to you and get some rest."

"I'll go to my bed, m'lord," the lad said. "But I can't make any promises about sleep or rest. That don't come easy."

"It does not come easily," he corrected absently.

"Right," said the lad. "It don't."

With that parting volley, his unwanted interloper promptly shuffled across the study and disappeared out the door.

Leaving Alessandro to stare after him.

And to realize, much to his chagrin, the boy was right.

Rest would not come easily to him this night.

Chapter Nineteen

"What is your favorite food?" Catriona asked her husband the next morning over breakfast.

Alessandro paused, forkful of eggs raised halfway to his lips, suspended in midair. "*Qué?*"

Catriona flicked a glance toward the butler, who had followed them from London and who, she had discovered, knew Spanish. *What* mouthed the butler.

Bless him.

"Your favorite food," she repeated, sending the domestic a grateful smile. "What is it?"

Her husband scowled at her. "Why are you smiling at the wall?"

He was in a dreadful mood this morning, was he not?

"I am smiling at Johnstone," she informed him, smiling at him now, with a cheer that was rather forced.

He had been gloomier than a storm cloud ever since she had first met him in the dining room for breakfast. After he had escorted her back to her chamber following their torrid encounter in the temple, he had simply walked away. She could only presume he had spent the night sleeping in the chamber adjoining hers, but she did not know for certain.

"You may go, Johnstone," Alessandro ordered without bothering to look in the butler's direction. "Lady Rayne and I shall finish the breakfast on our own."

"My lord," the butler began.

"That will be all," Alessandro clipped, interrupting what was sure to have been Johnston's protestation against not being allowed to dance attendance upon them.

Over her husband's shoulder, the domestic sent Catriona a long-suffering look. Her lips twitched, but she suppressed the urge to laugh.

"Of course, my lord," said Johnstone.

The servant was already much aggrieved by the state in which they had found Marchmont. But this breach of protocol would surely be viewed as an insult. She waited until the butler had gone, discreetly closing the door at his back, to raise a brow at her husband.

"Was it truly necessary to dismiss him?" she asked.

"Yes." He lowered his fork, glowering at her. "Why are you asking me about food and flirting with the butler?"

"Why are you so angry?" she countered.

She had not particularly appreciated being abandoned at her bedchamber door last night. Not after what they had shared. Not after he had kissed her. But she had understood all too well the struggle he was facing, an inner battle being waged between his past and his present.

Catriona had told herself to ignore his cool demeanor this morning.

She had told herself to try.

She wanted to please him. She wanted to make the best of their circumstances. Lord help her, she had believed, after last night, he may have begun to soften toward her. That his feelings for her had deepened, at least to the point where he no longer felt kissing her on the lips was a betrayal of his previous wife's memory.

But she had been wrong.

Dreadfully wrong.

On all counts.

"I am not angry, *querida*," he denied, assessing her with his molten gaze. "I am merely…perturbed."

"*You* are perturbed," she repeated, pursing her lips. "With *me*."

"Yes." He frowned at her. "What is this asking me about food? I do not like it. And then all these covert looks with Johnstone. This too, I distrust."

Had she thought him in a dreadful mood? How wrong she had been. He was being completely mad. That was what he was doing.

She settled her fork on her plate, ignoring the jarring clink it made upon the fine china—one of the few objects of value Alessandro's steward had not robbed. "I am asking you about what you like to eat because you are my husband and I wish to please you. I am planning our menus for the next week today, allowing for the organization of this undeniably lackluster household. The staff needs to acquire provisions as there is precious little stores here remaining. Perhaps I should have asked you what you do not like to eat."

"I do not like salmon," he informed her.

"Then I shall ask for it at every dinner," she returned.

"My lady." His tone was one of warning. Menacing. His expression was carved in stone. His jaw, rigid and flexed.

It was the first time in a long time he had referred to her by that name, and that he did so now was not lost upon her. They had shared intimacies. They had kissed. And yet, now, he chose to retreat.

She ought not to be surprised. "Is your dislike of all fish, or is it relegated to salmon alone?"

"If you must know, I grew ill after I ate salmon when I was a lad, and I have not had the stomach for it since." He paused. "What is this truly about?"

Catriona sighed. "It is about trying to please you, just as I have said."

"You please me well enough in the only manner I require," he said.

And there it was, in his gravelly velvet voice, the suggestion of passion. The reminder of what they had shared. Even as he sought to diminish their connection, she could not staunch the wave of need coursing through her. The familiar stirrings of desire settled deep in her womb.

But she was not going to allow him to so easily ignore that something between them had shifted last night.

"You kissed me." Though she had not meant to blurt the obvious statement, once she had, she was glad.

He stiffened. "Lust has made many a man before me weak."

"Has it made you weak enough to kiss another, or am I the only one?" she dared press him.

His jaw clenched. "Do not try to make more of what happened yesterday than it is. You are aware of our understanding. Nothing has changed."

How wrong he was. For her, everything had changed.

She loved him.

And he was intent upon maintaining a distance between them, keeping her at bay, withholding his heart from her. Intent upon leaving her.

"Our understanding, yes." She did not miss the way his eyes had dipped hungrily to her mouth. "You have a strange way of seeing the understanding to fruition, Lord Rayne."

He drummed his fingers lightly on the table. "Call me Alessandro, if you please. I dislike being called Lord Rayne."

"Why?" she demanded. "Is it because it reminds you of what you are?"

His lip curled. "And what am I, *querida*? Tell me."

"An earl," she charged. "A man who has been avoiding his duties."

He flinched as if she had struck him. "Enough."

"Why?" She had already come this far. She would not retreat now.

He was as immovable as a boulder. He needed to be pushed.

"You think I do not feel the guilt in my chest, heavy as an anvil, when I look around here?" he charged, his eyes darkening. "When I look at *you*?"

"You should not feel guilt for looking upon your wife," she told him, frustration lancing her. "You chose to marry me. But as for the guilt you feel when you look upon Marchmont, that I cannot deny. This estate, its lands, and its people, are your obligation. Yet you have been absent."

"*Suficiente!*" He slammed a fist upon the table, making the china and silverware rattle. "I said enough."

At last, she had shaken him, but his fury provided precious little comfort. She did not want his anger. She wanted his love.

"Do you feel guilty because you kissed me, my lord," she prodded him, "or because you liked it?"

He stood suddenly, throwing back his chair with such force, it toppled over. She rose to her feet as well, watching him as he stalked around the table. His anger enhanced the severity of his features, making him somehow more beautiful than he already was. She found herself in his arms, precisely where she wanted to be, one of his large hands splayed possessively on her lower back, the other caressing her cheek in the whisper of a caress. Her nipples went instantly hard, an ache beginning between her thighs and blossoming outward.

"I feel guilty because I want to do it again," he said grimly.

And then, his mouth was on hers. The kiss was not soft or gentle. But neither was it rough or angry. It was searing. Claiming. The way their lips fit together made her sigh. She kissed him back with all the fervent need rising within her to a brilliant crescendo.

A violent sweep of his arm on the table behind her upended the remnants of her breakfast, and she did not care. He moved them as one while he consumed her mouth. Her rump met the beveled edge of the table. He caught her lower lip between his teeth and gently nipped her, pulling back just a bit to gaze down at her.

His expression was inscrutable aside from the undeniable desire she knew he must see reflected in her own countenance. For a beat, she feared he would withdraw from her entirely. That he would push her away and resume the detachment he had been treating her to all morning.

But then, he guided her onto the expanse of table he had so ruthlessly cleared. His fingers tightened in the skirts of her gown and chemise, lifting them to her knees. He kissed her again, slower and deeper, and then he settled himself between her legs.

He was going to take her, she realized.

Here.

On the breakfast table, where they could be interrupted by a servant at any moment. She should be horrified.

Instead, heat coursed through her. A steady throb of want pulsed in her sex. Oh, how she needed him inside her. It was stronger than hunger or thirst. Powerful and wicked. He kissed down her throat, his long fingers tightening in her chignon and pulling her head back to allow his exploration.

His hand was hot on her skin, sweeping over the bare flesh above her garters and stockings. He sucked on her neck, and she felt it in her core. Her body was aflame, overwhelmed by sensation. His subtle dominance undid her. When his touch dipped between her legs, stroking her needy flesh, she moaned.

He found the sensitive nub hidden within her folds and teased it with slow, steady circles. It was too much. It was not enough. She jerked into his hand, wanting more. His lips moved to her ear.

"You want me," he murmured.

"Yes." Her acquiescence became a gasp when he sank a finger inside her.

But she did not want his lips grazing her ear. She wanted them on hers. Catriona grasped a handful of his cravat and yanked his mouth back to where she wanted it. On a growl, he kissed her harder. His thumb moved over her pearl.

A frisson licked down her spine. He curled his finger, touching a place inside her so deep and delicious, she lost control. Her body seized, a frenzied rush of release washing over her. She whimpered into his mouth, into his kiss, surrendering.

On a growl, he slid his finger from her channel. Between them, he undid the fall of his breeches with hasty, efficient movements. And then his thick tip was glancing over her folds. He thrust against her pearl, sending another miniature shower of spasms through her. His tongue was in her mouth, his hand still fisted in her hair as he ravaged her lips.

Movement in the hall beyond the door caught her attention briefly, sending a swift bolt of fear through her, followed by a wicked jolt of something else. Somehow, the notion of them being caught, of Alessandro about to slide into her body as the door opened, titillated her.

The near interruption did not matter.

Nothing mattered.

Because he guided himself to her entrance. One pump of his hips, and he was inside her, filling her. And it was good. It was so good. With his mouth on hers, his grip on her hair, his staff sliding in and out in a delirious rhythm, she could not control herself. She spent, the pleasure quaking through her almost violent in its intensity.

He thrust harder. Faster. The table, heavy as it was, shook beneath the force of his movements. Her fingers bit into his shoulders as more exquisite decadence rocked her. His lips clung to hers. On another low growl, he stiffened, the warmth of his seed flooding her as he lost himself as surely as she had.

But she had no time to luxuriate in the languor that overcame her whenever he made love to her. For he jerked away from her almost at once. With swift, efficient movements, he adjusted himself, fastening his breeches before restoring her skirts.

She sensed his inner withdrawal just as surely as she felt his physical one. "Alessandro," she said.

"Not another word," he bit out. "I have done my duty to you for the day, and now if you will excuse me, I must see to the rest."

"Alessandro, please," she called after him, hating the way he could not bear to face their intimacy without resorting to a cool, aloof stranger. Hating the guilt he felt. Hating the past he had known with another woman, the love he had given her.

But her husband ignored her pleas. He did not even meet her gaze. He merely turned on his heel and strode from the chamber, leaving her perched upon the table where he had placed her, the carnage of their abandoned breakfast all around her.

Wondering how they had gotten to this place.

Wondering if they could ever get beyond it before it was too late.

***

ALESSANDRO FOUND HIMSELF back in his father's study, this time by the light of day, a few hours of sleep none the wiser, and the ledgers his thieving steward had left behind laid out before him. Also, the heavy stone of regret lodged deep inside him.

Following his shameful inability to control himself at the breakfast table, he had spent the remainder of the day touring the estate. Discovering fallow fields, cottages in disrepair, others abandoned. The wing of Marchmont Hall that had been damaged by fire needed to be inspected by an architect. Rain had been pouring into the compromised roof in several areas, leaving the remaining walls moldy.

The ledgers before him offered incontrovertible proof that his steward had been swindling him for the last several years at least, growing bolder as time wore on. Perhaps the *bastardo* had even been robbing Alessandro's father, though he had yet to dig back far enough into the records to determine the veracity of his suspicions.

All around him was the undeniable evidence he had done exactly what Catriona had accused him of that morning. He had indeed been avoiding his duties. Marchmont had been going to ruin in his absence.

For the first time since returning to England, his obligations hit home. There was more, far more, he needed to accomplish aside from making certain his heir would inherit the line. He needed to restore Marchmont, or it would be destroyed. All the funds he had reserved to keep it running beneath his steward's careful guidance—so he had thought—had been depleted.

What he had on his hands was one hell of a mess of his own making.

He scrubbed a hand over his face, staring down at the ledgers, unseeing. He was beginning to fear his stay in England would necessarily have to be far longer than he had initially supposed. And that was a problem in itself, because he was also growing increasingly attracted to his maddening wife.

The mere thought of her was enough to make his cock go hard, even as he sat at his father's desk, wallowing in the depths of his own failures. He could still feel her lips beneath his, soft and pliable, giving and sweet. Could still feel the silken heat of her sheath, gripping him, pulling him deep into the depths of her body.

He had lost his head with her last night.

And then he had lost his head with her again this morning.

He told himself now it was merely lust that made him lose control in her presence. He was ravenous for more.

He could be in her presence without needing to toss up her skirts.

Sí, he could.

Beginning today.

Or perhaps, rather, tomorrow.

Or the next day.

Maldición.

This was not good. Not good at all.

Chapter Twenty

CATRIONA SNIFFED THE air. "You need a bath," she informed Olly.

They were working on the Marchmont library, which was in desperate need of something else. Organization. Books had been haphazardly stacked on the floor. Others appeared to have been thrown from shelves by someone in a fit of pique. With the household a bustle of activity and her husband once more avoiding her, she had deemed the library an appropriate task to tackle as it killed two birds with one stone.

She would set the room to rights and would also discover how literate the little scamp was.

"I doesn't need a bath," declared Olly, his bottom lip jutting out stubbornly.

And it was becoming apparent the answer was not very literate at all. The lad was able to discern letters, but he could not read. Nor could he speak properly.

"I do not need a bath," she corrected absently, tucking volume one of *Jortin's Erasmus* alongside volume two on a shelf she had emptied earlier.

"Are you sure you doesn't?" Olly asked, sounding suspicious. "If there be's something foul in the air, mayhap you need to look no further than the end of your nose for the source."

Rude fellow, wasn't he?

She looked over her shoulder at him, noting the grime coating his face and hands. It looked as if it had been present for some time. *"Are you sure you do not?* That is the proper way to say it, my dear Olly. And as I have recently bathed and there are no flies buzzing about my head as if I am a cow in the pasture, rotten with my own filth, I am sure neither myself nor my nose is the source of the stench."

"Here now, I doesn't see any flies." Olly tossed a book to the floor and crossed his arms over his chest, pinning her with a frown.

"Yes," she said grimly. "When was the last time you bathed?"

"Last week."

She did not believe him. "Olly."

Olly shrugged. "Last month, maybe."

She wrinkled her nose. "You are definitely the source of the odor. When one smells unpleasant, it is past time one removes the filth."

Olly's eyes narrowed. "I thought you wanted to get these books back on the shelves, my lady."

"I do," she agreed, taking up a volume of Shakespeare and settling it onto a different pile. "But not if I must suffer your smell all afternoon long. I am ordering a bath for you."

"No!" Olly hollered, an undeniable expression of fear crossing his features beneath the dirt.

"There is no harm in a bath," Catriona soothed, wondering why the poor child would possess such an aversion to cleansing himself.

"Perhaps the carpets is the source," the lad bit out hastily. "Or look there. Rainwater got into the wall." He pointed at a water stain marking the wall covering. "You smell rot from within."

The stain in question was dry. Catriona had already inspected the damage herself. Likely, it had been caused by the nearby window, which appeared to have been fixed. Either by someone other than the horrid steward or well before the man had grown so bold in his refusal to perform his duties.

"The smell has one source, and I am looking at him," she told Olly. "I will have my lady's maid prepare a bath for you."

"No," Olly denied instantly, eyes wide. "No bath."

His fear troubled her. "Come now, you must bathe at some point, and better now than before the flies circle you in truth."

"I'll be taking my chances," the lad insisted, scowling.

"No," she said sternly. "You will not."

Though she had no experience with children, Monty was her older brother, and he was something like the fully grown, man-sized version of one. Surely that had to count. She knew when to be firm, when to stand her grown, and when to concede the point.

If Olly wished to remain at Marchmont, he would need to win Alessandro's favor. He would also need to render himself far less pungent. She could not allow him to run about Marchmont covered in grease and grime, holding her nose each time she held an audience with him.

"I doesn't want no bath, my lady." Olly stood equally firm, just as determined.

For a young lad, he was certainly sure of himself. But then, she supposed he had needed to be. Heavens knew what manner of deprivations and suffering he had experienced at the hands of his departed guardian.

"I do not want a bath," she corrected gently, moving toward her quarry with slow, careful strides. Much as she would an untamed horse, lest she startle him. "You must learn the proper speech if you wish to grow up to a fine gentleman."

"I doesn't want to be a fine gentleman neither." He took a step back as she approached. Then another. "Take me to the village if you like. It's sure they has work for me there. Maybe in the tavern."

The thought of any child working in a tavern was enough to send a chill down Catriona's back. "No indeed, Mr. Olly. I am afraid that will not do. You must remain here. Lord Rayne is responsible for you now."

Not entirely true.

Certainly not what Lord Rayne wanted.

But Olly needn't know that.

"I doesn't want a bath," the lad insisted once more.

She caught his wiry arm in a firm but gentle grip. "Sometimes, Mr. Olly, life is not about what you want. Indeed, most times it is all about what you must do. Obligations and burdens, duties and requirements. I am sorry to tell you, but I cannot bear the smell of you for one moment more."

Olly struggled to escape, but Catriona was far stronger, and she held firm.

"Here now, you cannot make me do anything!" he protested.

A new wave of odor overtook her as she hauled him from the library in search of her lady's maid, a tub of warm water, and the requisite soap.

"Another sad life's lesson you are about to learn," she said grimly. "I can, and I will. You will thank me for it later, and so will Ashes. I should hate to have to feed him to my cat after all."

"I doesn't think so," growled Olly. "And you don't got no cat. Least not one I seen."

"I do not think so," she corrected again.

"Why not?" he asked.

Catriona sighed.

<hr />

THE STARTLED EXPRESSION on her maid's face was the first indication Catriona received that something was dreadfully amiss.

The second was her words.

"My lady, forgive me, but Mr. Olly is not…that is to say, he is a *she*."

Catriona blinked at Sadler. Being in possession of precious little experience with children, she had deferred to the domestic's expertise in matters of scrubbing. But she had been hovering in the hall beyond the guest chamber, waiting for the deed to be done.

"What do you mean, Olly is not a he?" she asked, even though the answer to her question was already apparent.

It made no sense.

Olly was a lad.

Short haired.

Ill-tempered.

Evasive.

Dirty.

Pretty beneath all that grime, however. Perhaps too pretty for a lad.

"Olly has…a bosom." The last was whispered into the silence of the hall, color rising to Sadler's cheeks in the wake of the word. "And, and…"

Catriona held up a staying hand. "You mean to say the lad is a girl?" How could it be? How could she have failed to notice? "A bosom? How?"

"Bindings," Sadler said simply. "I would guess her to be twelve or thereabouts. Dressed as she was, and covered in all that dirt, it was easy to mistake her for a boy of nine or ten. She is a slight thing, even for a girl. I would guess she has not been well-fed as a child ought to be."

Dear Lord.

This development rather complicated matters.

"What shall I do?" she asked, perplexed.

Part of her felt betrayed by Olly's deception. Part of her felt all the more concerned for the child's welfare. What had led her to hide herself as a boy? To pretend she was a young boy when she was in fact a girl on her way to becoming a woman? It certainly explained Olly's reluctance to bathe.

But it explained precious little else.

One thing was certain.

Catriona needed answers.

"You may want to ask her some questions, my lady," Sadler offered. "She seems rather distraught that I've made the discovery."

She sighed. "Thank you, Sadler. I shall see to her."

Sadler dipped into a curtsy. "Of course, my lady."

Hesitantly, she made her way to the guest chamber door, knocking soundly three times to announce herself before entering. Olly was seated on a chair by the bath that had been drawn earlier. Though she was once more clad in her breeches and shirt, the shorn ends of her hair sleek and wet, sans the layer of dirt obstructing her features, Catriona could see quite clearly that she was female rather than male. The soft, pretty lines of her face which had been mistaken for a younger boy's, along with her slight frame, now seemed painfully feminine.

Olly's legs were drawn up protectively against her chest, her chin resting upon her knees. "I told you I didn't want no bath."

"A bath," Catriona corrected, going to the child's side and dropping to her knees on the carpet, unmindful of her gown. They were eye to eye now. Nose to nose. "I did not want a bath."

"I know you didn't," said the scamp.

"Olly," she coaxed gently, resisting the urge to smile in spite of herself at the child's willfulness. "What is your true name?"

"Oliver."

She raised a brow. "*Olly.*"

"Fine." She huffed a sigh. "Olivia. My name's Olivia. But I prefer Olly. It's all I been for years now."

"How long?" Catriona asked, a maternal surge she had never before experienced coming to life within her. "And why?"

"Easier to be a lad than a girl," Olly answered.

Her heart gave a pang. "What do you mean?"

"Lads doesn't get touched the way girls do," Olly said quietly.

"Oh, Olly." Something inside her chest seized. She could scarcely imagine what had befallen this young girl in her life. "What happened to you?"

The child's face became shuttered. "You doesn't want to know."

"You do not want to know," she corrected gently. "And yes, I do. I care about you, Olly. If I know what happened, I will be able to better understand you."

Olly nodded, biting her lip. Slowly, she began to reveal her past. "When Mother died, I was sent to my aunt, her sister. Her husband, my uncle...he did not treat me as an uncle ought to treat a niece. I doesn't think Auntie Margery knew what he were about...if she had, he would have stopped. I knows it."

Dear God. What had the horrid man done to her, an innocent child?

"Olly," she began, "what did he do to you, your uncle?"

"He touched me," Olly admitted, ducking her head. "Made me sit on his lap and touch him."

Catriona felt ill. "Did he..."

She could not bear to finish the question.

The notion of a grown man forcing a child. *His niece.* It was repulsive. So horrible she could not even contemplate such a sin against an innocent. Such a blatant abuse of power and trust.

"Not like you think," Olly said quietly. "Not long after I took up with them, a lung infection claimed him and my aunt. I were on my own, once more. But this time, I was smarter. I knew being a girl wouldn't do me no good. I convinced everyone I were a boy."

"Oh, my dearest girl." She could have wept at the revelations. But she knew she must remain stoic for Olly's sake. "How did you find yourself here, Bramwell's ward?"

"He be a cousin of my uncle's. I doesn't know he were like him, but I feared it..."

"You do not need to explain yourself, child," she said, hating what had happened to Olly, or Olivia as she must come to think of her now. "I am so very sorry for what you endured. But please know you need not fear either myself or Lord Rayne."

"I doesn't fear you," Olly said reluctantly.

"I do not fear you," she corrected. "And good. That is excellent. Now do come along. The library can wait. We need to get you some dresses."

"I doesn't like dresses," the child argued, frowning. "Breeches is better."

"I do not like dresses." Catriona smiled, a new sense of purpose dawning inside her. "And you will. This, I promise."

IT WAS ALMOST dinner by the time Alessandro had finished poring over his mangled estate's equally mangled ledgers. He was weary to his bones, disgusted with himself and with his inept, thieving steward Bramwell, and oddly, he found himself missing the presence of his wife.

Catriona.

Just her name was enough to make the longing he had been tamping down burst forth again. His hunger for her was disturbing. But worse than his desire was the undeniable realization he was fond of her.

There was no mistaking it.

He *liked* his wife.

As the unwanted revelation sank in, Alessandro stopped in the portrait gallery. To his left and right hung a handful of paintings, those hanging within reach nothing more than dark squares on the wall coverings where they had once adorned the plaster. Perhaps Bramwell had not been able to secure a ladder in his haste?

He could only hope the devil would be caught.

And when he was caught, he would be cast into prison for the rest of his miserable life.

But whether or not Bramwell and the stolen paintings were ever located—for Alessandro had a sickening suspicion the money he had filched was long since spent—there was something more troubling than being surrounded by the evidence of his failures.

He liked Catriona.

He wanted to see her.

To kiss her again.

Cristo. What was wrong with him? He was not meant to make attachments here. He was meant to return to Spain, to fight Boney's forces, to honor the memory of Maria and Francisco. He was meant to go where he belonged.

Footsteps in the hall behind him predicated the arrival of his butler. "Sir?"

He turned to Johnstone, irritated for the interruption upon his solitude as much as furious with himself for the emotions swirling within him. "Yes, Johnstone?" he snapped. "What can it be?"

"Her ladyship has yet to return from her trip to the village, and I am wondering if we shall postpone dinner to accommodate her schedule," said the stalwart domestic.

He frowned. "I was not aware her ladyship was going to the village today."

Where had she gone and why? More importantly, why was she tarrying so long? She had not spoken one word of her plans to him. But then, he supposed she might not after what had transpired between them. He had proven himself a rutting beast, and then he had fled like a *cobarde*, a coward who could not face his own wife.

"Lady Rayne took Miss Olivia to the village," Johnstone informed him.

That his butler should know his wife's whereabouts and he should not seemed dreadfully wrong. It nettled.

"Who the devil is Miss Olivia?" he asked next, for that was not lost upon him either. He knew of no such person.

"The, er, young lad Lady Rayne has taken under her protection," the butler explained, for once at a loss for words. "He has turned out to be a girl. Named Olivia, my lord."

"Olly?" Alessandro stared, baffled by the revelation.

"Yes, my lord."

The *pícaro* was a female named Olivia. The discovery was only slightly less disturbing than the feelings he was beginning to develop for his wife. Of course, as his mind worked to make sense of the news, he had to admit, it made sense. He had been perplexed at the lad's softness of face and voice, his slightness of form.

"*La vida es loca*," he muttered to himself, passing a hand over his face.

"Indeed, life is mad, my lord," Johnstone droned, his expression impassive. "I quite agree."

He glowered at the domestic, irritated at the man's tenacity. "Do you know when Lady Rayne and Olly-Olivia departed for the village, and when we might expect them back, Johnstone?"

"They were in search of appropriate attire for Miss Olivia, my lord. I could not say," his butler replied. "But Lady Rayne did mention she ought to return before dinner when she departed."

Sí, when she had departed without telling him where she was going.

When she had departed without informing him the dirty little squatter she had taken under her wing had turned out to be an Olivia rather than an Olly.

Alessandro seized upon that, allowing his irritation with her to overtake his longing. "Postpone dinner for an hour, if you please, Johnstone," he directed. "Surely her ladyship will have returned from the village by that time. If you need me, I will be in the study."

Johnstone bowed. "As you wish, my lord."

"*Gracias*," he muttered.

"*De nada*, my lord." With that parting shot, the butler took his leave.

Alessandro glowered at the fellow's back before abandoning the somber gallery with its missing paintings and returning to the equally depressing study. When his wife returned, he would have a word with her. A rather severe word. He did not appreciate being left in the dark about matters within his household, and she would know it.

IT WAS WELL past the appointed hour for dinner when Catriona, her lady's maid, and Olivia returned from their impromptu trip to the village. They had managed to find some reasonably fine cloth and even a few dresses for Olivia. Fortunately, Sadler was a deft hand at sewing, and she was leading the charge in seeing the child properly clothed as befit a genteel young lady.

The grimy, breeches-wearing scamp would soon be no more. And Catriona was making it her mission to see Olivia properly dressed, educated, and given the chance at life she had deserved all along.

But when Johnstone greeted them at the front door, his aggrieved expression suggested the buoyancy of victory was about to plummet to the earth.

"Run along Olivia," she told her charge. "Sadler will see you are washed and dressed in one of your new gowns for dinner. I shall see you later."

Olivia doffed her cap, reminding Catriona that something would need to be done with her shorn locks and that her old habits would not leave her with the mere donning of a dress and petticoats. Sadler shared a look with her before leading the girl off to the massive staircase.

"Is something amiss, Johnstone?" she asked after her lady's maid and Olivia were beyond earshot.

The butler cleared his throat. "It is his lordship, my lady. Forgive me, but I fear I made an error. I had not realized Lord Rayne was not privy to the identity of Miss Olivia."

She frowned. "Do not worry yourself over it. The discovery was a new one, and his lordship was quite busy with his ledgers. I did not want to burden him with it when I was able to have it all in hand myself."

"Nevertheless, his lordship was distressed when I relayed the information to him. I am afraid he has—"

A loud bang, followed by a muffled male voice that was undeniably angry, interrupted the butler's words.

"What was that?" she asked Johnstone.

The domestic sighed. "That, I fear, is his lordship."

"What is he doing?" she dared query. Whatever it was, it sounded angry.

And violent.

The butler grimaced. "After my regrettable discussion with the earl, he discovered a portrait of his mother missing from the study."

Alessandro's beloved mother. Anguish sank through her along with dread.

"Thank you for the warning, Johnstone," she said sincerely. Though she had not been the Countess of Rayne for long, she had already come to deeply appreciate her husband's staff. They had welcomed her, and they were efficient and attentive. Most of all, they cared.

And she was grateful for them. All of them.

"Of course, my lady." Johnstone looked as if he was about to add something, but paused.

"What is it?" she asked, concern washing over her anew. "Is there something else I should know about?"

"No." The butler cleared his throat, casting his gaze to the floor. "Rather, I think you are good for his lordship, and I am pleased to see it. We are, all of us belowstairs, well pleased to see it. I am happy to serve you, my lady."

The prick of tears came to her eyes, filling them. She blinked them away lest she made a fool of herself. The butler's words were everything she wanted to hear. She wanted to believe them herself so badly she ached with it.

Yes, she wanted to be good for her husband.

Good enough to make him stay.

Good enough to win his love.

She swallowed down the knot of emotions clogging her throat. "Thank you, Johnstone. I consider that the highest of compliments. You pay me a great honor."

"The honor is all mine, my lady." The butler bowed.

Another loud crash echoed through the hall then, reminding her she had an irate husband to attend to. Exhaling on a sigh, she thanked Johnstone again before excusing herself and making her way to the source of the sound.

The study.

During her tour the previous day, she had discovered a great deal of dust, along with heavy, outmoded furniture carved with Greek deities. A handful of paintings had decorated the walls, along with some shelves and curiosities. The carpet had been faded and in need of repair, she had noted.

Aside from that and the chair behind the desk, the chamber had been fairly unremarkable. The chair bore a carving of a god she did not recognize, though she had noticed the nose appeared to have been lopped off and then reaffixed with glue, as perfectly imperfect as the rest of Marchmont.

As perfectly imperfect as her husband was.

She reached the closed study door to the dissonant music of another thud sounding within, followed by a curse she did not recognize. Spanish, no doubt. On a deep breath, she opened the door and crossed the threshold.

As the portal clicked closed behind her, she took in the panorama before her.

The study had turned into a battlefield. The floor was littered with ledgers. A chair was upended and broken glass glittered from the hearth. An entire sideboard, complete with decanters and glasses, had been left on its side, the crystal shattered.

In the midst of it all stood the man she loved, hands clenched, fury emanating from him. His dark gaze lanced hers. And she understood one fact. Her husband was livid.

"Alessandro," she said softly, hoping to blunt the swell of his rage. "What are you doing?"

"Where have you been?" he asked instead of answering her question.

His voice was low and guttural, a blade sheathed in velvet.

"To the village," she said, daring to close the distance between them by taking another step closer to him. "You did not answer my question."

"You do not have the right to ask me questions when you hide things from me," he said, his lip curling. "There will be no secrets in my household. Do you understand me, Catriona?"

She stiffened, for she understood quite well. She understood him better than he could imagine. Her beautiful husband was hiding more scars than she could count beneath his perfect exterior. And she was paying the price for every blade that had inflicted its mark upon him.

Losing his wife.

His son.

The battles he had fought.

Returning to his estate to discover it pillaged and on the brink of ruin.

Secrets.

It was a waterfall. Or perhaps, more precisely, a flood. But she was not about to allow either of them to drown in it.

"I understand," she said, crossing the chamber to him. "But you must, in turn, understand this, I did not keep anything from you."

He clenched his jaw. "The squatter is a female, which you neglected to tell me. You went to the village to procure her a dress, also without telling me. I learned these facts from the butler."

"You told me your duty to me was finished for the day," she reminded him bitterly. "Just before you walked away from me. Have you forgotten that, husband?"

He took a step forward, bringing him closer to her. They were nearly thigh to thigh, his angry heat radiating from his body into hers. He leaned down until his lips almost brushed hers. "I forget nothing when it comes to you, wife. Nothing."

She raised her chin. "Then perhaps you might remind yourself of the bargain you made with me. A marriage of convenience. You only remain here until you get me with child. I owe you nothing, not even fidelity, after I birth your heir. That is how you wanted our marriage to be, Alessandro. You chose those terms, not anyone else."

His nostrils flared. "You accepted them, my lady."

"Perhaps I do not accept them any longer," she told him, mustering the courage to be honest. "Perhaps I have changed my mind and now, I want something more."

A muscle in his jaw ticked. "Such as?"

"Such as a husband who will not abandon me one day soon," she dared to say before spinning on her heel. "Do not expect me at dinner, my lord. I find I have lost my appetite."

"Catriona," he called after her.

"Do not wait for me," she tossed over her shoulder. "I am exhausted after a long day, and I need rest. Good evening, Lord Rayne."

With that final shot issued, she slammed out of the study.

On the way to her chamber, the sounds of further desecration of the chamber her husband occupied ringing through the house, she recalled she had been meant to calm him rather than further infuriate him. But then she sternly reminded herself she could only offer so many olive branches. If he refused to take them, the choice was his.

Chapter Twenty-One

Catriona regretted her hasty decision to eschew dinner later that night as she rolled onto her stomach in her bed and flipped another page in *The Silent Duke*. The starving grumble echoed through the quiet of her chamber, further taunting her. Though the book was well-written and engrossing, she could not concentrate. The tumult of emotions roiling within her were rendering her enjoyment of the cleverly crafted words impossible.

As was her hunger.

How could she have been foolish enough to fall in love with a man who had done nothing but promise to leave her? With a man who had told her his heart would forever belong to another? He had given every part of himself to his first wife, and there was nothing left for her.

Closing her eyes against the tears, she released a heavy sigh. It seemed no number of attempts at distraction could change the truth. Her life was a series of mistakes. Of loving men who would never love her in return. How wrong she had been to believe marrying Alessandro would give her freedom. She would have been happier in Scotland, disgraced and ruined.

At least her heart would have remained whole.

A knock at the door joining her chamber to her husband's startled her.

What could he want? Had he come to exercise his husbandly

rights? The notion made heat unfurl through her, even as she knew she must not allow it. Her heart could not bear such intimacy tonight, not when he remained so removed from her in every other way. Not when he insisted upon maintaining the distance between them.

"I do not want company tonight," she called out, for it was the truth.

He had hurt her far too many times. Small hurts. Just enough to make her bleed.

The door opened despite her denial of his entry. He stood on the threshold, bearing a tray in his hands. In the warm glow cast by her candlelight, he was a half-shadowed mystery.

Her heart ached at the sight of him.

"I brought you some sustenance," he offered. "I thought you may be hungry."

As if on cue, her stomach growled.

She frowned and pressed a hand over it as if she could absorb the sound and make it cease to exist. "I am perfectly well."

"You must eat, *querida*." His tone was disapproving. He moved into her territory now, striding toward her, and as the light licked over his form, she was reminded of why she had not wanted him within her chamber.

He was temptation incarnate, and she could not resist.

But his irrational anger earlier could not be so easily forgotten. Nor could the cavalier manner in which he regarded their union. Theirs was a marriage of convenience.

A most inconvenient one.

She sat up in bed, clutching the bedclothes to her as if they were a shield which could protect her from his magnetism. "Go away."

She did not want his tenderness or his tray of food or the pretense he cared about her when she knew otherwise, and to devastating effect. The scent of roasted chicken reached her, and her stomach growled anew. Drat the traitor.

"I was forced to suffer through dinner alone," he said. "The scamp dined in the nursery, leaving me to hurl insults at Johnston in Spanish for entertainment. Did you know he understood them all?"

She was not surprised. "I have no wish to dine with a churl."

Uninvited, he seated himself on the edge of her bed as if he belonged there, lowering the tray between them. "A peace offering, *querida*. I am sorry for being curt with you earlier."

"I accept your apology, but you can take the food and go," she insisted stubbornly, for she knew she must not soften toward him.

He had taken his anger out on her without cause, to say nothing of his brusque dismissal of her in the wake of their passionate encounter at breakfast. Her heart was battered, and she must protect it now at all costs.

"Catriona," he said softly. "You must eat. If you are with child, the babe needs nourishment."

"Of course that is all you care about," she snapped bitterly. "How could I forget I am nothing more than a broodmare to you?"

"I have always been honest with you." He covered her hand with his.

She resented his touch, the effect it had upon her. The way it made her want him. "Yes, you have. But I am tired now, and I wish to be alone. Please go."

His jaw clenched. "He stole my mother's portrait."

"I am sorry." And she was. "I know how much you loved her."

"*Sí*. She was a good woman. A good person. Far better than I am." Idly, he stroked her inner wrist with his thumb.

She would be lying if she said it did not affect her. Lying, too, if she said the anguish in her husband's expression did not bring a fresh rush of tears to her eyes.

"Even if you are not able to find Bramwell and bring him to justice, and even if you do not find the portrait, he cannot steal your memories from you," she said softly. "Your mother will always be in your heart."

"You are a good woman too, *querida*," he said, his dark gaze intent upon her. "My mother, she would have liked you. Maria would have, too."

His words shocked her, sending an incipient rush of hope through her.

She quashed it. "Thank you for the dinner. Perhaps I will eat some after all. *Alone.*"

He nodded, removing his hand from hers before standing. "I will go, as you wish. I asked for some of the plum tartlets you like."

He had noticed she liked plum tartlets?

No, heart, she reminded herself firmly. *This man cannot be trusted.*

She swallowed. "That was most thoughtful of you, my lord."

He gave her a grim, lingering look before bowing. "Sleep well, querida. Tomorrow is another day."

Another day, she thought to herself as she watched him walk away from her for the second time. Another day of loving him, another day of knowing he would never love her back. She glanced down at the tray he had left her and snagged a tartlet.

It was bittersweet on her tongue.

FROM THE MULLIONED windows of his father's study, Alessandro had a perfect view of the overgrown gardens.

And his wife.

She was dressed to perfection, as always, in a sprigged muslin day dress that showed off her lush curves. The day was bright and brilliant with sun, glowing in the curls peeping from beneath her bonnet. She bent to cut a rose, and the sight of her luscious derriere made his breeches go tight.

He wanted her more with each passing day.

His lust for her was beginning to become a problem, in fact.

In the days following his apology to her, they had settled into a pax of sorts. Catriona had thrown herself into being the mistress of Marchmont with a fervor that pleased him, though did not surprise him. She was capable, determined, and resilient, all traits he admired.

Her efforts with the *picaro* were equally estimable. Olivia was at her side in the garden now, dressed as befit a young member of the fair sex. The dirty little squatter who had greeted him at the door had been replaced. Catriona had even hired a governess for the girl from the village, and the brat appeared to have begun learning her manners. It was remarkable, really, just how much his countess could transform in such a short amount of time.

Slowly, Marchmont was being restored. And slowly, day by day, the fractured pieces inside Alessandro were growing less sharp. Not precisely growing together, but getting smoothed soft, like a pebble in a stream. His anger was no longer as pronounced.

But she had yet to allow him back into her bed following their argument, and this, too, was a problem. A problem he would rectify today, for summer was giving way to autumn bit by bit each day, and he needed to travel soon if he wished to reach Spain before winter set in. He could not leave for Spain if he was not assured his wife was with child, and he could not be assured of a babe in her belly if he could not bed her.

Their impasse would naturally have to come to an end, and he had decided upon the means. Turning away from the window, he stalked from his study, in search of his butler. Johnstone, to his credit, was never far.

"Everything has been prepared as you required, my lord," the butler told him.

"*Excelente.*" He smiled. "Thank you for your assistance, Johnstone."

His butler bowed. "*De nada,* my lord."

He sighed as he turned on his heel, in search of his wife, for there was truly no argument against having an accommodating butler. Indeed, part of him suspected he would miss the fellow when he returned to Spain. Part of him would miss a great deal of things.

Including her.

Ruthlessly, he banished the voice inside him that reminded him the way his wife made him feel. He was not meant to feel. He was *El Corazón Oscuro*, and he was not just the dark heart. He was altogether heartless.

Which hardly explained what he was about to do.

This was for *him*, he told himself. He needed to bed his wife to get an heir, and courting her seemed the most advantageous means of achieving that goal. Also, the urge to return to the fancy of his youth undeniably drove him. Alessandro would never forgive himself if he returned to Spain without seeing one of the favorite places of his boyhood. For once he went back to war, he would likely never return again.

He found Catriona and Olivia not far from where they had been earlier in the gardens, cutting some roses. As his boots crunched on the gravel, his wife spun to face him. At such proximity, he could not help noticing the charming flush of her cheeks. Her eyes were startled, her lush lips firming into a line that was far from the welcoming smile he longed to see.

He bowed. "My lady. Miss Olivia."

To his amazement, the *picaro* dipped into a curtsy.

"Very good form, Olivia," his wife encouraged, smiling down at the imp.

Maldición, that was his smile, and he wanted it.

"Thank you, my lady." Olivia beamed up at his wife.

Though her shorn hair peeped from beneath her bonnet, the lass was otherwise looking the part of English gentility. His wife was a miracle worker. What were the odds a devil like him would have found another angel to wed?

And yet, he had.

"What do you think of Olivia's curtsy, Lord Rayne?" his wife prodded, her enthusiasm dimming noticeably when her regard was once more fixed upon him.

He cleared his throat. "Passable."

It was the wrong thing to say. He knew it from the way Catriona's brows drew instantly together.

"She has been working at it very diligently, my lord," she added through gritted teeth.

Could she not see he was not accustomed to this? His interactions with the *picaro* had been limited since his discovery she was a female. And he had been absent for much of his sister Leonora's life. He had just spent the last few in bloody battles, at war. What did she expect of him?

"It is better than passable," he tried again.

The child did not mince words. "You're bollixing it up, m'lord."

Catriona sighed. "Olivia."

He held up a staying hand. "The *picaro* is not wrong in this instance, I have no doubt. I am afraid I am woefully ignorant in such delicate matters. Forgive me, Miss Olivia, my lady."

His wife's lips pursed, and he could tell she was doing her damnedest to squelch a smile. "You are forgiven, my lord."

"Ah, but am I forgiven, or am I *forgiven*?" he could not resist asking her, gratified when her color instantly deepened and she averted her gaze.

She knew precisely what lay behind the hidden meaning in his words.

"Haven't you seen the way she makes eyes at you, Lord Rayne?" Olivia asked.

"Olivia," Catriona chastised, pinning her charge with a severe frown.

He found himself grinning. A lightness he had not felt in as long as he could remember settled over him. Perhaps it was brought about by the sun's rays. Perhaps it was the warmth of the day. Or the prospect of surprising his wife and the *picaro* with the endeavor he had planned. Perhaps it was just the way he felt when he was in Catriona's presence. Near enough to touch her. To kiss her.

Dios, he missed those lips.

The way she tasted.

The way she kissed him back.

But he could not afford to linger upon any of that, for he had a plan to put into motion. Still, he could not resist taunting his wife, who had been doing her best to keep him at a distance these last few days, making him want her all the more.

"How does she make eyes at me?" he asked.

"Rayne," Catriona snapped.

"Wife," he countered, still grinning at her. "You have something you wish to impart? Some gem of wisdom, perhaps?"

She tilted her head and raised a brow at him. "I do not make eyes at you." And then she cast a glance toward the *picaro*. "I do not *make eyes* at him, Olivia."

He winked at the imp. "She does."

The imp grinned back, revealing a gap between her two front teeth. "Aye, she does."

It occurred to him this was the first time he had seen the child smile. And this, too, filled him with a curious happiness.

"Why are you here, my lord?" his wife asked acidly.

"Marchmont is my country seat," he told her seriously. "I am in residence."

She blinked, looking distinctly unimpressed at his attempt at sarcasm.

Well, it had been a long time, and he was out of practice. He could not recall having been so inclined to joke. Levity had been lost upon him for many years. Indeed, this odd sensation swirling within him now was something he had not felt since…

Not since Maria.

The reminder of his past, juxtaposed with the false brilliance of the day, was enough to sober him. To force his mind back to his original plan.

"What I meant," probed Catriona pointedly, "is what are you doing in the gardens, Lord Rayne? I have not seen you out here often."

She had all but implied his absence in the gardens was her reason to linger there. Beyond his reach. Out of his presence.

"I have a surprise for you and Miss Olivia," he told her, all the more pleased with himself for his idea.

Why had he not thought of it sooner?

"A surprise." His lady wife did not appear impressed.

The *picaro*, however, was a different story. She began bouncing, quite literally, on the overgrown path. "I love surprises! What is it, my lord? What is it?"

Perhaps not all her lessons in manners and deportment had yet taken effect, he thought wryly. But her enthusiasm proved rather infectious, all the same.

"Fishing," he told her.

One of the females before him wore an expression of instant joy. The other, one of distinct suspicion. At least he was certain to win one of them over.

"Come along," he told them. "I have everything prepared."

※

FISHING WAS A gentleman's sport.

But Catriona had not bothered to douse her husband's enthusiasm with her disapproval. She had been keeping him at a distance enough ever since their row days before. And so, she found herself being charmed by him all over again—albeit vicariously—as she stood on the sun-stained banks of the river cutting through Marchmont in a peaceful bend just before the dams, watching him teach Olivia how to manage her fishing tackle.

"This is a rod fashioned of bamboo," he was telling the girl, "held together with screws of brass. It is a beautiful contraption, really."

"I've fished in my day, but we never had nothing so fine as this," Olivia confessed, wonderment in her voice.

"We never had anything as fine," she and Alessandro corrected in unison.

Their gazes met and held for a beat, and she could almost imagine, gathered as they were, the blissful sunshine of late summer upon them, the peacefully flowing river before them, that they were parents teaching their child.

Together.

But that was just a fantasy. A fiction her heart longed to believe.

For in truth, Olivia was not their daughter, and the Earl of Rayne had no intention of lingering after he had planted his seed in her womb. Her jaw clenched at the thought.

He inclined his head toward her, seemingly in deference, before returning his attention to Olivia. "This is a fly I made when I was a lad, Olivia."

"It must be dreadfully old," remarked the incorrigible child.

To her amazement, her husband laughed. How rare and precious a gift it was, that sound. It rang, clear and deep and beautiful, touching all the parts of her heart she was do desperately determined to keep from him.

"It is almost an antiquity, *picaro*," he told Olivia. "But I promise you my flies can catch fish, and as we are about to engage in a tournament, you will be grateful indeed I have lent them to you. Lady Rayne is not so fortunate."

"A tournament?" Olivia asked.

"Indeed," Catriona added, her eyes narrowed. "What manner of tournament have you in mind, Rayne? I have no wish to fish, you realize."

"No wish to fish, why, Lady Rayne, you are a poetess," he teased.

She frowned at him. Her husband was a breathtaking, beautiful man. But when he smiled and teased her, her every defense against him dissipated, and he was even more impossible to resist.

"What lure are you providing me that is so inferior to Olivia's?" she asked, forcing herself to be concerned with more important matters than admiring her husband's looks. She did that readily enough every time she was in his presence.

Even when she was angry with him.

And yes, even when she was doing her best to keep him at a distance.

"Not inferior. Merely different. For you, I have a lob worm," he told her.

The word *worm* made her wrinkle her nose in distaste. "Is it alive?"

"Of course." He grinned. "Until I hook it."

Her heart did strange things inside her chest. All the stranger for the subject matter. "No thank you," she told him. "I shall watch you and Olivia have your tournament. That shall do quite nicely."

"No indeed," he denied, shaking his head. "I am afraid that will not do, will it, Miss Olivia?"

Olivia—the dratted traitor—had eyes only for the savior who intended to provide her with a superior lure for their impromptu fishing tournament. "You must join us, Lady Rayne. How can we have a tournament with nothing but two people? Lord Rayne will hook the worm for you, will you not, my lord?"

Her husband's gaze was upon her, dark and fierce and burning, touching her deep inside where she wanted to keep him from trespassing. "My lady, would you prefer to set your lure?" he asked solicitously, holding up a long, wriggling creature for her inspection.

"No, thank you," she declined, quite disgusted at the prospect. "I am certain fishing is generally considered the sport of gentlemen for a reason, Lord Rayne. Whilst I applaud your efforts to bring us here and show us the land, perhaps we would be better served to return to the main house."

"I doesn't want to go anywhere," Olivia protested instantly, holding her fishing tackle in her small right hand as if it were a weapon she was capable of wielding.

"I do not wish to go anywhere," both Catriona and Alessandro corrected simultaneously once more.

They stared at each other.

"That's what I said," Olivia argued stubbornly.

"Come," her husband said then, gifting her with one of his rare smiles.

She stared at his outstretched hand, distrust curdling her every thought.

"I caught fish here when I was a boy," her husband said softly, his gaze burning into hers, finding all those places she never wanted him to see. "It will be a few mindless hours of entertainment, and I know all three of us could benefit from just such a thing if you will but allow it. Tell me you will."

Catriona cast a glance toward their charge, mindful to keep the girl from overhearing their exchange. "Alessandro…"

"*Querida*," he returned, his voice knowing.

Oh, how he could find his way beneath her every defense.

"I am not touching a slimy fish," she informed him. "Nor will I touch a wriggling worm."

His grin deepened, rendering him even more beautiful than before. "I knew you would see to reason."

She succumbed to a lesson she had learned some time ago. When the Earl of Rayne smiled, resisting him was futile.

Chapter Twenty-Two

After dinner, Alessandro found himself at the door joining his chamber to Catriona's. He had not attempted to come to her since the night he had brought her the dinner she had missed. But the afternoon had proven a resounding success.

The *picaro* had won the tournament, albeit with a little help from Alessandro's lures and knowledge of the best places to fish in the river. Not much had changed at Marchmont since his last time in residence there, save the incompetence of the steward he had once trusted. They had brought home half a dozen trout. Olivia had been grinning from ear to ear.

But the greatest victory of all had been his.

He had won back his wife's approval.

The way she had gazed upon him all dinner had been enough to make him want to kiss her, then and there, before the servants dancing attendance upon them and Olivia, who had been invited to the table to enjoy the fruits of her labor.

It had been only the presence of the *picaro* which had kept him from doing what he wanted. What he was going to do now. She had chanced to whisper in his ear she would be expecting him later, and he had not needed to hear the invitation twice.

He rapped on the door once.

Once, as it happened, was all he required.

"Come in," his wife called.

Her husky voice sent an unexpected ripple of longing straight through him. Her mouth had been taunting him all day. Kissing her had become an obsession of his. Bedding her was not far behind.

All in the name of obtaining his heir, *por supuesto*.

He opened the door, crossed the threshold, and stopped when a wall of lust came barreling down upon him with the force of a herd of wild horses. Catriona's brown curls had been unbound, falling around her shoulders, and she wore a night rail that was the wickedest combination of innocence and decadence he had ever seen.

It was a virginal white, but the fabric was transparent. He could see all of her through that wispy veil, from the pink buds of her nipples to the dark curls of her sex. The décolletage revealed the creamy swells of her full breasts, the seductive curves of her waist. She was beautiful to him, from the inside out. So beautiful, she almost brought him to his knees.

"*Querida*," was all he could manage to say, desire rocking him. Need was a living, breathing creature. Demanding he give in.

Duty and obligation were far from his mind as he ate up the distance keeping him from her sweet, jasmine-scented skin. It had been too long since he had last been able to touch her. And fortunately for him, his wife was suffering from a similar affliction of desperate longing.

For she met him halfway across the chamber, and she was in his arms as though it were the most natural place in the world for her to be. And indeed, in that rare, unfettered moment, it was. She belonged to him. Belonged in his arms. Every swell and dip of her sweetly feminine body fitted perfectly against his.

His hands found her waist, mooring her to him, while hers went around his neck. Her breasts crushed into his chest, her hungry nipples prodding his chest in erotic promise.

He was hard and ready for her slick, tight sheath to take him to oblivion. He was a head taller than she was, which meant his cock was pressed into the soft swell of her stomach. Not where he ultimately wanted to be, but any part of her would suffice for now.

She was warm and soft, her flesh supple and delicious. She burned into him, her head tipped back to watch him. His fingers tightened on her, lest she try to slip away. He was a greedy bastard when it came to this woman. And he could not let go.

"Thank you for this afternoon," she said softly.

There were a hundred different things she could have said to him in that moment, and yet, the one she had chosen, affected him as no other could.

"No," he returned, devouring her upturned face with his gaze. "Thank you. I know fishing is not the manner in which you would have preferred to spend several hours, but I do think the child liked it."

"Yes." A smile curved his wife's full lips. "She did."

Cristo, how he wanted to kiss her. "Did *you, querida*?"

Somehow, even as every part of him charged him to claim her mouth, to kiss her into oblivion, he did not. He wanted to prolong their interaction. And some part of him enjoyed the intimacy of their conversations. There had been a time when he had believed himself incapable of ever accepting another woman's touch. His grief had been too strong, too all-consuming.

The fierce woman in his arms had changed all that.

She had changed him.

"I enjoyed watching the two of you," she admitted, gazing up at him. "I do not think I have ever seen you so at ease, as if you had nothing weighing down upon you."

It was how he had felt, as well. The glorious sunshine, the beauty of the river, the return to something which had once given him great joy but had been somehow forgotten in the madness of his manhood, the joy of watching the child take to it, seeing the happiness it brought his wife.

"It was a good day." The best day he had experienced in as long as he could recall.

Best of all was being able to hold Catriona in his arms at the end of it.

"And you are a good man, Alessandro," she said then.

How wrong she was.

"I am not a good man," he felt compelled to correct her. "Taking a wayward orphan fishing cannot ameliorate the sins I have committed in my life."

Her fingers were sifting through his hair now, her nails lightly traveling over his scalp. He had never before known such a touch would be pleasurable, but it was. *Dios*, how it was.

"And what sins have you committed in your life?" his sweet, innocent wife asked.

How trusting she was. How trusting she had always been with him, from the first moment, almost, they had crossed paths. She was hesitant of him, that much was undeniable, but she always enabled herself to get close enough to the dragon that it could breathe flames upon her and consume her whole.

He lowered his forehead to hers, staring into her eyes. "I have spent the last few years at war," he began, even though he knew he should not. She already knew he had been fighting in Spain.

He had come this far. She was in his arms, warm and soft and willing. He should simply take what was his to take. He could have his desire fulfilled without this conversation. He could empty himself inside her without thinking about where he had been, what he had done, who he had lost.

"Many good men have been to war," she said, tipping up her chin so their lips were only a breath apart. "Many good men have fought and spilled blood."

"I was ruthless," he blurted, and he did not know why. "There was a time when I had lost everything, and the French invasion began, that I did not care who I killed or why."

"You were fighting in a war." Her response was swift, soothing. Her hands had somehow found their way to his face, the moons of her palms cradling his jaw in the most reassuring caress he had ever known.

"Yes. But some of my men were even more ruthless than I was. Some of them committed atrocities I cannot begin to describe," he admitted.

"We are not the sums of our pasts, Alessandro." Still gently caressing his face as if he were beloved to her, her gaze burned into his. Searing in its violet intensity. "We are our futures. We cannot change what has happened, cannot undo what has been done. All we can do is live for tomorrow rather than for yesterday."

She was right.

The rightness of it, the acknowledgment, settled in his bones. Worked straight through him. Found its unerring path to his heart. To the husk he had believed long dead. As if she could hear his thoughts, her hand was there, splayed over his steadily thumping heart, absorbing each beat.

"You do not know what I have done," he rasped, compelled to warn her. To dispel her notions there were any lingering traces of goodness in him.

"I know the man you are," she insisted. "You are a man compelled to fight for what he believes in, a man who loved his wife and son with a dedication I admire, a man who—"

He could not bear to hear any more. He silenced her by taking her lips with his. On a growl, he claimed her mouth. And with a heady feminine sigh, she kissed him back. He deepened the kiss, savoring the way she tasted, like the sweet, red wine from their earlier dinner and like something more mysterious and delicious.

Catriona.

He did not deserve her, but he was greedy when it came to this woman he had wed. And he was going to take anyway. Take because he could. Because he had to.

Deber, he reminded himself as he walked them to her bed, kissing her all the while.

Duty. He had a debt of obligation to the title, just as he had to this land.

But a small voice inside him said he was lying to himself. The blood coursing through his veins, the rampant desire stiffening his cock, the urge to drive himself home inside Catriona—none of these had anything to do with duty. Nor did the way he dragged his lips down her throat, or the way he cupped the inviting fullness of her breasts. Or the way he stopped everything to stare down at her, his breaths ragged.

Her lips were reddened and full from his kiss, her eyes glazed with passion. Her hair was a bewitching cloud falling around her shoulders, calling attention to the elegance of her fine-boned face. The freckles on the bridge of her nose called for his attention, and he could not resist dropping a kiss there, as if in so doing he could claim these tiniest parts of her for himself, too.

He wanted all of her.

Everything she had to give.

The knowledge astounded him as much as it terrified him. But he would not think of it now, for his need was monumental, bursting forth, demanding satisfaction. He tore at the belt keeping his banyan in place, and then he shrugged it from his shoulders, allowing it to fall to the carpet. He kissed her cheek before withdrawing enough to remove the sinfully tempting night rail.

She aided him in drawing it over her head.

She was nude before him, and though it was not the first time by far, he devoured every satin-smooth bit of skin. He could see her thus a hundred thousand times, and still his ardor would not be quelled, he was certain. His hands were on her, learning the hollows and dips, the curves and swells, the heat and the womanliness of her.

A different word stole into his wild thoughts then.

Delicious.

Everything about Catriona was worthy of worship. The flare of her belly, the beauty of her hips, the sweet mound between them. He had tasted her there before, but he wanted her again, just as much as ever. Perhaps more so. He kissed her, slowly, softly at first. Then with growing hunger. His fingers dipped into her sex, and she was already slick, the bud hidden within her folds swelled with her own need.

He played with her, listening to the quickening of her breath, drinking in the new urgency of her kiss. With his knee, he urged her legs wider apart, to grant him greater access to the honeyed cove he wanted most. He worked her pearl in slow, steady circles, all while making love to her mouth. What a beautiful mouth it was, and his, all his, just like the rest of her.

Hushed, hungry mewls were sounding from his wife's throat now. He could feel her climax pulsing to life, ready to burst open. But he wanted to prolong the pleasure for both of them. He sank one finger inside her. Instantly, she tightened, jerking against him to bring him deeper.

He caught the pout of her lower lip in his teeth and tugged. "Not yet, *querida*. I am going to make you mad with wanting me first."

ALESSANDRO DID NOT have to make such a promise to her, for he had already made her mad with wanting him. He was all she could breathe—his spicy, masculine scent—and he was all she could feel—his lips against hers in the most decadent kisses she had ever known, his finger teasing her.

After keeping him at a polite distance for the last little while, she could not get enough of him now. She was ravenous. But if his actions were anything to judge by, so was he. Somehow, they wound up in the bed together.

Alessandro was pressing sweet, unhurried kisses all over her body. Down her throat, over her breasts. He flicked his tongue around a nipple. Her fingers sank into the thick, lustrous strands of his hair. The rasp of his beard against the underside of her breast made her quicken between her thighs.

He kissed down her belly, settling himself there. And then his tongue was on her. In her. Her body bowed from the bed, seeking more of his splendid torture. The pleasure was too great. It exploded within her, like fireworks erupting brilliantly across the night sky. Dazzling and brilliant and filled with color.

As the violence of her spend subsided, leaving her with a sated glow, a new determination rose within her. He kissed his way back up her body, but when he settled himself between her legs, she stopped him with a staying palm on his shoulder.

"No," she said.

He froze, frowning down at her. "No, *querida?*"

"It is my turn," she elaborated, pushing at him with the heels of both hands now.

His brow still furrowed, his eyes darkened with passion so they were the same color as his hair, he allowed her to guide him onto his back. She had not forgotten the day he had told her, seemingly a lifetime ago, that he was a broken man. He carried the pain and the scars of his past within him, a burden he refused to share.

She wanted to show him, in the only way she could, how thoroughly she worshiped him. How deeply she loved him. And maybe, just maybe, she could take away some of that pain. Maybe she could heal those wounds. One kiss at a time.

"Catriona, what are you..."

The manner in which his words trailed off gratified her as she threw herself into her task. His body was beautiful and strong. She kissed his shoulder first, the smooth, strong curve of it. Kissed her way to his throat, burying her face there, where he smelled most like himself. Across his strong jaw she traveled next, to his firm chin, loving the abrasion of his whiskers on her lips.

She had only just begun. His heart may belong to another, but his body was hers, and she was staking her claim upon it. Upon every part of him she could. Down his chest, where his olive skin was dusted with dark hair. Over his thumping heart. Down the ridged slab of his abdomen. Her hands found his thighs, her nails raking lightly over his skin.

She kissed his hip bone, inhaling the muskiness of his flesh.

"*Querida*," he growled.

But she ignored the warning in his tone, for she had found his thick length. She took him in her hand as he had shown her before, kissing the blunt, velvet-smooth tip where a drop of liquid had escaped him. She licked her lips to taste it, and it was salty and sweet at once.

He growled. "Catriona."

"Tell me how to please you," she said, kissing him again. "I want to bring you pleasure the way you have pleased me."

For a moment, she thought he would protest. She stroked him, meeting his gaze.

"Take me in your mouth," he said, his voice low. Guttural.

On a surge of answering pleasure between her thighs and a surge of primal satisfaction, she did as he told her, drawing him into her mouth. Just the head of his cock at first, spurred by instinct to flick her tongue over him. His hips pumped, and she took more of him.

He was whispering things in his native tongue. She was sure they were wicked, and she loved them. Loved every growl, every hiss of his breath, each twist of his body as he showed her what he wanted. Faster. Deeper. His fingers sank into her hair, guiding her in the rhythm he wanted. Using her hand and mouth, she worked over him.

How she adored having this big man at her mercy.

Giving him pleasure made her achy with her own need. She

sucked and licked and moved with him, giving him what he wanted. What they both wanted. He surged inside her deeper still.

"*Cristo*, I am going to come in your mouth if you do not stop," he grunted. "You must stop."

She liked the notion of him being powerless to stop the rushing tide of his pleasure. To know he was mindless in his need for release, that his control would break, that she would be the cause...

It was heavy.

Potent.

She surrendered herself to the act of pleasuring him, refusing to stop. She wanted him to fall apart. To submit to her. To give her his release, even if he would not give her anything else. He could deny her his heart, but this, this was hers.

"Fuck," he said, thrusting again, taking her mouth the way he took her cunny.

And then he stiffened beneath her as he surged into the back of her throat, stealing her breath as a torrent unleashed.

"*Querida*," he said afterward, his voice melodious, robbed of all the hard edges it ordinarily possessed. He looked relaxed, almost boyish with one arm thrown over his forehead. "You should not have done that."

"I wanted to," she told him softly, falling to the bed alongside him and curling against him.

He was warm and reassuring and strong. His arm banded around her, holding her close. "*Gracias*."

She pressed a kiss to his chest. "*De nada*."

And she realized, as she lay there with him, it was not just his pleasure that was hers. *He* was hers.

All she had to do was prove it to him.

Chapter Twenty-Three

From the study window, Alessandro watched absently as the new head gardener he had hired from London and his laborers set about the Herculean task of shaping the Marchmont gardens back into the image of grandeur they had once been. He was pleased by how much he had accomplished in his time in Wiltshire. Over the last few weeks, he had thrown himself into the task of righting the wrongs which had been perpetrated upon his estate.

He had also dedicated himself—with singular devotion—to getting his wife with child. He had been bedding Catriona at least twice a day now that they had settled once more into a truce. His countess's appetite for pleasure matched his, and one of his favorite missions was plotting when and how he could get her alone so he could lift her skirts.

Thrice in the library.

Once in the gardens.

Yet again in the Temple of Artemis.

Two times in the drawing room.

Four times in the portrait gallery. The chairs in that room were generous and quite accommodating. He had discovered there were few greater joys in life than convincing his wife to sit upon his lap and ride him whilst he suckled her nipples.

He frowned, scarcely taking note of the panorama before him, one of the laborers pruning a particularly wild rosebush. The endless lust he felt for his wife was becoming something of a problem.

It never diminished as he had imagined it would.

Instead, it grew.

And it was growing still, every minute, every hour, every day, with a persistence that concerned him. He was not certain what he could do about it, save continue bedding her as often as possible in the hopes she would soon be carrying his heir and he could move forward with his life.

A sudden commotion from the hall beyond the study reached him. He spun on his heels, about to investigate the source, when the door burst open, and there stood Olivia, her face pale, eyes wide.

"Come quick, m'lord! Something has happened to Lady Rayne!" she said.

Dios.

His heart was instantly hammering, fear clenching his gut. "What do you mean something has happened to her, child? What is it?"

"She swooned, and she won't wake up," said the child.

As he moved closer, he detected the faint shimmer of tears on her cheeks. He had seen his wife only hours ago, and she had been hale and hearty, her cheeks painted a sweet pink from the exertion of their morning lovemaking. What the devil could have happened?

"Take me to her," he said grimly.

SHE WAS GOING to lose him.

It was all Catriona could think as she watched the doctor Alessandro had summoned to her side take his leave of her chamber. How strange the heart was, to be capable of bursting with happiness and breaking all at once.

She had been so busy these last few weeks, between the endless tasks occupying her at Marchmont, taking Olivia on as her charge, and navigating the complex marriage she shared with her husband, she had failed to notice she had missed her courses.

But miss them, she had. She had been due for them a fortnight after Alessandro had consummated their marriage. How had she failed to note all the signs? The sudden churn of her stomach in the mornings? The extra urge for dessert? The dizziness which sometimes assailed her, as had happened earlier.

All of it normal, the doctor had assured her, for a woman who was with child. The reason she had failed to come to initially was that she had knocked her head upon the floor in her fall. But though she had a throbbing ache in her skull to show for it, the doctor assured her that after a day of rest, she would be fine.

How wrong he was. For she would not be fine. Not when this discovery meant her life as she had come to know—and love—it was about to change irrevocably.

Catriona closed her eyes against the swift prick of tears. A strange barrage of emotion pounded down upon her, like a punishing hailstorm. Maternal longing, a rush of awe, followed by regret and a bittersweet, searing pain.

For if she was going to bear him a child, Alessandro would be leaving her.

Soon.

It was not enough time.

And while she had spent every moment since falling in love with him with that horrible knowledge impinging upon her happiness, it had never felt as final or as real as it did now, as she lay in her bed, the new life they had created together growing inside her.

The door to the chamber opened, but she kept her eyes closed. She already knew who had entered without bothering to look, for she had become so attuned to her husband, she recognized the sound of his prowling walk. The bed dipped as he sat upon the edge.

"Catriona," he said softly. "Look at me."

Hot tears scalded her eyes, sliding from beneath her lowered lashes. Still, she would not obey. Nor would she speak. She did not think herself capable of it in this moment.

"Dr. Sheffield has told me," he said at last, his accent more pronounced, his voice deeper, darker.

Even his beloved, familiar scent seemed to take on a new note with her eyes closed. Her every sense was painfully heightened, her heart a painful danger she had worn on her sleeve for far too long. Always, always belonging to him.

And never, ever had he given himself in return.

"I suppose you are happy," she managed to whisper. "You have what you wanted."

"*Sí.*"

She inhaled sharply at his acknowledgment, for it cut her as surely as any blade. "When will you go?"

"Dr. Sheffield says you must rest for a day or so to make certain all is well with the babe after your fall," he told her. "I will begin the preparations for our return to London."

"London," she repeated, her lips feeling numb. She opened her eyes at last, unashamed of her tears. They tracked down her cheeks. "Why London?"

"I will not have you alone here. My sister and your mother will attend you for your lying in, and you must be wherever they are." His dark gaze burned into hers, a frown on his beautiful lips. "Why tears, *querida*? Are you ill? Is it the babe?"

Tears because you are leaving me, you foolish man.

Tears because I love you, and you will never love me in return.

"It has been a trying day," she lied. "I am emotional and tired. I wish to rest."

"Are you certain you are well? The doctor assures me you are in fine health, but you must promise to tell me, Catriona, if anything is amiss," he pressed.

How tender he was. How caring.

But of course, none of it was for her.

"When are you leaving for Spain?" she asked.

He clenched his jaw. "I will see you settled in London, and then I will leave. You will send word to me upon the birth, and if the child is not a boy, I will return if I am able."

There it was, the blow she had been anticipating. The final confirmation of all her fears. How could she have forgotten she was nothing more than a broodmare to him?

"Of course," she managed to say, though her heart was breaking.

It felt as if a dagger had been lodged in her chest. And it was—a dagger of her own making.

"*Querida*," he began.

But she could not bear to hear another word from him. "I do not wish to talk more now, if you please. I am tired, and I must rest."

He pressed a kiss to her brow. "I will have your woman attend you."

"No," she said. For as much as she enjoyed the company of her lady's maid, she could not bear it now.

All she wanted was to be alone.

"Catriona." He frowned down at her, his gaze searching. "You are not acting as your normal self. Is something hurting you?"

Only my heart.

"Nothing." She forced a smile for his benefit. "Thank you, Alessandro. Please, all I need is some rest. My head is aching from the fall. A little quiet, and I shall be fine."

"Very well." He frowned down at her, looking for a moment as if he were about to say more.

But in the end, he simply stood and walked from the chamber, leaving her alone in a grim echo of what would soon be a far more permanent departure.

She waited until the door clicked closed before rolling onto her side and curling into a protective ball. Burying her face in her pillow, she wept, both with joy for the new life inside her and with despair for the man who would never love her.

⚜

HE WAS GOING to be a father.

Again.

Alessandro walked from Catriona's chamber, uncertain of where he was going. All he knew was that his feet were going. His legs were striding. He was moving forward, hurtling to a destination.

A myriad of emotion assaulted him. Happiness. Awe. Fear. Regret.

Someone was speaking to him, but he was so caught up in the tumult of his thoughts, he scarcely heard their words. Female, he realized. Olivia.

He stopped halfway down the massive, spiral staircase which was the center of Marchmont, one of its crowning glories. Also, where his sister had taken a fall in her youth, so severe it resulted in the fracture of her limb. Such stately elegance, carved mahogany shining once more, and yet also the source of great grief.

How fitting.

He turned back to find the *picaro* at the top of the stairs, her young face pale, her countenance worried. "My lord, how is Lady Rayne?"

Before him stood evidence of his wife's innate goodness. This child, whom no one had loved or cared for, was now fuller-cheeked and well-dressed and groomed. She was now loved. If he had ever harbored concern about Catriona's capacity for maternal care, it was long gone.

"She will be fine, child," he told the girl, though he was not as certain as his words suggested.

There had been an undeniable sadness in her demeanor. She had reassured him, repeatedly, that all was well with her. And yet, her eyes had told a different story. The haunted look he had recognized deep within their blue depths had returned. This time, he very much feared he was the source.

"She is not going to die, is she?" Olivia asked, an unmistakable tremble in her voice.

Cristo.

The child's question took the air from his lungs. Instantly, he was catapulted back to the day Maria had breathed her last. How pale she had been. How still. Just like their son.

Everything within him seized. He could not speak. Could not allay the child's fears. Because he had seen death before. He had lost a wife to the childbed. Had lost a son. And for some godforsaken reason, he had never before contemplated the full implications of getting Catriona with child.

That she would face the same dangers and risks Maria had.

That she, too, could perish.

"Come now, Miss Olivia," said his wife's lady's maid, appearing in the hall above. She cast a gentle arm about the picaro's slim shoulders, drawing her into her form for reassurance. "Lady Rayne shall be just fine. Is that not right, my lord?"

"Yes," he forced himself to say, but the word was like a splinter in his tongue, with a matching one every bit as sharp in his heart. "She will. *Perdóneme.*"

Without waiting for a response, he turned back to the stairs. Somehow, he made his way down them. Blindly, his breath arrested in his chest, his heart thumping wildly. Bleak emotions stronger than ever churned through him.

By the grace of God, he reached the bottom of the stairs without toppling down them, and without recalling a moment of how he had gotten there. But his legs had a mind of their own, and they were moving still. Carrying him to the door. As far away as he could go. As fast as he could get there.

Johnstone appeared at his side. "Lord Rayne, is something amiss?

Algo anda mal?"

"*Sí*," he bit out, striding past the butler, scarcely even taking note of his attempt to speak his language. "Everything is wrong."

He did not bother to wait for a response. He could not bear it. He needed to escape this house, these walls, all the reminders of who he was, what was expected of him. Marchmont felt as if it were strangling him. The obligations, the pain of his past, all his losses, his sins, the battles he had fought, the depravities he had committed, jumbled together into a sickening knot in his gut.

For a moment, he feared he would cast up his accounts.

And then, he was out of doors, gulping in the fresh Wiltshire air.

But he was still moving, still going.

Where, he could not say, only that he needed to leave.

Chapter Twenty-Four

THE JOURNEY BACK to London had proved even more arduous than the trip to Wiltshire had been. Perhaps because this time, Catriona was with child, and the rocking movement of the carriage, coupled with the biliousness she could not seem to shake, made her stomach heave every few miles. And perhaps because the pace they had set—she, Sadler, and Olivia—was grueling. And most certainly because her heart had been dashed into a million tiny, jagged shards by her husband.

Even breathing hurt. Her eyes were red-rimmed, and her nose was puffy from all the tears she had cried between Marchmont and the sooty, foggy, busy streets of Town.

By the time she reached London and the Mayfair front door of Torrington House, she was sure she looked a dreadful sight. She had not been able to hold down a bite to eat since Basingstoke, and the last decent meal she had consumed before that had been a meat pie of questionable culinary delight in Salisbury. Even the tea she had attempted to consume had revolted against her in disgusting fashion, leaving her weaker and more miserable than she had been at the onset of her journey.

Worse, she was sure there was at least one vomit stain upon the hem of her traveling gown, and it was entirely possible the sour stench assaulting her nose on the odd breeze originated from her.

Thankfully, she was known to the butler, who showed her into the blue salon to await Hattie with an unperturbed smile of welcome. If he thought it odd she made her call accompanied by her lady's maid and a child who clutched a small cage in one hand bearing a pet mouse, he said not a word.

But then again, he was in the employ of Torrie, and everyone know the Viscount of Torrington was a ne'er do well of the first order. Or, at least, he had been. Until the accident. Hattie's letters to Marchmont had been sparse and spare of word concerning her brother, and Monty, being Monty, had not bothered to write her more than a handful of lines, none of which contained any news of note. Even her mother's letters had been laden with unimportant meanderings on the weather, which seemed a favorite subject of hers.

She could only hope Torrie had improved, and that she was not about to thrust too great an encumbrance on an already burdened household. When the butler took his leave, Catriona commenced pacing, wringing her hands as she worriedly wore tracks in the thick Aubusson.

"Do sit down, my lady," urged Sadler. "You've had so much upset these last few days, and what with all the travel and your sicknesses, it is not good for the babe. You look frightfully pale."

But Catriona could not bear to sit after having been forced to ride for two days across the countryside once more. Alessandro's carriage was well-appointed, it was true, but not even the most expensive traveling vehicle could atone for hours spent upon one's rump.

"I am fine, Sadler," she reassured her. "Thank you for your concern."

"You does—*do*—look like you may be about to cast up your accounts," added Olivia, her lip curling in distaste.

The mere mentioning of vomit was making her feel as if she may have to empty her stomach all over again. She pressed a hand over the sickly swirl and swallowed against a sudden knot of queasiness.

"I am fine," she reassured everyone, which was all she seemed to be doing since discovering she was with child.

And which was always the worst sort of prevarication.

She was not fine.

Indeed, she was the furthest from it. She was miserable, physically and emotionally. Drained. Terrified. Elated. Lonely. Lovesick. Grief-stricken. Awed. Tired yet unable to sleep, hungry yet unable to eat. Overjoyed at the tiny life beginning inside her, yet despairing over what it meant for her marriage. She longed for the man she loved, and yet she could not have him.

"You doesn't—ahem, don't—seem fine," Olivia countered, still having quite a lot to learn about her manners. "Have they got any cats here? Ashes can't live beneath the same roof as those furry little killers."

It occurred to her, rather belatedly, that Hattie *did* have a cat. A great, fat, snowy white beast called Sir Toby. The creature was most disagreeable. It only liked Hattie and not anyone else.

"There is one," she managed to say past a fresh wave of sickness. "But fret not, for the thing never leaves her chamber. It's a most disagreeable cat."

"Tell me you are not speaking of Sir Toby Belch," Hattie said as she swept into the room, looking utterly fetching in an evening gown of pretty pink silk with a rich floral motif overlay in gauze.

The contrast between her dark hair and the pale pastel of her gown was arresting. Her hair was artfully curled around her heart-shaped face, and she had never looked more beautiful. Catriona took one look at her beloved friend and burst into tears.

"Oh, my darling," Hattie crooned, sweeping her into a violet-scented embrace. "Why are you crying?"

She could not seem to find the words, nor to form them. The tumult of the last few days descended upon her all at once, and here, in her friend's arms, she felt the first bit of comfort she had known since the moment Alessandro had informed her he would be returning to

Spain as soon as possible.

That everything they had shared meant nothing to him.

That she meant nothing to him.

Whilst he meant *everything* to her...

"I am abysmal at choosing men to fall in love with," she managed through her sobs.

"There, now." Hattie passed a soothing caress over her back, calming her. "Shrewsbury was a rotter, I will own."

She had forgotten all about the marquess.

"It is not Sh-Shrewsbury," she sobbed, aware she was making a mess of her dear friend's elegant gown.

Her emotions were as unpredictable as the weather.

"I gathered as much." Hattie drew back, her brow knitted in a frown as she studied Catriona's face. "I was only attempting to make you smile. You look as if you have just left a grave. Tell me what Rayne has done, and together, we will come up with a fitting punishment. I would say Montrose should meet him at dawn, but we all know how that went the last time round."

Monty. Wild, madcap, beloved Monty, who was the reason for all this, indirectly. She loved him and she hated him, all at once.

"This is all Monty's fault," she said on a sniffle. "If he had not been sotted—"

"You do realize every bad turn in Montrose's life begins with just such a phrase, do you not?" Hattie interrupted with a small, sad smile.

"How is the viscount?" Catriona asked then, reminded, instantly, of one of Monty's most egregious sins.

Hattie's smile vanished. "He is not yet himself. Though whether or not that is a boon or a curse remains to be seen. But enough of our scapegrace brothers. Tell me what has brought you here. Is your honeymoon over?"

"What's a honeymoon?" Olivia asked.

Hattie's attention was diverted to the child for a moment, her eyes narrowing upon the cage. "Who is the miscreant, and why is she carrying a rat about? Has she no notion of the pestilence they carry?"

"Here now, Ashes ain't no rat," Olivia said, forgetting her lessons in her umbrage.

"Ashes is not a rat," Catriona somehow found the presence of mind to correct her charge. To Hattie, she added, "Ashes is a mouse. Olivia's pet."

Hattie raised a brow, her gaze flicking back and forth between Catriona and the child. "And who, precisely, is Olivia again?"

"Olivia is Rayne's ward," she explained, though it was perhaps not entirely legal just yet. It *would* be legal, she vowed. She would not be separated from the child. Olivia needed her.

And the truth of it was, she needed Olivia, too.

"I see." Hattie's frown returned. "That is not the reason, surely, for your upset?"

"No." She took a deep breath. "I am leaving Rayne. Before he leaves me. And I do not wish him to find me, should he attempt it. That is why I am here. If I go to Riverford House, he will find me, and if I go to Hamilton House, he will find me there as well. I hope we might be able to remain at Torrington House until Rayne returns to Spain. I cannot bear to see him again. If you cannot accommodate us, I understand. After what Monty has done…"

"What Montrose has done will be his to answer for, one day," Hattie said coolly. "You are like a sister to me, and you are welcome here regardless of your scoundrel brother, as ever. Now tell me, if you please, why you have come. What has Rayne done to chase you from your very home before he leaves for Spain? I thought freedom was what you wanted most."

"It was," she agreed on a sniffle. "Until I fell in love with him. Until I realized he will never be able to love me in return. I can only blame myself. He never wanted anything from me but an heir, and now he is returning to Spain."

"Poison seems a fitting punishment," Hattie said. "Not enough to kill him, of course, but enough to make him virulently ill."

Her friend was not serious. Was she?

The room was beginning to spin about Catriona before she could contemplate anything else, and she knew what was going to happen next.

She recognized the signs. Her body went hot, then cold. She tried to take a deep breath, to regain her calm. But just as before, the weakness caused by her inability to keep sustenance where it belonged made her all too susceptible.

"Catriona!"

"My lady!"

"Lady Rayne?"

Blackness overtook her. The concerned trio of voices were muted by the sudden roar of oblivion. She pitched forward into the darkness.

HIS WIFE HAD left him.

Alessandro could scarcely believe it even now, two days after the discovery, as he rapped on the London door of Hamilton House. Of course, Catriona had not been in residence at Riverford House, where he had expected her to retreat. When he had reached his townhome and found it empty save the servants he had left behind, a blinding sense of despair had hit him for the first time.

She could run so far, so fast, he could never find her.

And he had only himself to blame.

The door opened to reveal the stern butler he had faced on many occasions. "Lord Rayne," he greeted.

"Is Lady Rayne within?" he asked, daring to hope.

The butler frowned. "No, my lord. She is not."

"What of Montrose?" he tried next.

The butler's stony expression did not alter. "I am afraid His Grace is not currently at home."

He would be willing to bet Marchmont that Montrose was passed out in a stupor somewhere. The hour was unfashionably early.

"Please convey to His Grace this is a matter of grave import concerning his sister, Lady Rayne," he told the domestic, not about to be dismissed.

Time was too important. Each moment that passed was another without Catriona, and each moment took her farther and farther from him.

The butler inclined his head. "Do come in, my lord."

Gratefully, Rayne stepped into the entry hall of Hamilton House, watched over by the stern visages of a half dozen marble busts. All of whom seemed to cast judgment upon him, and he could not blame them. He had been a fool, and he knew it.

"Thank you, sir," he told the domestic. "I cannot stress the import of an audience with His Grace enough."

"Of course, my lord," the butler intoned before bowing and taking his leave.

Alessandro paced, reminded of the last time he had felt so helpless. When he had been losing Maria. But unlike then, he had a fighting chance to keep from losing the woman he loved.

Sì. Loved.

He ran a hand over his jaw as he paced. On the day he had learned Catriona was carrying his child, he had been so overwhelmed by the discovery, he had walked. Walked and walked until he reached the village. The time and distance had led him to some realizations he'd been previously unable to face.

Somewhere between the day he had first happened upon her in the Hamilton House library and the moment he had kissed her lips in the Temple of Artemis, Catriona had stolen his heart. How he had failed to see it until he had walked two miles—the last half mile or so in a driving rain—he could not say.

Stupidity?

Pride?

Fear?

Likely, a combination of all three.

Whatever the cause, he could see everything now, and with a clarity he had never before possessed. Everything had changed because of her. Ironically, it had been the words of the oft-drunken Duke of Montrose which had returned to him in his lowest point, as he had been soaked to the skin, attempting to dry himself at the inn.

Montrose had accused him of spending his life running.

And he had not been wrong.

Alessandro had run from England. From the losses of Maria and Francisco. And finally, he had been running from Catriona. The answer had hit him with the force of a cudgel to the head as he sat at the battered table. There was only one place he wanted to run, and that was to the woman he loved. His heart had not died with Maria and their son. Rather, he had closed it off.

But Catriona had opened it up once more, and he knew that now.

Just as he knew he wanted a family.

He wanted to be a father.

He wanted to be a husband.

He wanted Catriona at his side as they restored Marchmont, along with the *picaro* and even her damned rodent. He wanted it *all*. But first, he needed to find his wife.

The letter she had left him told him she was returning to London on her own, but she had not specified where she was going. She was ready, she had said, to seize her freedom, and she wished him happy in his return to Spain. By the time the rains had stopped, returning to Marchmont on a darkened, muddied road had been too treacherous. He had spent the evening in the village, returning home by borrowed carriage the next morning.

But he had been too late. Catriona had already been gone, nothing but her elegant words on a page left behind.

The Duke of Montrose appeared before him suddenly, leaning on a crutch, looking more gaunt and pale than he had when last their paths had crossed. "What the hell is the meaning of this, Rayne?" he demanded. "Where is my sister?"

"I am hoping you can aid me with that," he told the duke, swallowing his pride.

Montrose's eyes narrowed. For once, he did not appear inebriated, though there was something else about his mannerisms which seemed decidedly off. "Satan's earbobs, do you mean to tell me you have *lost* my sister?"

"She left me," he admitted. Nothing mattered but Catriona. He had to know where she had gone.

"Left you," Montrose repeated, sounding suspicious. "What the devil have you done to her to make her leave you?"

"I…" he paused, struggling to find the words. Where to begin? The truth, he supposed. "I left her first."

"You devious scoundrel," the duke bit out, charging forward, though the effort of hobbling with his crutch rendered the effect less than fearsome.

Alessandro remained where he was. If Montrose wished to hit him, he would not defend himself. Indeed, if there was anyone deserving of a sound drubbing, surely it was he.

"Go ahead. Hit me," he said. "But after you do, tell me where she may have gone. She is not at Riverford House, and she is not here."

Montrose grimaced in pain as he reached Alessandro. "Cursed ankle."

"Perhaps you ought not to have been searching for whisky after the bone had just been set," he offered.

"And perhaps you ought not to have left your wife and then lost her," the duke spat. "If anything ill has befallen her because of your stupidity, Rayne, I will challenge you to a duel. And this time, I will be prepared."

"If anything happens to her, I will deserve to be shot," he returned bitterly. "*Cristo*, she is everything to me. I know I do not deserve her, but I love her."

They stared each other down.

Montrose nodded. "Damned right you do not deserve her, Rayne. She is too good for you."

"*Sí*," he agreed.

"Always has been," Montrose added.

He could not argue. "*Sí*."

"Always will be."

He gritted his teeth. "*Sí*. Are you going to help me, Montrose, or not?"

"My best guess is she is at Torrington House," Montrose said. "She and Miss Lethbridge are bosom bows. Closer than sisters, those two."

Ah, yes. The friend who had looked upon Montrose as if he were a worm at dinner. Why had he not thought of her?

"*Gracias*, Montrose," he said. "Do you have the direction?"

Having been abroad for so long, he could scarcely find his way around Town.

"Never mind that," the duke said. "I shall accompany you."

Chapter Twenty-Five

"Finish your tea," Hattie ordered Catriona. "And eat another biscuit. You are still looking so horridly wan."

"Yes, Mother," Catriona grumbled, taking another hesitant sip of tea. Fortunately, her angry stomach was beginning to settle, and the brew did not make her instantly want to retch.

"You cannot go about swooning all over London," her friend added.

"This is the second time she's swooned now," Olivia added around a mouthful of biscuit.

Catriona frowned at her charge. "Ladies do not speak whilst they are chewing, Olivia."

"Sorry," she said, crumbs flying from her mouth.

"Second time swooning?" Hattie's eyes narrowed upon Catriona. "What is the matter with you, dearest? You have one of the heartiest constitutions of anyone I have ever met."

Ordinarily, she did. But it would seem she was making up for her good fortune now.

She sighed. "I am perfectly well. It is merely that I am—"

"She's having a babe," interrupted Olivia.

"Olivia," she chastised. "Ladies do not interject during the dialogue of another lady."

"I ain't no lady," Olivia said with a gamine grin. "Can Ashes have a biscuit? She's hungry."

"I am not a lady," she corrected. More lessons in deportment were in order, clearly. "And I suppose Ashes may have a portion of a biscuit, as long as Miss Lethbridge does not mind."

"But you *are* a lady," Olivia argued, true to form.

On yet another sigh, Catriona turned her attention to Hattie. Her friend gawked at her.

"Do you mind?" she asked hesitantly. After all, it was rather uncommon to take tea with a mouse.

Hattie flew from her seat and gathered her in a tight embrace. "Catriona, how dare you not tell me I am going to be an auntie? You should have said so from the moment I saw you!"

"Forgive me for not relaying the news sooner," she said, hugging her friend back with all the strength she could muster. "It has been a long few days of upheaval and travel, and I am afraid not even someone with the halest of constitutions can withstand the rigors of being in a delicate condition."

"It is more difficult for some women," Sadler chimed in with an air of authority. "My own mother was terribly ill each time, in the early months."

"Splendid," she said weakly, wondering how she would survive months of biliousness and dizziness.

And carrying on without the man she loved.

Hattie pulled away, glancing down at her with a quizzical air. "Does Rayne know?"

"Yes," she said softly, feeling a fresh rush of tears coming on. "It is why he is leaving me."

"God's fichu, what a spineless weasel," Hattie said distastefully.

God's fichu.

Catriona found herself frowning at her friend. "That is one of Monty's nonsensical curses."

Hattie's cheeks flushed. "Of course it isn't. I heard it from someone else, I am certain."

Before Catriona could pursue the matter, the butler arrived on the threshold of the chamber. "The Earl of Rayne and the Duke of Montrose, Miss Lethbridge," he announced.

Alessandro was here.

With Monty.

Her traitorous heart pounded faster, and hope rose within her against her will.

"Tell them we are not at home to mendacious curs," Hattie announced.

"Tell us yourself, Miss Lethbridge," came the cool, almost detached voice of her brother.

And just behind him stood the beautiful, beloved form of her husband. His dark stare met hers and held. "*Querida*, all I require is a few moments of your time."

She gazed back at him, terrified he had only sought her out to tell her goodbye. Foolish enough to know that she loved him so much, even a few more minutes in his presence would be worth the pain.

"You do not have to go with him," Hattie told her quietly.

She gave her friend a sad smile. "Yes, I do."

"I understand, dearest." Hattie gave her a stern look. "Holler if he upsets you in any fashion, and I shall come charging to your rescue."

Catriona gave her friend a quick embrace. "Thank you."

She hoped she would not need rescuing, but that, like her heart, was ultimately in Alessandro's hands.

ALESSANDRO FACED HIS wife in a small morning room across the hall from the salon where he had initially found her. Love for her, so profound and strong, overwhelmed him.

All he could think, was that he had found her.

Thank *Dios*.

And then, he realized how pale she was.

"How are you, *querida?*" he asked softly.

"Why have you come?" she returned instead of answering.

"You left me." He took a step closer to her. "Where else would I go but where you are?"

"Spain, perhaps?" Her lips tightened.

He did not miss the bitterness lacing her dulcet tones.

He deserved that bitterness and her distrust both. He had wronged her. Again and again.

"I am not going to Spain." As the words left him, he felt indescribably light, as if the weight of a cartload of bricks had been lifted from his shoulders, from his heart. "Not now."

She frowned at him. "When, then? Tomorrow? Next week? Next month?"

"I do not know," he answered honestly. "Spain has been a home to me for all my life, and I want to return one day. But not without you. I am not leaving you, *querida*. I cannot leave you or the *bebé*."

"I do not understand, Alessandro." Her gaze searched his. "What does all this mean? Mere days ago, you could not wait to see me settled in London so you could go. Here I am, settled. You are free. I am free. It is all done. I will not try to keep you here, where you do not wish to be."

He reached her then, and he could not resist drawing her against him. She was trembling, but then, so too, was he. Alessandro buried his face in her soft, sweetly scented curls, inhaling deeply. "There is nowhere else I would rather be than here, with the woman I love."

She stiffened. "Do not toy with me, Alessandro. I cannot bear it."

"I would never toy with you." He drew back enough to gaze down into her upturned face. "I love you, Catriona. I was a blind fool for not realizing it sooner. You brought my heart back to life. You have filled my darkness with your light. I love the way you tease me, the way you laugh, the way you kiss. The way you care for Olivia, the way you are as stubborn as an ox, the way you rose to the task of restoring Marchmont alongside me. Cristo, I even love the way you snore. So, you see? I cannot bear to be without you. Not for another hour, not for another minute, not for another second."

Tears shimmered in the blue-violet depths of her eyes. "Oh, Alessandro."

He caressed her cheek. "The night we married, *querida*, you said I was to be your darling, and yet you have never called me by that name." He paused. "I do not deserve it, I know. But in time, I will prove myself to you. Grant me the chance to be that to you. To be your man. Your darling."

"I was horridly sotted on brandy that night," she said softly.

"*Sí*," he agreed, grinning down at her as he recalled precisely how sotted she had become. "I love your hiccups, too, *mi amor*."

She bit her lower lip. "Did you truly liken me to an ox?"

"Only the stubborn streak in you," he said, "and I am grateful for it. You have been good for me. Good to me. A lesser woman than you would have given up on me long before now. I only pray I did not come to my senses too late, that you can forgive me."

She covered her hand with his, smiling up at him even as tears rolled down her cheeks. "I do not need time to know my heart, for it is already yours. It has been for some time now. I love you, Alessandro Forsythe."

"*Dios*," he said, relief washing over him, along with love. So much of it. "How I love you, *mi amor*. Thank you for the gift of your love, which I do not—"

"Hush." She pressed a finger to his lips, stilling further words. "You *do* deserve me, just as you deserve love and happiness. Now kiss me, my darling."

Smiling, he did just that.

Epilogue

Vicente Francisco Alessandro Forsythe, Viscount Stewart, future tenth Earl of Rayne, had only been in the world for a few days, and already, his mother and father were hopelessly in love with him.

Catriona rested her head upon her husband's shoulder as they sat together in her bed, no less than a dozen pillows plumped up at their backs. She had just finished feeding her son, and Alessandro had been impatiently awaiting his turn to hold Vicente, who seemed to sleep best in his father's arms.

Love swelled in her as she watched father and son. Vicente's eyes were closed, his perfect little lips parted as he slumbered peacefully. Gently, she caressed the tuft of dark, silky hair atop his head, so like his father's.

"It hardly seems fair that he prefers you to me," she complained. "After I carried him in my body all these months and grew to the size of a cow."

"You never resembled a cow in the slightest, *querida*. You were beautiful carrying my babe, just as beautiful as you are now. And he does not prefer me."

She watched as he caressed Vicente's cheek. "You are a charmer. But it is all very well. I know he prefers his papa, and I have accepted it."

"He does not." Alessandro glanced up at her with a rakish grin.

"He loves us both equally. It is merely he knows his papa has a soothing voice for lullabies. He prefers them in Spanish, you know."

She smiled back at him. "Of course he does. He is your image, Alessandro."

"He is *perfecto*." Her husband dropped a tender kiss on her cheek. "Just like his mama."

"I am far from perfect." She leaned into him, following up with a peck on his sinful mouth. It was too soon for them to be intimate again following their son's birth, but that did not mean she did not want her husband just as much as ever. More so, in fact. "But I thank you for loving me anyway."

"No, thank you," he said, his gaze burning into hers, "for loving me. I do not know why such a black-hearted sinner has been blessed with so much, but I am a greedy man, and I will take it all. You, Olivia, and Vicente are my world."

"As you are ours," she told him.

Much had happened over the last few months. Bramwell had finally been brought to justice. Many of the stolen paintings had been recovered—most importantly, the portrait of Alessandro's mother, which now hung proudly in the gallery once more. Alessandro's architect had rebuilt the east wing. The estate was once more robust and profitable. Olivia was officially under Alessandro's legal guardianship.

And even Spain was free of Napoleon's tyrannical rule. Word had reached England not long ago of the Treaty of Valençay, releasing King Ferdinand from captivity. It was, in all, a dawn of new beginnings, the commencement of a bright future.

A knock sounded at the chamber door.

"Mama?"

Catriona recognized the sound of Olivia's voice. Though it had taken a great deal of time for her to completely gain the girl's trust, she had finally won her over.

"Come in," she called.

The words had scarcely left her mouth when the door popped open, and Oliva burst over the threshold in a profusion of energy and muslin skirts. Her hair was finally growing, and her diction had improved greatly, but some things would never change.

"I have escaped Miss Grimsby for the day," she announced.

"You have not locked her in the Temple of Artemis again have you, imp?" Alessandro asked, taking the words from Catriona's mouth.

Though Miss Grimsby was an accomplished governess, she was rather strict. Olivia and rules did not always go well together. It would not be the first time she had resorted to such tactics to free herself from the governess's charge.

"I would never do such a thing," Olivia said with a grin. "May I?"

"*Por supuesto*," Alessandro said, patting the bed at his side. "Your brother is missing you. He told me so himself before he fell asleep."

"Babies cannot talk, Papa," the girl said, rolling her eyes at Alessandro's whimsy.

But the twinkle in her eyes told another tale entirely.

"You do not have Ashes in your pocket, do you?" Catriona asked next, for the special mouse-sized pockets Olivia had convinced Sadler to sew into her gowns had led to a series of surprises, not all of them the welcome variety.

"Johnstone is watching her for me," Olivia reassured her. "Mice do not like babies, you know."

"I did know that," Alessandro said, giving their daughter a wink. "Ashes told me."

"Papa!" Olivia exclaimed.

But then she started to laugh. And then so, too, did Catriona and Alessandro.

It was a moment—the rare and precious sort of moment in life—that seemed too wonderful to be real. Catriona gazed upon her beloved family, her heart so full, it ached.

"Do you want to know what else the mouse told me, *mija?*" Alessandro asked Olivia.

She rolled her eyes again, still smiling, *"Qué?"*

"That I am the luckiest man in all the world."

About the Author

USA Today Bestselling author Scarlett Scott writes steamy Victorian and Regency historical romances with strong, intelligent heroines and sexy alpha heroes. She lives in Pennsylvania with her Canadian husband, their adorable identical twins, and one TV-loving dog.

A self-professed literary junkie and nerd, she loves reading anything but especially romance novels, poetry, and Middle English verse. When she's not reading, writing, wrangling toddlers, or camping, you can catch up with her on her website. Hearing from readers never fails to make her day.

LINKS:
Website: www.scarlettscottauthor.com
Facebook: facebook.com/ScarlettScottAuthor
BookBub: bookbub.com/profile/scarlett-scott
Instagram: instagram.com/scarlettscottauthor
Pinterest: pinterest.com/scarlettscott
Twitter: twitter.com/scarscoromance

Printed by Amazon Italia Logistica S.r.l.
Torrazza Piemonte (TO), Italy